ANNAPOLIS TO ANDROMEDA

by
Grant Carrington

Brief Candle Press titles
by Grant Carrington

TIME'S FOOL, AND OTHER STORIES

Coming soon from Grant Carrington
DOWN IN THE BARRAQUE

Brief Candle Press titles
by G. David Nordley

TO CLIMB A FLAT MOUNTAIN

THE BLACK HOLE PROJECT
(with C. Sanford Lowe)

AFTER THE VIKINGS: TALES OF FUTURE MARS

AMONG THE STARS

PRELUDE TO STARS

ANNAPOLIS
TO
ANDROMEDA

Brief Candle
Press

Publishing History
Previous versions of these stories were published as follows:

"The Pied Piper of Gotham" (*Plume & Sword*, November 9, 1964)
"Yours For the Future" (*The Diversifier*, November 1977)
"Night on Old Baldy" (*Weirdbook 14*, 1979)
"A Shakespearean Incident" (*Fantastic*, October 1975)
"The Interstellar Ragtime All-American Jazz Band" (*Eternity*, 1979; *The Diversifier*, May/July 1978)
"Ask Lafferty" (*At the Sleepy Sailor, A Tribute to R.A. Lafferty*, 1979)
"A Simple Twist of Fate" (*Eternity*, 1980)
"The Key" (*Amazing*, June 1992)
"Younger Than Springtime" (*Best Erotic Fantasy & Science Fiction*, 2010)
"Hark, Hark, the Quark!" (*Isaac Asimov's SF Magazine*, March 1980)
"There's No One Left to Paint the Sky" (*Amazing*, May 1972)
"His Hour Upon the Stage" (*Amazing*, March 1976)
"Nothing Personal" (*Eternity*, 1973)
"Carrara" (*Eternity*, 1975)
"Half Past the Dragon" (*Fantastic*, November 1974)
"On the Planet Planet" (*The Diversifier*, October 1976)
"World's End" (*Night Voyages*, Fall 1981)
"Timid Bank Clerks and Other Writers" (*Knights 20*, March 1979)

All other material is original to this work and is printed with permission of the author and publisher.

First published in 2014 by Variations on a Theme

Cover Design by Rob Kroese
Thomas Point Shoal Lighthouse photograph courtesy of Jay Yourch

First Brief Candle Press edition published 2015
www.briefcandlepress.com

ISBN: 978-1-942319-12-2

Dedication:

To the memory of my sister,
Marilyn Carrington Esposito,
1934-2013

Table of Contents

Annapolis to Andromeda...

PAST AND PRESENT

I'd like you to meet some of my stories...
—Grant Carrington

Pied Piper of Gotham

"And furthermore they cause some kind of disease," Al asserted.

"How do you know?" I asked.

"It was in the paper."

"Since when have you started reading the paper?"

"Bede told me about it."

I looked at Bede to see if it was true. She was busy floating one of her sandals in the fountain. Her dirty blonde hair nodded affirmation without looking up.

"Why, those damn pigeons are walking around in filth all day. They say several people have died already and I bet if they really look into it, they'll find out pigeons cause all kinds of disease."

"Al, I think you're going just a little bit off the deep end."

"What do you mean? Just look at the crap they wallow in."

"So what? You walk in it all day; so do dogs and cats, and you don't scream your head off about them."

Al gave me a dirty look. Bede gave no indication that she was even listening but I knew that she never missed a words that passed between any of us. Red was sketching and his eyes were glazed in concentration. Yet it was Bede who first noticed him.

"Say, Al, look at that man over there."

We saw a tiny man dressed in green talking to some tourists. He was nervous and excited.

"Now I've seen everything," Al commented, making a significant glance at Red's ample beard.

"He keeps walking around like that and the cops'll be hauling him in," observed Bede.

Al nudged Red. "Hey, O Great Bearded One," he intoned, "dig the goofball."

Red looked down at Al's grinning face with smoldering fire in his eyes. Al pointed to the subject of his interruption. Red followed the line of his finger and his jaw dropped in unfeigned astonishment.

"I'll be goddamned," he intoned. "It's a friggin' brownie, a real honest-to-Christ fairy." There was no second meaning in his voice.

The subject of Red's astonishment was short, not even five feet tall, with a big bulbous nose and green eyes that glittered over a wide grin;

a profuse shock of red hair waved excitedly and agitatedly although there was not the promise of a breeze over the Square. He was wearing a pastel green pullover that was open at the collar so that the flaming red hair of his chest showed at the throat; the pants were a brilliant green and tapered down to a pair of pointed shoes, which, thank God, were brown. Not one of these particular items of clothing was particularly strange for the Square but, put together on the little man, they gave him the appearance of a leprechaun or, as Red put it, "a friggin' brownie."

He had a pen and pad in his hand and, as he talked to people, he jotted down what they had to say. When he reached us, Al greeted him. "Hi, there! What's your racket?"

"Oh. You've been watching me?" He did not seem the least bit surprised.

"Sort of."

"Well, I'm taking a survey. It's a personal project, you might say. What I'd like to know is, of all the things you can think of, what don't you most like about the city?" We must have all looked quite blank, for he added hastily, "What I mean to say is, what do you dislike most about the city? Surely there must be something."

Red muttered something under his breath about the park commissioner and the little man wrote it down quite accurately, even putting down Red's correct given name. He turned to me and I shrugged my shoulders. Bede shook her head.

"Oh, come on, now, there must be something you don't like." He turned to Al, who was standing impatiently. "Don't you have something?"

"I certainly do. These damn pigeons."

A broad smile lit the man's face. "Ah, yes. They are way ahead. You would like to see the city free of pigeons, would you?"

"I most certainly would," agreed Al.

"Yeah," Bed said, "let's start a Get-Rid-of-the-Pigeons campaign."

"I take it then that you agree with your friend?" Bede nodded. "And you?"

I thought about it a moment. "You say a lot of people would like to see the place free of pigeons?"

"Yes."

"Well, don't add my name to the list. Just call me, uh, uncommitted. Yes, uncommitted."

"Well, maybe we can do something about it. Thank you. Good day."

He continued on to the next group of people and Al turned to Bede and me. "Boy, what a weirdo."

"Yes, doll." (That was Bede, not me.)

"What did you think of him, Red?" Red was busy sketching. "Red?"

"Huh?"

"What did you think of that guy?"

"In the green? Very interesting, very interesting."

I looked over his shoulder to see what he was sketching—a very strangely dressed little man.

)OOO(

A few days later we were back at the fountain—Red was sketching as usual, Bede was...well, anyway, it wasn't much different. Al was still complaining about the pigeons.

"I wonder if that guy really meant what he said about getting rid of them?" I asked.

"That guy in the green the other day? Hell, no. He was some kind of a crackpot. Don't you think so, Red?"

Red looked down loftily. He was having trouble getting absorbed in his work. "I hope so. It might not prove an unmixed blessing."

"What do you mean? Tell me one good thing that the pigeons do. Just one."

"Well, they eat bread crumbs for one thing, " I interposed.

"I'm serious, Will. You can't name me one really important thing, because they don't serve any purpose. They're useless. Life would be a lot better in this miserable city if they weren't around."

Red looked down at Al with something close to annoyance. "Well, if they do any good, we'd certainly know it if they left. But, seeing as how there's not much chance of that, you'll just have to learn to live with them, Al baby."

It was Bede, absorbed in her sandal sailboats, who first heard it. "Hey fellas, do you hear music?"

When she mentioned it, I realized that I had been hearing it for several minutes.

"Hey, yeah," said Al. "Somebody's playing a flute."

"Or a piccolo or a recorder," I amended.

"It's a pipe," Red informed us tonelessly.

"Yeah," agreed Al. "We know it's a pipe. What we want to know is what kind of pipe it is."

Red looked down at him scornfully. "It's a Pan's-pipe."

"Hey you guys, shut up!" I said. "Listen!"

Everyone in the Square was aware of the pipes now and it was difficult to hear the piquant melody over the babel of querulous voices.

"Don't you hear something else?" I asked.

"Yeah. Hey! It sounds like a herd of elephants," Al said.

"Or buffalo," added Bede.

Red took a deep draw on his pipe, closed his sketch book, and stood up. As he glanced up at the sky, the pipe almost fell out of his mouth. He was as excited as I had ever seen him: down Fifth Avenue, over the Arch, was a black shifting funnel.

"Run," I cried. "It's a tornado!"

"That's not tornado," Red said quietly. "It's birds."

"It's a bunch of friggin' pigeons!" Al yelled.

"It's that little green man!" Bede screamed.

He was marching down the middle of Fifth Avenue playing on his pipe and the birds were following him. I realized that the Square was empty of pigeons. A few forlorn English sparrows were sitting on the ground, chirping bewilderedly, and there were a number of other birds flying around the funnel of pigeons, as if trying to lure their comrades away, but the pigeons ignored their strident cries and those of the crowd of people who were following the piper.

The little man circled once around the fountain, waving to us for a moment, then continued on down West Broadway, his retinue of birds and curious people trailing. We watched dumbfounded as the birds began to dwindle and disappear behind the buildings of the Village until Al finally broke the silence.

"Well, Red, it looks like I won't have to learn to live with them after all." He had a very broad grin on his face. "It looks like somebody finally figured out a way to get rid of them pesky pigeons, pardner." Red wasn't listening. He was looking at the rapidly disappearing cloud and his brow was furrowed. Al nudged our apartment mate. "What do you say, Red?"

Red looked slowly down. This time there was nothing of amusement, anger, or disdain in his look. "I'm worried, Al. And, if you remember your fairy tales, you'll be worried too. "

Al snorted.

)OOO(

When I returned from class a couple of days later, I discovered Al looking disconsolately out the window.

"Hi," I greeted him, trying carefully to be neither too cheerful nor too glum. "Where's Brigitte?"

"Huh?"

"Bede. Where's the beautiful mistress of Usher Hall?"

"Oh. She walked out on me."

Bede walked out on Al average of twice a week. "Where's Red?"

"Who knows?"

Our bearded apartment mate could be anywhere from Astoria to the Bronx. He could have been in the kitchen, for that matter, and Al, in the mood he was in, would not have known it.

I had almost run the length of my opening conversational gambits. "Why did Bede run out on you?"

"It's those damn pigeons."

"The pigeons? But they haven't been around for days. That little green man lured them all away."

"Yeah, I know." The smoldering burst into an open fire. "That's the bastard who's responsible for the whole damn mess. If it wasn't for him, the pigeons'd still be here and so would BEDE!"

"I don't understand. What do you mean?"

"Look, do you know where Bede's gone?" I shook my head. "She went home. She took a train to Paterson. And do you know why?" Obviously I did not. "Because she can't stand it, that's why. And I don't blame her one bit. It's unnatural; that's what it is."

I was beginning to comprehend vaguely what he was trying to say. "Now that you mention it, Al, I've been kind of uneasy about it myself."

"Uneasy?" Al exploded again. "Look, I walked all around the Square today for two hours and it just didn't seem the same. It was like a morgue; there were a few sparrows peeping and some kids shouting but, outside of that, it was dead silent."

Al was exaggerating of course but there was truth in what he was saying. We take many sounds for granted: the dull roar of traffic, running children, quiet conversations; all interweave until they become a meaningless rumble. The constant cooing of the pigeons and the roar of their wings in flight are among these noises and we didn't realize it until they were gone.

Al had whipped back to the window again in a rapid movement that told me he had no desire to talk any more. I went into the kitchen to begin making our supper: tonight it would be canned beans and frankfurters instead of one of Bede's exotic, if sometimes inedible, meals.

It took me five minutes to maneuver a can into an open position but thereafter things went smoother and I had the beans simmering by the time Red crept up the back stairway.

"Where's Al?"

"Last I saw of him he was staring out the window."

Red looked at me for a moment, as if he had not comprehended what I had just said. "That's what he was doing when I left this morning."

"Were you here when Bede left?"

"No. They went for a walk together just after you left for class, and Al came home alone."

"Do you know what's the matter with him?"

"The same thing that's wrong with the rest of us." I accepted that as a simple explanation without comprehending its full meaning. "Have you seen a paper today?" Red waved practically every New York daily in my face. I shook my head and went back to preparing supper. Red laid the Times out on the table and pointed to a box on the front page in the lower corner. The headline read: ORNITHOLOGISTS PUZZLED OVER SUDDEN DISAPPEARANCE OF GOTHAM PIGEONS.

I laughed. "We could tell them the answer to that."

"Read it."

Underneath was a secondary headline: Sociologists Blame Pigeons. "The disappearance of Manhattan's pigeons several days ago has not proved to be an unmixed blessing. Although many of the city's residents and workers hailed the disappearance, members of the city's cleaning department have found a great deal of debris still remaining. As street sweeper Ben Heath said, 'I didn't realize them pigeons were such good vacuum cleaners.'

"Assistant Park commissioner Milton Newbolt has had park cleaning crews working overtime in an attempt to remove the extra trash, which is composed primarily of decaying food. Mr. Newbolt is afraid that if an attempt is not made to keep the streets and parks clean that the decaying organic matter will become a menace to the public health.

"The disappearance of the pigeons has yet to be explained. Ornithologists at the Museum of Natural History have been unable to discover any cause for it. According to Camille Day, head ornithologist, the pigeons have only quarantined Manhattan island. The pigeons are still to be seen in Brooklyn, the Bronx, and the other boroughs as well as all other cities in the United States. There has been no detectable increase in other pigeons populations.

"The disappearance of the pigeons has saddened many park visitors, those who enjoyed feeding their feathered friends. Such a man is Franz Dalbey, worried about his poor friends, who he is afraid are going to starve. Many such people have had a very important daily ritual taken from their lives.

"But, according to Dr. Sigismund Scott, a Park Avenue psychiatrist, it is not only the pigeon feeders and park maintenance crews who have been affected by the birds' mysterious disappearance. 'It affects us all,' said Dr. Scott. 'People need an outlet for their frustrations, a goat to blame it on when they do something wrong. The pigeons have provided this outlet. How often have you heard people complaining about the pigeons? Now, with the pigeons gone, people have to either find a new object to take their frustrations out on or realize that their shortcomings are inside themselves. This is not always easy.'"

I chuckled. "Yeah, that's pretty good."

"Look, it doesn't say a damn thing about that little green man."

"Well, maybe they didn't see him."

"Look, you know as well as I do that at least hundreds of people saw him come down Fifth Avenue. And if they didn't see *him*, how could they miss seeing that mass of pigeons in the air above him?" Red was serious. "Look, *you* remember him, don't you?"

"Of course."

"And Al?"

"Sure. We were just talking about him an hour or so ago. Al said he didn't want to hear anything about him."

"What about Bede?"

"Gee, I don't know. Al said she's gone home to New Jersey."

"New Jersey? Why?"

"I don't know. Something about not being able to stand the city without any pigeons."

"Yes, it all fits. Don't you see how it all fits?" I shook my head uncertainly. "Look, let's go for a walk."

"But supper..."

"Oh, bull! You can heat up the beans when we come home."

)OOO(

"Do you notice any difference?"

"Well, now that you and Al and the newspapers have brought it to my attention, I realize that I don't hear any pigeons cooing or wings flapping."

"That's a beginning. Is there anything else you don't hear?"

I listened carefully. The only sounds were the ceaseless roar of the city traffic and the wind whispering through the fire escapes.

"No one's talking!"

"Right!" Red whispered exultantly. "It's as if the whole city is cowed—there aren't even any children playing."

"But people have to talk!"

"Yes, they do." We turned into a residential street. "Listen."

For a moment there was that same silence then a strident voice cried out, "Don't shout at me!"

"I wasn't shouting at you! For Chrissake, can't I have a little peace around here?"

It was a catalyst—suddenly we were surrounded by shouting men and women, their phantom voices rippling out from the windows.

"You see? People aren't just talking—they're arguing, shouting, complaining. But when they're where pigeons ought to be and aren't, they're silent and scared, awed even. You didn't foresee this, did you? Not any of you!" The anger in his voice surprised me. "Did you?"

"Not exactly. But I didn't want to jump into it like the rest of you."

"Come on." Red led me to one of the ice cream vendors in the Square. "You were here the other day when the birds left, weren't you?" Red asked.

"What birds?"

"The pigeons. Don't you remember when they came flying down Fifth Avenue, through the park, and out to Brooklyn?"

"Mister, you must be off your nut. I ain't seen no pigeons for a long time and I ain't seen them flyin' off to Brooklyn. And I been here every day since last Thursday."

We talked to all the vendors in the park and the answers were the same.

"You see? Nobody remembers. Nobody but us. Surely out of all these peddlers, one of them must have been here when the pigeons flew the coop."

)OOO(

When we returned to the apartment, Al was gone. We ate in silence—I was too confused to say anything and Red was lost in musings of his own. We left a couple of hot dogs and some of the beans for Al, and I went to the front room to study while Red went to his studio to paint and think.

I was working over my theme for Advanced Compositional Studies when the door opened carefully and Al peered in. He looked at me and whispered, "Where's Red?"

"In there." I motioned to his studio.

"Shh. Not so loud. I don't want him to know I'm here. Come on. I want to show you something."

I was beginning to become accustomed to whispers and bizarre invitations and lack of explanations, so I followed Al for several blocks in silence until he stopped in front of an ancient building with the white crosses of destruction in its windows. "It's cruel, that's what it is," he informed me as he started climbing the fire escape.

"Hey, wait! What the hell are you up to?"

"Shh. Not so loud! Come on. I want to show you something."

I leapt for the overhanging ladder and followed him to the top floor. "There!" He pointed his finger at something in the darkness on the cement ledge of the building.

I leaned over and in the waning light of dusk I saw a scraggly conglomeration of sticks and feathers that held three dead squabs.

"Yeah. That's too bad. What about it?"

"What about it"? It's Red's fault, that's what about it."

"Now wait a minute, buddy boy. As I remember, it was you who wanted to see the city rid of pigeons."

"Me? I never said no such thing."

"What do you mean? Don't you remember when that little green man came into the Square?"

"Little green man? Have you flipped your wig?"

Our argument was interrupted by an imperious voice. "Hey, you two, what are you doing up there? Get down here immediately."

"Christ, it's a cop. How the hell can we get out of here, Al?"

"Get out of here? I'm going to show him this. It's a disgrace and the police ought to do something about it." Gingerly he picked the nest up off the ledge.

"Are you coming down or not?"

"Coming, officer," Al yelled.

As we neared the bottom of the escape, the policeman yelled, "What's that you've got in your arms?"

"You'll see. You go first," Al said to me, "and I'll throw it down to you."

The officer watched us warily and he twitched as Al threw the nest to me. "What is that thing?"

Al took it from my arms and walked over to the policeman. "It's a nest."

"A nest? What are you, some kind of nut?"

"Look at that, officer. Don't you think it's a disgrace that the city would allow this to happen?"

The policeman looked at the dead pigeons. "What are they?"

"They're pigeons. I bet there are millions of them, all over the city—maybe some of them are still alive, if we can get to them in time."

The officer scratched his head. "It's sure a shame, all right. Is that what you were up on that fire escape for?" Al nodded. "Well, I can't do nothing about it. Go see the mayor or something. But don't let me catch you on that fire escape again."

After he left, Al threw the nest with its pitiful burden into a trash can and muttered "That dumb oaf!"

"What are you going to do now?"

"What can I do? Nothing. So I'm going to go live with Bede's folks in New Jersey. If you think I'm going to stay here while it's like this, you're out of your mind."

"But what about your classes?"

"To hell with my classes."

As we turned the corner, I bumped into Red. "Hey, where have you guys been? I've been looking all over for you." I started to explain but he interrupted. "Never mind. Come with me."

He started racing toward the Square and I followed him. Al just kept walking toward the apartment. When we reached the Square I saw the reason for Red's excitement—our little green friend was in the strangely vacant park.

"Hey, what's he doing back here?"

"That's what we're going to find out."

As we started walking toward him, the little man turned around and saw us. "What has happened? What went wrong? I thought that if I got rid of the pigeons for you, everyone would be happy."

"No, my little friend, it's turned out just the other way."

"But I don't understand."

"It seems that human beings need some kind of a scapegoat for their own weaknesses and failings. The pigeons of the city have provided that until now, and people had come to depend on them.

The little man looked at Red uncomprehendingly then he slowly nodded his head. "Yes," he said sadly, "I think I understand. But isn't there something I can do?"

Red took a mental puff on the pipe he had left in the apartment. "No, I don't think there's anything."

"Thank you." The little man turned and walked toward the new student union building. As he turned the corner, about to disappear from our sight, he paused and waved at us, smiling wanly.

"What are we going to do now?" I asked Red.

Red shrugged his shoulders. "What can we do?"

Al was packing when we returned to the apartment. "I'm leaving," he said. "I'm going to see Bede in New Jersey. Is there anything else you'd like to know?"

"Yes. Why?"

"He's pigeon happy," I explained.

Red's answering smile was not unlike the one which the little man had given us. "We just saw the little green man," he told Al.

"What little green man?"

Shock rippled over Red's face and was replaced by an understanding. He helped Al pack.

)OOO(

"Well, it's like old times, isn't it?" Red said as we ate alone that night.

"He'll be back."

"I don't know. I don't want to make any predictions. At this moment I don't understand anything about the world, not the tiniest little thing."

There was a scream from the front room as the door burst open. "Hey, is anybody here? The pigeons are back! The pigeons are back!"

We followed an excited Al down the stairs and, even before we had reached the Square, we were aware of their cooings in the lofts and buildings of the Village. People were gaily chattering again and pointing, and the other birds had taken up the chants they had forgotten.

)OOO(

"Hey, Red, tell us about that little green man again," Al coaxed. I looked up, hoping that Red would comply—it's the best of Red's stories, so good that, when Red tells it, you could almost believe it had actually happened. But Red just stared into space, deliberately ignoring Al's request. It was Bede who looked loftily down at Al with a touch of amusement.

Just a Five-Dollar Man

The first time Warren Mitchell saw her was in the old Green Griffin coffeehouse in San Francisco in November of 1966, about eight months before the Summer of Love. He was watching the door as he played, checking out newcomers so he saw her as soon as she entered. She looked right at him and smiled. Warren had always thought the saying "a smile that lit up the room" was just a lot of hyperbole but it seemed to him that the room suddenly got brighter.

She immediately walked to the front of the tiny stage and stood there, as if appraising him. His fingers stumbled briefly then he looked away from her, unable to stand that knowing look. She nodded and walked back to the tables opposite the kitchen at the front of the coffeehouse, where Claymore was brewing more of his evil coffee.

Henderson, who was playing bass behind him, said, "She likes you, man."

Warren took that with a big ounce of doubt. Henderson was about six foot two and weighed a little over one-forty. He pursued women with the clumsy passion of a Russian wolfhound, slavering all over them until he had driven them into the arms of someone else. More than once, Warren himself had been that someone else. In fact, if it weren't for Henderson's puppy dog eagerness, Warren would have had no girlfriends at all.

There was smattering of applause from the smattering of an audience when he finished his butchering of Robert Johnson's "Terraplane Blues." But probably none of them had even heard of Robert Johnson, so it really didn't matter.

Warren saw Claymore, in the kitchen, hold up a finger to indicate that he was only to do one more song.

"I'd like to finish my set tonight with an original."

Henderson looked at him questioningly.

"But stick around if you really want to hear the blues. Rick van Damm will be up in about twenty minutes and he'll give you the real thing." Warren then launched into "Hey There Pretty Mama," in which he tried to cajole a woman in the audience into going out on the road with him. It had never worked in the past and it probably wouldn't work this time either. Nevertheless he sang most of the song at the chick who had just come in.

He stepped down from the stage and began putting his guitar away as Claymore began passing the bucket around the audience.

"Hey, man," Henderson said. "Aren't you going over and talk to her?"

"Who?"

"You know who, man. If you ain't gonna do nothing, I sure will."

Warren shrugged. He wouldn't know what to say to her and he didn't want to look as clumsy and awkward as Henderson did. "Go ahead."

Henderson shook his head. "You're crazy, man." He walked over to the chick's table.

"What's shakin', Warren?" Rick van Damm had been sitting at a side table.

"Oh, Henderson's got the hots for a chick who just came in."

"Henderson's got the hots for anything that's female and walks on two legs. And he'd probably settle for one in a pinch. You're talkin' about the one that just came in? What's with her?"

Warren sat down across the table from Rick. "I don't know. Never saw her before. As far as I know, she's new in town."

Rick nodded very slightly. Like Henderson, he had a beard, but Rick's was neatly trimmed. "Mind if I tune my guitar while you talk?"

"There's nothing to talk about. When are you goin' to show me that Lightnin' Hopkins riff?"

"Come on over tomorrow afternoon. You put on a good show tonight, Warren. You might be playin' at the Avalon soon."

"Right. Me and the Beatles. You haven't played the Avalon yet. So why would they want me?"

"Different strokes for different folks. And them folks don't care for my strokes. But I think they'll dig you."

"I ain't holdin' my breath." Warren took out a cigarette and lit it.

"Those things'll kill you, man."

"Not for a long while. And I plan to die of something else first."

Rick winced at the sound of his B string. It was nearly a full half-step off. He began cranking the peg. "Damn things. I don't know what it is about B strings."

Claymore left the bucket on the table in front of Warren. "Not a bad haul," he said as Warren took out a bunch of ones and a handful of change.

Warren looked over to where Henderson was trying to put moves on the chick. She was smiling but it wasn't the hundred watt beam she had turned on when she had entered the Green Griffin. For a moment, her gaze flicked over Henderson's shoulder and met Warren's stare, and the full smile flashed briefly.

"What's the matter?" Rick asked.

"Huh?"

"You seemed to be off in the ozone somewhere, man."

"Oh, nothing. Just thinking."

Rick glanced over in the chick's direction. "Uh-huh." He played an E chord and stopped to tweak the G-string. "Henderson doesn't seem to be doing too well with the lady."

"Really? She was smiling at him."

Rick smiled. "I thought so." He played a few chords and arpeggios then put his guitar down. "Come on, I'll buy you a cup of espresso."

"Buy me a cup? Coffee's always free for the performers."

"I didn't say a cup of Claymore's swill. I said espresso. Come on." Van Damm set his guitar down and began walking toward the counter. As he approached the table where Henderson and the young woman were sitting, he said, "Nice going, Henderson. You're getting pretty good."

"Really?" Henderson smiled broadly at the compliment. "You want me to play with you?"

Van Damm put his hand on Henderson's shoulder. "I didn't say you were that good yet." He looked over at the young lady. "Did you enjoy it?"

"I just got here," she said. "But what I heard, I liked."

Rick reached his hand over to her. "I'm Rick Van Damm. And your name?"

"Samantha."

"Sounds like something out of a Bing Crosby movie."

"Wait'll you hear Rick," Warren said. "He really plays the blues."

"Are you learning from him?" she asked, smiling brightly again at Warren.

"As much as I can."

"Then I'll have to pay attention. I definitely would like to know who your influences are."

"Well..."

Van Damm pulled up a chair and sat down. "You're new in town?"

"Uh-huh." She suddenly seemed nervous.

"Relax," Rick said. "I'm only gonna be here a few minutes." He motioned toward the stage with his head. "I've got to go to work." He looked toward the counter. "Claymore! Two espressos. Put it on my tab."

"When are you gonna pay that bloody tab?"

"As soon as you pass the bucket." He turned back to the young woman. "I hope you like espresso."

"I don't know. I've never had it."

"Really?" Rick raised one eyebrow, a trick Warren wished he could learn. "You must have come from another century then."

Samantha looked startled. "I... I guess you could say that. Yes. Yes. You could."

Rick looked at her a moment. "A small town girl then. Iowa. Nebraska. Where people still live in the Nineteenth Century."

"Something like that."

Rick got up. "Well, I've got to go entertain the multitudes. I hope you and Warren enjoy your espresso."

"Hey," Henderson said. "I thought that was for me."

"Since when have I ever bought you anything?" Rick turned and headed back toward the small stage.

Samantha turned to Warren. "I'm really very pleased to meet you, Mr. Mitchell."

"Warren. Please."

"Yes, of course. I really liked what I heard... I mean, the little I heard tonight, that is. I'd like to hear more. Soon."

"Well, I'm here every Monday and Thursday. And usually at the open mike on Sunday night."

"I'm here then too," Henderson said. "Anyone who wants to have bass behind them."

Warren got up. "Excuse me, but I always like to watch Rick up close. Sometimes I can figure out what he's doing."

"I'll come with you. Don't forget your espresso."

)OOO(

Even this far away from Haight and Ashbury, the streets were alive with people in gaily-colored clothes when Warren and Rick and Samantha left the Green Griffin.

"Now I think I understand," she said.

"Understand what?" Rick asked.

"Where Warren got... I mean..."

"Yes?" Warren prompted.

"Well, I can see the influence that Rick's had on you."

"After one song?"

"Two songs. That last one. That's one of yours, isn't it?"

"Yes. How did you know?"

She smiled. "I'm psychic."

Rick gestured around them. "Half the women within ten blocks of here think they're psychic."

They continued down the street for two blocks then stopped at a corner. "I'll see you tomorrow afternoon then, Warren?" Rick asked.

"Tomorrow?" Warren asked dumbly.

"Right. Lightnin' Hopkins. Remember?" Rick was smiling broadly.

"Oh, yeah, yeah. Lightnin'. Sure. Three o'clock okay?"

"Fine. See you then." Rick tipped an imaginary hat. "Nice meeting you, Miss Samantha," he said, in a broad parody of a Southern accent. "Hope to see you again. Soon."

She smiled brightly. "I hope so too."

As Rick walked away, Warren turned to Samantha. "Uh, do you have a place to stay tonight?"

"Not yet."

"Would you like to crash at my place?"

"I thought you'd never ask." She put her hand in his, and Warren thought he would fly all the way home.

She didn't stay long, though. A few days later, she said, "I've got to do some research."

"Research?"

"You know. Look some things up."

"Like what?"

"Oh, nothing much. People. People you haven't heard of, at least not yet. Maybe someday you will."

"Hey, I'm not just a dumb musician, you know."

"I didn't mean... Look, I'm sorry, Warren. I'll be back. I promise. But this is pretty esoteric stuff, you know? Like biogenetics."

"Bio what?"

"You see? It's edge of the world stuff. You don't need to know about it. All you need to do is play."

"But..."

"I'll be back. I promise."

There was some yelling back and forth, mostly from Warren, and some making up but, in the end, she was gone and Warren was alone again. But this hurt more than any of the other women he had been involved with.

"It's like she took a piece of my soul away with her. It hurts, Rick, it hurts."

Rick closed his eyes, took a drag from the joint, and passed it to Warren. "Yeah. I know."

"Do you? Do you, really?"

Rick opened his eyes and looked straight at Warren. "Yeah. There's always someone who'll take away a part of you that you never knew was there until she took it."

For the first time, Warren saw the pain in Rick's eyes. "That's why you sing the blues."

"That's why anyone sings the blues. You know what the blues is, Warren?"

"Well, yeah. I mean, you've showed me how to play them."

"I've showed you the mechanics, Warren, but the blues comes from inside. 'The blues ain't nothin' but a ten-dollar woman and a five-dollar man.' Patrick Sky. You know what I'm sayin', boy?"

"I'm not sure. It doesn't sound good. It doesn't sound right."

"The blues is women, Warren. Can't live without 'em and can't live with 'em."

"I'm going to miss her, Rick. It hurts. It hurts bad."

Rick shook his head and smiled ruefully. "Yeah. I know."

)OOO(

Warren didn't see her again for nearly two years. By then, he'd gone through Ledbetter, McTell, and Sonny Boy Number One, and was working his way through McGhee and Terry. He scratched out a living from one town to another, having no fixed address, playing with some people who made his days at the Green Griffin look like primo Hopkins and others who would've played Rick Van Damm into the ground in fifteen seconds flat. There were some harp players who could've doubled for Sonny Boy, bassists, fiddlers, and mandolin players. Once he even played with an accordion player. The money was just as good as the money he got for the blues and there was quite a bit more of it. But that lasted for one night in a Polish park outside Seymour, Connecticut, and he was back on the road again.

Now he found himself in a blues house in the nowhere land of Iowa, somewhere on the outskirts of Dubuque. Although the bar was packed and the cigarette haze was thick as Los Angeles smog, only a few people were listening to him and he had already given up trying to cut through the constant chatter.

Despite the dim lighting, he had no problem spotting her the minute she walked in the door. She flashed him a quick but uncertain smile. He could swear she was wearing the same clothes she had worn the day he had left her, as though no time had passed from when she had walked out on him until she walked into this blues house.

He quickly finished his song and started up "Hey There Pretty Mama." He hadn't played it since she had left San Francisco and all that he'd learned since went out the door, and he played as simply and as poorly as he had then, worse even, because he kept stumbling as he tried to remember how the chords and the words went. No one appeared to notice the sudden downshift in manual dexterity, not even the handful who seemed to be listening to him.

When he finished, he put the guitar in its stand and stepped down from the tiny stage to a smattering of applause.

"I told you I'd be back," she said as he sat down opposite her.

"You ain't back. This ain't San Francisco."

"But it's where you are, and that's all that's important." She pushed her beer towards him and he took a drink from it. It tasted good and it was nearly half gone by the time he put it down.

"Where have you been?" he asked.

"Waiting for you to get here."

Warren rested his face and knuckled his eyes for a moment. "You're still giving cryptic answers, aren't you?"

"I can't tell you the truth, Warren. If I did, it would ruin everything."

He looked at her for a long moment before letting out a heavy sigh. It worked on a lot of women but of course it didn't work on Samantha. It never had.

"Try me. Don't you think maybe you owe it to me? Let *me* decide whether or not it ruins anything."

She took his hand. "Warren, if I had stayed with you, where do you think you'd be now?"

He looked around. "I don't know. But probably not in this dump."

"This dump is a good place for you to be right now."

She got up and Warren immediately got up too, the chair clattering to the floor behind him.

"Where are you going?"

"I don't know, Warren, but I'll be back. I promise you that. I'll always be back."

"Wait. I love you, Samantha. I mean that. I do."

She smiled sadly. "I know you do. I know that more than you could possibly understand. But I also know that I'm not good for you. You'll accomplish a lot more without me around all the time."

Warren started to follow her but the manager stopped him. "It's time for your next set. Get up there."

The blues poured out of him, raw and untamed, his voice filled with anger and hurt, betrayal and sorrow. His fingers, trained by many hours of practice, found the notes easily, bent the strings, slurring and sliding. The bar became nearly silent. Occasionally there'd be the clink of a bottle or glass, murmured comments. If someone dared to raise their voice, they were soon silenced by those around them. At the end of each song, there would be silence for a moment then the applause would thunder out. From time to time, someone would set a bottle or a glass of whiskey in front of Warren on the floor of the stage.

At last he sat there, drained, holding his guitar limply, not knowing what to do next, barely aware of where he was. No one in the audience approached him. Some left the bar; others turned to resume their conversations, softly at first then getting louder until the bar was back to normal.

An old man approached him, wiry, his face full of deep seams. He handed Warren a glass of whiskey. "Here, boy. You've earned this."

Warren tried to smile at him but the smile went only so far. It never reached his eyes. "Thanks."

The whiskey went down smooth and easy. It was probably the finest brand in the house.

)OOO(

Word spread and, even though he never approached the power of that one night, enough bitterness and hurt remained that his performances were still strong enough to hold most of his barroom audience. He was held over for another week and he immediately got another gig in Cleveland then one in Memphis until finally he found himself playing in a smoky blues club in Manhattan's Bowery, where he nervously mounted the stage where so many blues legends had performed before him. His first set that night was the worst he had done since his first nights in Dubuque and the audience, primed to hear another incipient legend, soon grew bored. Depressed and angry, his next set brought them back and he continued to build. Several small blues labels vied to record him.

And from there it snowballed, until he found himself no longer playing in clubs and high school auditoriums. He played in concert halls and stadiums, he played with some of the legends, and he amassed a retinue of agents, hairdressers, and hangers-on, until the pain and anger and hurt were covered over and became a rarely-felt ache.

Inevitably, the audiences turned against him and he began the long slide back down to clubs and bars, where Samantha showed up for the third time. The years had been far kinder to her than they had been to him. His face was lined and seamed and creased in a dozen places; his voice was hoarse from thousands of shots of whiskey and thousands of cigarettes. She, on the other hand, looked as she hadn't aged a single day.

"Go away."

She reached out to touch him and he moved away.

"Have I treated you so badly?"

He looked up at her. In the bar mirror behind her was a face that was lean, nearly haggard, a face that had been shaped by life until now he closely resembled many bluesmen who had gone before him.

He looked at her steadily for a long time before he finally said, "You left me."

"I had to."

"Why?"

For the first time that he could remember, she turned her face away from him. "I can't tell you. I wish I could."

"Then we have nothing to talk about."

"Warren, if I'd stayed with you, you wouldn't be where you are now."

The twisted grin said what he thought of where he was now.

"You needed to grow and I would've held you back. You couldn't see it. I don't think you can see it now. But it was clear to me and it was clear to Rick."

"Rick." Warren hadn't thought of him for years. "I wonder what happened to him."

"Do you want to know?"

"You know?" For the first time in their conversation, he showed an emotion other than bitterness.

"He's married with two kids and teaches in a high school where he also conducts band practice."

"Rick? Band practice?"

She nodded.

"Tubas? Bass drums? Halftime shows at high school football games?"

"All of that."

"Rick? I can't believe it. Not Rick. Why, he was practically a god to me."

"Even gods have to make a living, Warren."

"Are you saying that would have happened to me if we'd stayed together?"

"Maybe not that. Maybe something else. But I don't think you'd still be playing music. Not like you do now."

Again, Warren looked at the room around him. "Like I do now?" He looked down at his hands. "No. What I do now..." He put one elbow up on the table and placed his forehead in his hand. "Christ, I've lost it, Sam. It's gone. I threw it all away." He now had both hands on his forehead, the heels of the hands rubbing his eyes.

She reached out to touch him. "No, Warren, you haven't lost it. Not yet. It's still there. You just have to reach into yourself and find it again, pick up the pieces and start over again. You can do it. I know you can."

"How do you do it, Sam? How the hell do you find me in these places just when it seems I most need someone like you?"

She was quiet a moment. "It's not that difficult. You leave traces. Anybody who wanted to find you wouldn't have any trouble at all."

He smiled weakly. "I guess nobody wants to find me then. Can't say that I blame them."

She took both of his hands in hers and he marveled at how anything so small could have so much power and strength.

"Stop feeling sorry for yourself, Warren. You haven't lost anything yet. Just think of this as..."

"Experience. Yeah. I know." There was bitterness in his voice. He slammed his fist into the table. "Damn."

"Warren..."

He pulled away from her. "I've wasted so much fucking time."

"Maybe you needed to."

He looked at her, his eyes seeming to bore holes in her. "You know, Sam, what I've been through... it's just a drop in the bucket compared to what those old-time blues guys went through. You know that, don't you?"

"Is that what you're trying to do? Live *their* experience? You can't do it. It's a different time and you're not them. And a lot of them had it pretty good, as I remember."

"Yeah. When they were too old for it to do them much good."

"And they remembered their youth as a good time. They didn't try to kill themselves with alcohol."

Warren buried his face in his hands again. "But I'm not young any more. I'm nearly forty."

She took his hands back in hers. "That's not exactly old either."

)OOOC

They spent the next week together. Samantha was right. Once he had dried out, most of his ability came back. When his gig at the bar was over, he had two weeks before the next one, in Eugene, Oregon.

"I ought to tell them to go to hell," he said.

"Don't," she said.

"Why not?"

"If you're going to make a comeback, Warren, you'll have to start here, where you are now. You can't very well make a comeback at the top, can you?"

He grinned. "I'm not going to make a comeback."

"No?" There was concern in her eyes.

"No. I'm just going to have fun, like it used to be. It's become work now, just a job, like digging ditches or working in a steel factory. It's what we weren't going to do when we started out." He paused then said in a near-whisper, "So long ago."

She smiled but the concern was still in her eyes. "Good. You're right. That's what it should be. But you have to do that gig in Eugene."

"Why?"

She looked away from him, evading his eyes. "You have to, that's all. It's important."

"Eugene, Oregon, is important?"

She faced him again. "You never know what will happen." She placed both of her slim white hands over one of his brown and mottled ones. "You've got to start again somewhere, don't you? Why not Eugene? And you don't want to get the reputation of being undependable. If you make a commitment, you should keep it. That's all I'm saying."

Warren grinned. "Wow. That was quite a speech for you."

"It's important," she said firmly.

"Will *you* be there?"

She hesitated but finally said yes.

"*That*'s what's important. Okay. Let's go."

"Now? But you've got two weeks."

"I want to visit San Francisco first."

)OOO(

It was a disappointment. It had been many years since Warren had been there and there was nothing left from those wonderful days. Franchised coffee shops and fresh-faced college students walking the streets, most of them probably not even knowing what had gone down here so many years ago. Bland female singers and rap music blared from the speakers outside a CD store. The Green Griffin was boarded over, with used needles and other trash in the narrow alley alongside it.

Rick van Dam was living in a small town outside San Jose and seemed genuinely glad when Warren called, inviting them over and meeting them at the door.

"So you two are back together again, huh? It's good to see some things never change."

Rick had put on a lot of weight and was beginning to get bald. The goatee apparently was long in the past. Warren wondered if he would've recognized him if they'd met on the street.

Rick stopped them before they entered. "Uh, Warren, it's all right to reminisce about the past, especially the music. But, uh, don't talk about drugs, okay? I've got kids now."

Rick's wife was a pleasant nondescript woman, making Warren think of the wife in some Sixties TV sitcom. Bright and pleasant and totally forgettable. She seemed impressed to have Warren Mitchell in her home and their grammar-school age children enjoyed it when Rick and Warren played together after dinner.

Rick shook his head. "Man, Warren, you've gone way beyond me."

It seemed to Warren as if Rick had forgotten a lot but he said nothing about that. All he said was, "It's a lot easier when you do nothing but play music all day long."

"Yeah, I guess. You have no idea what it's like in the... workaday world. I sure didn't. Boy, we sure had some dreams, though, didn't we?"

"We sure did."

)OOO(

They were quiet as they drove back to their motel in Warren's six-year-old car. Finally Samantha said, "What are you thinking?"

"I don't know. All kinds of things are running through my mind. Wishing I could go back to Haight-Ashbury twenty years ago and keep Rick from making this mistake."

"It didn't seem to me like he felt it was a mistake. He seemed pretty happy to me."

"Yeah. I guess. But it scares me, when I think of all of what I threw away. I blew it, Sam. I had it and I blew it."

"It isn't over yet, Warren."

"Yeah. I know. The fat lady hasn't sung yet."

"The fat lady?"

"You know. Yogi Berra, I think." But she didn't seem to know what he was talking about. "Christ, Sam, where have you been all these years?"

"I... I've been doing research."

"Right. You and your research."

)OOOC

His gig in Eugene was extended another week and, by the time it was over, Sam was gone again. It hurt but not as much as it had in the past. Warren had been half-expecting it.

The years flew by as he became a senior statesmen of the blues. His voice became harsher but that only added authenticity. His fingers eventually lost some of their dexterity but no one else seemed to mind. He learned to compensate for it by holding notes longer, letting one note do the work of three. "He only played one note," someone once said of another guitar player, "but it was the right note." Warren had learned to play the right notes.

Every once in a while he thought he saw a familiar face in the crowd but he was never able to reach her before she disappeared.

The final time he saw her, he was lying in a hospital, an old man who had seen much of the world. He'd like to see still more, learn more songs, but he was in many ways satisfied.

"Your granddaughter is here, Mr. Mitchell," the nurse said.

"My granddaughter?" As far as Warren knew, he had no daughters, much less any granddaughters.

But it was *her* again, looking as fresh and as young as she had more than fifty years earlier, wearing the same jeans, the same halter top, the same love beads.

"Hello, Warren," she said. "May I call you that?"

Why not? He had never seen her so tentative before, so unsure of herself. He nodded his head.

"I hope you don't mind that I masqueraded as your granddaughter."

He tried to nod his head yes but his muscles didn't seem to want to work that way. He settled for the only sound he could make, like he was clearing his throat.

"I just wanted you to know that you're not going to be forgotten, that you're going to be remembered for a long time." She took his wrinkled hand in both of hers and brought it up for a brief kiss. "I hope you don't mind."

He shook his head no again.

"It doesn't upset you?"

He tried to smile and settled for another shake.

"Good." She smiled at him then rummaged in her purse for a moment. He felt something as searing as ice against his forearm briefly. "It won't be long now," she said, as she took his hand in hers again. "You'll always be with me, Warren. I want you to know that."

The world began to slip away from him until all that was left was that warm, adoring smile. Then it too was gone forever.

Yours For the Future

The recent untimely death at the age of 98 of the great science fiction pioneer Isaac X. Greenback, the founder and sole editor of *Amazing Galactic Science Fiction and Analogous Fantasy Magazine,* was a blow to all of us, reader and fan alike. How well so many remember sitting on his knee while he told us stories of "Herbie" Wells and "Julie" Verne. The MassCons in his hometown of Yazoo Junction won't be the same without him.

In his effects were found a number of unmailed rejection slips which indicate how this great master of science fictional editing worked with and influenced so many of the great science fiction writers of our time. We would like to share with you some of the wisdom of Mr. Greenback found in these letters.

Dear Mr. Asimov:

Thank you very much for allowing me to have a look at your latest short story, "Nightfall." I enjoyed it very much but I'm afraid it is not for the readership of AGSF&AAF. We are not a market for anything in the style of the so-called "New Wave." Most of our readers are intimately involved in the scientific and engineering community and are interested in stories that revolve around technological ideas. Nor is there any reason to suspect anyone would enjoy a story that has no human beings in it.

From a logical point of view, it is hard to visualize a society that would evolve the high civilization portrayed in your story that would then fall apart simply because of a few minutes of darkness. On the other hand, your expertise in handling the concept of a world in the midst of a multiple star system is to be admired. If you could give me more such hard science in a future story, I would be most eager to give it serious consideration.

Yours for the future
Isaac X. Greenback, editor
Amazing Galactic Science Fiction
and Analogous Astounding Fantasy Magazine

Dear Mr. Leiber:

I have enjoyed all your recent submissions but I am afraid they are not right for AGSF&AAF. While we do like to publish a sword & sorcery story every now and then, we like ones with more believable characters. We like the s&s that appears in AGSF&AAF to be a little different from the run-of-the-mill s&s, with interesting characters. I think our readers would have a hard time identifying with rogues, thieves, and cutpurses, such as your Fahfrd (please, Mr. Leiber: characters with unpronounceable names do not an s&s story make) of the Gray Mouser (frankly, it sounds more like a cat than a human being). The names should be closer to reality, perhaps even suggesting some historical person. This is true even for place names: Cimmeria, for example, brings to mind Sumeria. But Nehwon, Mr. Leiber? It is a piece of nonsense, having no connotations inherent in the word, no references, no inferences. Please try to use names that have associational references.

Yours for the future
Isaac X. Greenback, editor
Amazing Galactic Science Fiction
and Analogous Astounding Fantasy Magazine

Dear Mr. Blish:

Please do not send me any more of your so-called "Okie" stories. The premise on which they are based is just too slim to sustain a short story, much less a full series. The very use of the term "Okie" is a good example thereof: such a term is part of our past; in the future a term such as "Terries" or "Earthies" might be used, but not such an archaic term as "Okies." The series also suffers from the lack of strong central character, but its most serious defect is the ludicrous terminology you choose. "Spindizzy," Mr. Blish? Indeed. Pseudogravitational warp generators perhaps or gravitic repellors. Bone up on your scientific terminology and leave such gibberish as "spindizzy" to the amateurs.

I also wish you would study up on your use of the language and the craft of writing. You are appalling in this area. It's a shame we don't have a good critic of science fiction whom you could learn from but you might start with Strunk's *Elements of Style*.

Yours for the future
Isaac X. Greenback, editor
Amazing Galactic Science Fiction
and Analogous Astounding Fantasy Magazine

Dear Mr. Bradbury:

Your novel, *The Martian Chronicles*, is just not for AGSF&AAF. Our readers are looking for strong, lusty, bigger-than-life heroes that they can identify with. Your characters are too weak, too insipid; they have no dimension. You should read more Burroughs and Wells, even (if I may go outside the bounds of science fiction) Melville. You could learn a lot from a book like *Moby Dick*. Your plot (which is nonexistent) needs a central character to revolve about; this is a series of bland and unexciting episodes, Mr. Bradbury, not a novel.

Give my readers flesh-and-blood human beings and real-life aliens they can sink their teeth into, and you will be rewarded with an avid following, perhaps even outside the science fiction field itself.

All things considered, I'm afraid I must pass this one up, but thanks for giving me a look.

Yours for the future

Isaac X. Greenback, editor

Amazing Galactic Science Fiction

and Analogous Astounding Fantasy Magazine

Dear Mr. Clarke:

I regret to inform you that your novel *Childhood's End* does not suit our present needs. What we are looking for here at AGSF&AAF are exciting stories of the future with realistic alien cultures. But, above all, we are looking for optimism fused with technological innovations, which I'm afraid is lacking in your novel. Your characterizations of human beings are quite good but you need to spend more time developing your science, so that your extrapolated backgrounds will be more real. Also, your view of the future of the human race, as expressed in this novel, is just too bleak for my taste.

Have you thought of writing for the movies?

Yours for the future

Isaac X. Greenback, editor

Amazing Galactic Science Fiction

and Analogous Astounding Fantasy Magazine

Dear Mr. Bester:

I'm afraid I am going to have to return *The Stars My Destination* to you. It's an interesting idea but one that's been done too many times, and you have brought no new insights to the concept of teleportation (not "jaunting," please, Mr. Bester). This Gullivern Foyle character is far too unbelievable and your method of developing his teleportative powers in a life-or-death situation is just too far-fetched. No scientist would *dare* use such an experimental method. Furthermore Foyle is not the type of person readers of AGSF&AAF are interested in; I need more heroic and cerebral characters. I could continue listing faults in your conception of a future civilization (the idea of the Scientific People, for example, is not only absurd but flies in the face of all science fictional tradition and is anti-scientific), the characters (caricatures, rather) you have drawn, and so on, but I think I have made my point.

Thank you for letting me see it however.

Yours for the future
Isaac X. Greenback, editor
Amazing Galactic Science Fiction
and Analogous Astounding Fantasy Magazine

Dear Mr. Heinlein:

I am returning your novel *Stranger in a Strange Land*, as I feel it is too improbable. A society where such a man as your Michael Valentine Smith could exert such an influence could not with any rationality exist. People are *rational*, Mr. Heinlein; they are not about to follow any so-called messiah, guru, or whatever, who comes over the horizon. And the communistic style of living portrayed could never become popular in America. Finally, the violent assassination of Mr. Smith that occurs in your novel could not happen to any public figure in today's America.

I'm sorry, Mr. Heinlein, but the whole novel is just too improbable. Please try me with your next, but keep your imagination within bounds.

Yours for the future
Isaac X. Greenback, editor
Amazing Galactic Science Fiction
and Analogous Astounding Fantasy Magazine

Dear Mr. Ellison:

I am returning your story "Repent, Harlequin! Said the Tick Tock Man" for obvious reasons. The title itself is absurd: a simple "The Harlequin" or "The Tick Tock Man" would have been sufficient. There is no need to insult the intelligence of my readers. However there is much more wrong with this story than a mere title. Its flaunting of properly-delegated authority is something I simply cannot condone, not even in a short story. It sets a bad example for my readers, many of who are young and impressionable. And the notion that a handful of jellybeans could bring technological machinery to a halt is utterly laughable.

On the plus side, the happy of the rehabilitation of the Harlequin shows that, if you view this story properly, it can be salvaged with severe reworking.

By the way, have you read any of the young writers coming out of England these days, such as Moorcock or Ballard? You could learn a lot from them, Mr. Ellison; they're the Wave of the future. Don't stick your hand in the sands of the past, as you have done with this story.

Yours for the future
Isaac X. Greenback, editor
Amazing Galactic Science Fiction

Dear Mr. Niven:

AGSF&AAF is not in the market for such "New Wave" writing as your novel *Ringworld*. My readers want good hard science writing, steeped in fact and current up-to-date cosmological theory. The idea of a so-called "black hole" at the center of the galaxy is ludicrous, to say the least and contradicts all the current cosmological theories that I am aware of. And the construction of your ringworld, while an interesting exercise in imagination, is just too far-fetched for me. I suggest you bone up on your astrophysics, Mr. Niven. A few classes at Caltech might be helpful.

Yours for the future
Isaac X. Greenback, editor
Amazing Galactic Science Fiction

Although Isacac X. Greenback is no longer with us in the flesh, he still lives in our hearts and dreams and, most importantly, in the work and words of the many writers he influenced. We have so much for which to be grateful to him.

Night on Old Baldy

Jim Garvin lay in the grass on the top of Old Baldy, watching the clouds floating by, making animals and castles out of them as he had as a child. Below him, the splendor of the North Carolina October mountains spread out in a crazy quilt of reds, oranges, browns, and yellows, with the occasional dark green of a pine for contrast. The small brown spire of the Methodist Church in Jim's home town of Jackdaw Valley was barely visible if you knew just where to look.

A hawk wheeled in the air over one of the other peaks and the scratching of autumn birds and their calls formed a muted background to Jim's musings. Far away a crow's cawing echoed over the valleys.

It had been well over ten years since Jim had been home during autumn. He had gone to college in September of his eighteenth year and that was followed by seven years of school, culminating in a Ph.D. in entomology, and then he had gone to work in a laboratory near the South Carolina coast. Other than summers and holidays, the only times he had been home were for his mother's funeral a few years earlier and that of his father only six months ago. But he had never been home in autumn before. He hadn't realized how much he had missed the cool brisk promise of the season until now. All his cares and worries seemed to have flown away like ghosts on the autumn breeze here on top of Old Baldy. Even his father's death seemed natural and inevitable and perfectly acceptable; his father had had a good life and he had known many mountain autumns.

At last the chill air of evening replaced the mere briskness of the autumn afternoon and drove Jim, sweaterless, back down the mountain, past the deserted mill pond at its base by the road, to his sister's home. The walk felt good and he was glad he had stopped off on his way back to the lab after the American Entomology Society meeting. But he wished that he didn't have to drive back the next day; he wished he could stay a little longer.

The jack o'lantern that Jim had made for Julie's children the night before was glowing in the window, barely visible in the still light of early evening. His niece and nephew, Dora and Donnie, met him at the door.

"Hurry up, Uncle Jim. We've been waiting dinner on you, and we can't go trick or treating until then."

Halloween, or Hallow's Eve, as they called it in Jackdaw Valley. What memories that brought back! After visiting all the houses in Jackdaw Valley, everyone would go to Dick McLeod's general store, where Dick would hold a jamboree with cold country cider, bobbing for crisp McIntosh apples, and prizes for the best costume, which Jim had never won. The children would scream and run and yell and play in their own age and neighborhood groups, while the womenfolk sat to one side, comparing their sewing and canning, and later the menfolk would go off somewhere till late at night, drinking and carousing. Jim had never gone off on those excursions because he had been too young and had left before he was of age. Now he was above such things, and that felt kind of sad. His hard-won sophistication seemed a sad replacement for the earthiness of country life.

After washing his hands, he sat down at the table with Julie, Dora, Donnie, and his brother-in-law, Marcus Whitfield. Although barely past thirty-five, Marcus already had the weathered look of a mountaineer, the seamed and leathery face, the thin gaunt body, the weariness in his pale blue eyes. His thick shock of pure white hair made him seem even older.

"Donnie," said Julie, "do you want to say grace tonight? And do it right, because this is Hallow's Eve, you know."

Donnie squirmed a bit then said, "Dear King of Grace, we thank you for our food and all the good things, for the beauty of the mountains, and we thank you for the deer and the rabbits and the corn and the squash. And thank you for the beautiful weather this evening. Amen." He said it in a toneless voice and didn't rush it but said each word clearly, knowing that his mother would make him say it over if he said it too fast.

As soon as everyone had said amen, Julie and Marcus began passing around the bowls on the table. There was late squash and yams, lima beans and corn, and, especially for Jim, Julie had taken some sweet venison steaks out of the freezer, which normally they would have held for Thanksgiving and Christmas. When Jim had protested, Marcus had said, "Nonsense, Jim. It's been a good year. They've extended the hunting season another week and allowed us to take two more deer. We'll have plenty this year."

The men of Jackadaw Valley, the Whitfields, the Garvins, the McLeods and the Evanses, always got their allotted number of deer each year and usually a few extra. The game warden was aware of their poaching but did little about it except to hint every now and then that he was aware of it, so they didn't overdo it. No one wanted to take on the families of Jackdaw Valley; they still told the story of the warden who had tried to arrest Gabe Whitfield and Tom Evans forty years earlier, who had been found drowned in the Yellowgage River while the entire Jackdaw Valley was having its Hallow's Eve jamboree. Since then, no one had challenged them and they had never taken more than they needed. Nor would they ever.

After dinner, Julie took the kids out in their costumes, while Jim and Marcus stayed home, smoking cigarettes over their coffee.

"You're coming down to the store with us later, aren't you?" Marcus asked.

Jim grinned. "Wouldn't miss it for the world. Things don't change much around here, do they?"

Marcus flicked an ash off the cigarette. "Not much. You ought to know better than that, Jim."

Jim shook his head. "I'm afraid I'm not part of the community any more, Marcus. I've been out in the outside world too much."

"You're still a Garvin."

Julie and the kids were back an hour later and they all went to the general store Tom McLeod had inherited from his father. All the forty-odd families that made up the town of Jackdaw Valley were there, most of them named Garvin, McLeod, Whitfield, or Evans.

The tall thin schoolmaster, a man by the name of Thorburn, his thick shock of red hair a distinct contrast to that of the other men, approached. "You're Jim Garvin, aren't you?"

Jim took the proffered hand and said yes.

"It's really odd seeing a stranger here."

"Jim's not a stranger," Marcus said quietly.

"Not to you. But he is to me. I'd like to talk to you sometime, if you don't mind, Mr. Garvin."

"Not at all. But I'm leaving tomorrow. What would you like to talk to me about?"

"I'd like to find out why you left Jackdaw Valley. There are so many good students here who should go to college but none of them want to leave, and I was hoping maybe you could help me."

"I'm afraid I don't have much time, and I don't see how I could help you, anyway."

"Just a few minutes. After the jamboree, perhaps."

Marcus put a broad mountaineer's hand on Jim's shoulder. "Jim's coming with the rest of the men after the jamboree, aren't you, Jim?"

Jim felt a strange thrill go through him, like a little boy going out for a smoke with the big boys for the first time. He grinned. "Sure. Of course. I've never been here for the doings after Hallow's Eve."

"We all know that," Jim said softly.

The schoolmaster had a strange look on his face. "I wish you wouldn't. I really need to talk to you."

"Why don't you come along then? We can talk wherever everybody else goes."

"I'm afraid not, Jim," Marcus said. "This has always been a family thing. You know that."

"But..."

"You're a Garvin, Jim. Don't forget that. I know your father wanted you to go away to college. Don't make him regret it."

Despite the fact that his father was dead and never again would regret anything, Jim felt a pang of remorse, as though he would have to face his father and tell him he'd let him down. He shrugged helplessly. "I'm sorry, Mr. Thorburn."

The look of pity on the schoolteacher's face puzzled him. "So am I, Mr. Garvin."

Instead of the sharp crisp cider he had tasted as a child, Jim was treated to Marshall Evans' homemade hard cider, and all the men were slightly tipsy when the jamboree broke up, although Jim was feeling it more than the others.

Old Al Whitfield, his white hair shining in the moonlight, clapped Jim on the shoulder. "Good to have you back, Jim. You've been gone too long." His pale blue eyes seemed to twinkle.

"I'm leaving tomorrow, Mr. Whitfield."

"That's all right. Come on. We're all set to go up to the mountain."

As Jim climbed into the back of Tom McLeod's pickup truck, he could still see Mr. Thorburn's red hair in the patch of women left behind, herding their children home as the jamboree broke up. The night air whistled past, fresh and invigorating, as the truck hit the highway out of town. Jim noticed several of the younger men in the truck with him, apparently going out on their first Hallow's Eve shindig with the men, their sandy hair waving in the wind like Jim's. He felt strangely at peace and at rest, as though he had been waiting all his life for this moment. The worries and problems of the laboratory seemed distant and inconsequential.

"Where are we going?" he asked at last.

"Old Baldy," said the man on his left, Ken Evans, whom Julie had played with when they were children. Julie had written Jim a couple of months earlier that Ken had lost his wife in childbirth. He wanted to say something, to offer condolences, but he could think of nothing to say. Perhaps it was just as well to say nothing and let the memories lie fallow, to be covered over and lost to memory.

How quickly the dead were forgotten. It seemed to Jim as if his own father, only six months dead, was already just a memory that had never really existed, as if he were only a ghost, a phantom, that soon would pass away into oblivion as if he had never been.

The night was clear as crystal when the truck stopped at the foot of Old Baldy. Other men climbed out of other trucks and started the long hike up the path, their hair almost aglow in the moonlight. Some of the men had banjos and guitars with them; Old Al Whitfield had his fiddle. It had been a long time since Jim had heard their music and he longed to hear Al's country fiddle again.

The moon was full and bright and Jim had little trouble following the path to the top of Old Baldy. It had been less than twelve hours since he had been up there earlier in the day but everything looked different now. Nothing looked familiar in that pale unearthly light. There was no wind, no calling birds, and the men were silent as they climbed the path. Jim wanted to say something to break the silence but the very idea seemed sacrilegious. He was still an outsider, despite what Marcus had said. He was no longer wholly a Garvin, no longer a resident of Jackdaw Valley. He didn't really belong with these men any longer; he was here only by an accident of blood. Yet, deep down at another level, he knew he belonged, and he felt at peace and at home.

The silence was so stifling it seemed that he scarcely drew a breath until they reached the top of Old Baldy. The world below them now was dark; not a glimmer of light penetrated the trees below them. Jim wondered about that; he could have sworn he had seen lights from Old Baldy when he had been up here during summer evenings as a teenager, and then the leafy screen was far more dense. But there were no more lights below them than there were words on Old Baldy.

Old Al Whitfield took out his fiddle and drew a long quavering note that reached up toward the moon. He was joined by a couple of banjos and two guitars, and soon four of the men were on the top of Old Baldy, solemnly dancing, their white hair flopping in the still air as the rest of the men stood around them in a circle, clapping in time to the music.

The full moon rose higher and higher, reaching toward the zenith, and the intensity of the music seemed to rise with it. Man after man got out and danced, one man retiring as another entered the circle. Like the three young men who were here on the mountain for the first time at a jamboree, Jim stayed on the outskirts, occasionally drinking from the jugs that were passed around, his amusement tempered by the solemn silence of the occasion. He felt the urge to join in but he was unable to figure out the cue by which one man would enter as another left.

Marcus Whitfield entered the dance, dancing to the music of his great-uncle's fiddle, his face calm and emotionless. He looked at Jim for a moment as though he were looking right through him, his pale eyes almost pupilless in the moonlight.

As the moon reached zenith, Jim thought he saw something in his peripheral vision. He turned to look but saw nothing. There was another flicker of movement at the edge of his sight, a pale white ghostly wisp of nothingness, perhaps just a wisp of cloud settling toward the mountain and the valley in the chill air of night catching an errant moonbeam. Other milky wisps were settling toward Old Baldy, rippling across the night sky like pale auroras, taking on cloudlike shapes in the night, castles and horses and dancing men and women. Several of the wisps drifted closer to the circle of men, whirling and spinning, almost human in their shapes.

Jim became aware that the banjos and guitars had stopped playing and that only Old Al Whitfield's fiddle was still playing, although it seemed to have been joined by a new instrument, one that wailed thinly like no instrument Jim had ever heard, a sound that cut through his flesh and bones like a sharp knife through soft butter.

There were other dancers in the circle now, their forms wavering and obscure, yet somehow familiar, that seemed to glow and flicker a pale blue, the color of cloud and mist glistening in the moonlight. He felt hands at his back and he was being pushed into the circle even as other men retreated. He felt his feet moving in rhythm to "The Crippled Kingfisher," as if they had an existence of their own. To his left, he saw one of the youngsters who was also up here for the first time, dancing smoothly.

There was a cold touch on Jim's shoulder and he turned to find his father opposite him, a wraith of cold pale blue flesh, a phantom from beyond the grave. There was a sadness in his father's cold dead eyes, now bulging from the skin that had drawn back, the flesh that was beginning to rot. His chin and cheeks were covered with a long ghostly stubble and his lips were drawn back in an involuntary death's-head grin. Behind the pale almost luminescent skin, Jim felt he could see the skull, the eye sockets, the nasal cavity.

His father's rotting hand was on his shoulder, a cold palpable presence that seemed to penetrate a centimeter or so into Jim's flesh but no further. There was no pressure, no yielding of flesh against flesh, just a presence, a cold and chilling presence.

Jim looked about wildly. He and the three youngsters who were also making their first men's jamboree on Old Baldy were the only ones in the circle, which seemed tighter than it had been when the other men were dancing. In the center of the circle with them were three silent specters, the ghosts of the three people had died in Jackdaw Valley since last Hallow's Eve: his father, one of the McLeod girls that Julie had told him had drowned, and Ken Evans' wife.

Jim could feel a larger, brooding presence beyond the circle, a dark misshaped demon that sat in the woods, a charcoal-gray satyr at the edge of the treeline where it was barely visible, drawing its darkness from the luminescence of the dead spirits.

The cold hands of his father turned Jim around and he found himself looking into those cold pale sad eyes. Then the cold palpable hands pulled him forward, pushing him toward the other wraiths. Their grave-clothes, their shrouds, hung on them like rotting rags, and their flesh, their luminescent flesh, seemed to hang on their bones as the clothes hung on their bodies. The McLeod girl, barely in her teens, once a young lively girl with flashing dark eyes of allure and mystery, was a glowing body with breasts that already were beginning to sag and flow. Her once-abundant hair was stringy and thin. She was an ugly hag with the decaying body of a teenager.

Like Ken Evans' wife, she was stripping off the remnants of her grave-clothes, even as the men in the circle stripped the clothes from two of the young men, and then the young men were enfolded by the wraiths, pulled to the ground, the grotesquerie of the action heightened by the mechanical zombie-like movements of the young men.

Jim felt hands at his clothes, the solid hands of everyday flesh, undressing him even as the third youngster began to copulate with the McLeod girl-wraith, seemingly supported in mid-air inches above the ground by the blue-white ghost.

He wanted to say no but the word died in his throat, strangled, would not come out past his lips. He wanted to fight his way free from Old Baldy but his limbs wouldn't obey.

His father seemed to want to say something to Jim but there were no words, just the sad mournful pale eyes, which tried to tell him that it was all right, that it was just something he had to go through, something his father had had to go through, that Jim's sons and grandsons would have to go through when their time came, all his descendants to the last tick of recorded time, but that it was all right, that it would all soon be over, just a dream, a fantasy, and that everything would be all right.

He looked about for Ken Evans, found him, and saw nothing in his face—not love nor hatred nor compassion nor anger—as Jim found himself pushed by both living and dead hands toward Ken's wife, found himself mounting her, the chill all over his body, reaching root-deep into him, pulling his entire being out and spreading it on the grass of Old Baldy.

And the dark shape at the edge of the woods seemed to grow larger, smiling darkly at the scene enacted in front of it.

From a far distance, Ken heard the crowing of a rooster, then another, and he found himself on the hard ground of Old Baldy. Solid material hands were helping him dress. The morning star was high in the still dark sky and the moon was on the western horizon.

Slowly, silently, sullenly, they trudged back down Old Baldy. When they reached the foot of the path, Jim walked over to the old mill pond and looked in. His eyes were the pale blue of the autumn haze, his hair as white as the first snow of winter, and there was an aching emptiness in his breast where his soul should have been.

A Shakespearean Incident

It was a dismal tour, but beggars can't be choosers: at least I had to fortune to be playing Hamlet. Me, a thirty-year-old bits-and-pieces actor, playing the indecisive teenager. Well, if Olivier could do it at sixty, I guess Erskine Callaway could do it at thirty.

I had just finished an off-off-Broadway spear-carrying role when my agent came up with this tour, sponsored by an educational foundation. They had rigged some kind of deal with Equity, as educational foundations will do, and, for each Equity member, there were three college drama students. And now we were stranded in East Hicksburg with half the troupe down with the flu.

Ed Stortz, our Claudius, had it the worst and was lying up in our grubby fleabag of a hotel, delirious with a hundred-and-two-degree temperature. The rest of us were staggering through rehearsal in the rundown old East Hicksburg Palladium.

"The show must go on," the director had said. He was a drama professor from some unknown university and he was full of platitudes. While the pros groaned, the college students cheered... and the show went on.

From somewhere in East Hicksburg, Bob Hantover came to take the part of Claudius. I had to admit that he wasn't half bad, better, in fact, than most of the pimply-faced students.

"Okay," Professor Kirchner said. "Let's take a ten-minute break then we'll do a dress run-through before dinner break."

After dinner break would be the real thing, if anything happening in East Hicksburg could be said to be real. Bob Hantover came over to talk to me. He was a tall, gangly fellow with parchment skin and fine white hair. His beak of a nose gave him a superficial resemblance to Olivier.

"Do you always have a full dress rehearsal at every place you stop?" he asked. "I should think you would have this thing down cold by now."

"I'm afraid so," I said. I jerked a thumb in Kirchner's direction. "The professor there thinks we have to get familiar with each new theatre, as if they're all drastically different."

"I see." Hantover smiled with easy camaraderie.

I have to admit he did have a noble profile, a good man to play our king, better even than Ed Stortz.

"I hope you don't mind my saying this," I said, "but you surprised me there."

"Oh? How?"

"You're a pretty good actor. I hadn't really expected it."

He smiled easily, not taking offence. "Oh, well, I've been doing this sort of thing for forty years now. I played Hamlet once here myself. Of course, it wasn't as professional a production as yours but we did pretty good."

"Did you ever try to make the professional stage?"

"No." He looked off into the rafters. "I wanted to once, but... but things just didn't work out."

"Something personal?" I asked, not really caring much.

"No, not really. Just marriage and the usual things. My wife wanted to stay here."

At that point, Kirchner came up and, insinuating between us, clapped us both on the shoulder. "That's what I like to see. Teamwork. None of these little cliques. We're all professionals her, right, Ersk?"

"Right," I said, punching him in the arm.

"How's your flu coming along?"

"I'll survive," I said, half-wishing I wouldn't. Like half of the other actors, I was running a temperature. At times, the room wavered and I felt dizzy.

"Fine. Hang in there. We can't afford to lose any more actors." He left and I excused myself from Hantover's presence, drew myself a cup of coffee, and chased down some more aspirin with a cup of water. By that time, Kirchner had called places and it was time for dress rehearsal.

We stumbled through the first few scenes until it was time for me to meet Hamlet's father's ghost. I couldn't believe the makeup job they had done on Willy Rubano, the college sophomore who was playing the ghost. It was better than anything they'd ever done in our earlier performances. But I guess they'd had nothing else to do while we were running through Bob Hantover's scenes. Still, it was eerie. There were times I could swear that I could see right through him. I wanted to say something about it to him but it would have interrupted the flow of our run-through and, knowing Kirchner, he'd have made us go all the way back to the beginning of the play and start all over.

And then Willy spoke. Frankly, I didn't think he had it in him. His first words, "Mark me," were said in a quivery voice that sent shivers up my spine. Maybe it was partly my fever but he really had me. I thought my heart would jump out of my mouth when he talked about his own murder: "If thou didst ever thy dear father love, Revenge his foul and most unnatural murder." If I had had to say more than "Murder?" then, I'd never have been able to do it. But the word tumbled out of my mouth and the words of the following speeches as if I were saying them for the first time, not parroting memorized speeches.

Then, with "Adieu, adieu! Remember me," he was gone. Somehow I got through the rest of that scene and the next one and, when the ghost said "Swear," I could have sworn the voice came from above me rather than from under the stage.

I stumbled off at least, my eyes watering, my forehead burning, and my head aching. I leaned against a doorway, glad there were several scenes to play before I had to go on stage again. I looked up into Willy Rubano's ashen face.

"What happened, Mr. Callaway? Who took my place out there?"

I looked at him, puzzled. "What do you mean? Wasn't that you out there?"

"No, sir. I went out to get a couple of pizzas for the other kids and, when I came back, the scene was almost over."

"But then who was it?" I asked.

"It must have been one of the other kids."

"No, it wasn't." We both turned at the voice. It was the theatre janitor, a man whom we'd all seen at work but had never bothered to get to know. "It wasn't anybody in your company."

"What was it? Some kind of joke?" I was too lightheaded then to think of how difficult it would be to play such an elaborate joke. What if Willy hadn't gone out for pizza just then?"

"It was no joke. It was the ghost." The janitor's voice had become a conspiratorial whisper.

"Ghost?" Willy asked.

The janitor nodded his head slowly. "Twenty years ago, one of the local actors was killed in here and he's been haunting the place ever since."

"Well, that sure make a nice story," I said.

"But what's he still haunting the place for?" Willy asked. *He*, at least, had been taken in by the janitor's story.

"They say he's looking for his murderer. You see, the mystery was never solved."

"You watch a lot of TV, don't you?" I asked.

"I usually watch *The Lucy Show* and things like that."

I nodded. "Stick to it. It's a lot safer than putting silly ideas in kids' heads."

"Ask Bob Hantover. He'll tell you. He was here then."

"Sure. I'll do that." I had no intention of doing so, however. Hantover seemed like a level-headed sort but you never can tell. If he believed in the East Hicksburg ghost, he'd leave the cast and we'd be in trouble again. Though, come to think of it, maybe then Kirchner would have to cancel the performance.

That line of thinking came to a halt when one of the stage managers dragged me back to the wings for my next entrance.

)OOO(

The rest of the rehearsal passed, however slowly, without any more such incidents. When the ghost appeared again in Act III, it was Willy Rubano in his ludicrous phosphorescent makeup.

At dinner break, I stumbled to my hotel room, set the alarm, and flung myself on the bed. My stomach was in no mood for food and I was feeling miserable. I groaned and tossed, unable to get to sleep immediately, feeling beads of sweat forming on my forehead, until at last I fell into a fitful slumber.

When I awoke at last, the room was dark. I jumped out of bed immediately and was immediately sorry. My head throbbed mercilessly and I fell back onto the bed, momentarily dizzy. I took a painful deep breath that made my head throb even more strongly but at least cleared the dizziness away and turned on the light. That didn't help my headache either and I had to squint at the alarm clock. It was ten o'clock! The show was already almost over. I couldn't understand it. I felt the alarm. Apparently I had turned it off in my sleep. Still, someone should have come to wake me up when I hadn't signed in before curtain.

I dressed as quickly as possible and staggered over to the theatre. The janitor let me in the side door, saying nothing, a strange look on his face.

"Mr. Callaway!" It was Willy. "What are you doing here? Shouldn't you be out on the stage?"

"What do you mean? Who's doing my part tonight?"

"Why, you are. I mean, aren't you?"

"No. I've been asleep since dinner break."

"But I saw you putting on your makeup. I mean, if that's not you out there, who is it?"

I stumbled into the wings, leaving a confused stage crew behind me. They were already well into the last scene. People in the wings gaped, looking from me to the stage and back again. There was someone out there in my costume but it didn't look like me. Not to me, anyway.

"The King, the King's to blame," Laertes said.

"The point envenomed too?" There was bitterness and triumph in Hamlet's voice. "Then, venom, to thy work." And he stabbed the king, Bob Hantover.

Hantover's eyes opened wide and he stared at the new Hamlet with sudden recognition. "Walter!" he said, departing from the script, and fell over. The stage erupted in pandemonium. "The curtain! Pull the curtain!" the stage manager cried, and the curtain slowly, ponderously came down.

The stage looked like a New York street after someone had been hit by a car. Practically everyone standing around, dumbfounded and unwilling to get involved, while two or three actors (all college kids, I noticed) were trying to revive poor Bob Hantover. When I joined the crowd, someone asked me how I had gotten into my street clothes so fast.

That's when we all noticed the Hamlet costume lying on the stage next to Bob Hantover.

Hantover was dead, of course. The local doctor who examined him found only a slight scratch from the sword. The police chief confiscated the sword and reported a day later that there was no poison on it. Official cause of death: heart attack.

So I was clear, even without the testimony of the stage crew that I had been in the wings when it had all happened. The similar testimony of the janitor, of course, counted for much more. The townspeople accepted the incident much more easily than the cast did.

Kirchner was forced to cancel two performances of *Hamlet* in East Hicksburg but, when we left, we left the flu behind us.

I learned from the janitor that Bob Hantover's wife had previously been married to the man who had been murdered twenty years earlier. I guess that put the lid on things. If you believe in ghosts, that is.

The Interstellar Ragtime All-American Jazz Band

It couldn't last, of course. It was a good thing while did last, but eventually someone like The Potomac River Ice-Breaker had to turn up and Fred Harmon was out in the cold again.

Here's these four guys, see: they call themselves The Potomac River Ice-Breaker. A drummer, a bass player, and two electric guitars. Hardboxers, for Christ's sake! But that's where it's at these days and an old-time blues player like me is out on a stick. The folk music scene is nowhere.

"What you oughta do, Fred, is join a group." Steve Hughes, the Alley Cat's owner, took a hit and passed the joint to me. "Shit, man, you got the talent. Playing one of those electric axes is no sweat."

"I've told you before, Steve, I'm a loner. I can't play with anyone else."

Steve shrugged. "Well, I'm sorry, Fred. But I've got to make some bread too, you know. I've been running awfully thin lately. If the Ice-Breaker can pack them in for just one week, I'll be running in high black."

"Skip it, Steve. Thanks for the use of your stage for the past few weeks." I picked up my guitar, hiked my knapsack up on my shoulders, and took one more look at the stage, where the folk-rock group was doing things that Leadbelly never dreamed of in his raunchiest stud days.

"Here, take this. It ain't much, man, but if a word from me will help you get a job, let me know." He slipped me a fiver and, if you think I gave it back to him, you're out of your ever-loving God-twisted mind.

As I started for the door, some yo-yo said to me, "Was this your last riff, Charley?"

I looked at him. He was straight from the mags, so help me, all decked out in the latest hip-Playboy garb, looking and sounding like a touriste trying to come on like the genuine article. But what the hell, I've got a fan club of one.

"'Fraid so," I said. "From here on in, it's The Potomac River Ice-Breaker in this coffee house."

"And what's to become of you?"

"I don't know," I said, trying to play it straight. "I guess I'll head for The Village. There's still a few basket houses trying to keep alive."

"Need a ride?"

My guardian angel must have been drinking again. I looked at him. Hard.

"You're not putting me on, are you, babe? A ride? All the way to New York City?"

He smiled one of the most innocent smiles I've seen in my whole ever-loving life and shook his head. "I'm a big fan of yours, Charley. I might be able to help you."

That really tops everything, I thought. All I need is a queer on my fan club. But he wasn't coming on swish, so I figured I might as well take the ride for as long as it lasted. I could always jump out if he made a grab for my lily-white bod.

)OOO(

The dude took me took to a '48 Hudson, bomb smooth and shiny, reflecting the streetlight overhead.

"Man, that's some machine," I said. "I haven't seen one of these in a long time. You must have kept good care of her."

He laughed. "We picked up this A-1 used car at Honest Joe's with a one-month warrantee on all parts, and then followed the E-Z instructions on a Do-It-Yourself mail order kit to do our own customizing."

I stared at him. He didn't really look that flaky. What kind of a put-on was this? Then he took off, peeling pavement and kicking up gravel like a mule on hash.

"Who's we?" I asked weakly.

"Some real cool friends of mine. I've been watching you, kid. You've got style." He looked over at me like a heavy in a 1940 B-grade movie. "You know you're really Number One on my Hit Parade. I'd like my friends to hear you play."

I was really sweating it now. Take it easy, I kept telling myself, or he's liable to bash you over the head and dump you in a ditch someplace.

"That's a shame," I said. "They should've dropped into the Alley

Cat while I was there."

"That's not their style. They can't be seen in public."

"What's the matter, they got smallpox or something?" My nervous laughter seemed too loud in the car.

"No, no. But these cats're liable to start a riot or something." Oh, God, no, a bunch of freakin' rednecks or black nationalists! "So maybe we could stop at my place? They'd really love to hear you play. I've told them so much about you."

"Hey, man, I've got to get to New York. I can't play around with a bunch of tourists."

"This'll only take a few minutes."

"No, really, man, I . . . "

"Please. I promise. Then I'll drive you to New York. Cross my heart."

And, so help me, the mother did.

)OOO(

The guy left me in the front room of an old farmhouse. It was pretty barren, an old rickety table, a battered console radio, and several straight-back chairs the only furniture. An overhead lamp cast garish shadows across the room.

He came back alone.

"Where are your friends?" I asked.

"They've got their ears glued to the radio, Charley." He took a microphone out of his pocket and plugged it into a wall socket. "Just flail away and let the mike pick up the sounds and send out the airwaves."

I figured I'd better humor him, so I started playing "Saint Louis Tickle," an old-timey piano tune that Dave Van Ronk had transcribed for guitar.

After I got past the intro, to the first F-sixth chord, I heard a bass note come in on the D, moving down the scale as I played. It seemed to come up under the chin and roll around in the mind, touching memories and sensations. It was followed by what sounded like a tabla, but with more delicate variations: first a rhythmic tattooing then slow, laconic, the tension on the head varying so that the instrument covered more than an octave.

Finally came The Axe: try to hear an oud crossed with Jack Sheldon's throatiest trumpet. Then give it the richest tones of the best classical organ. Taste an Italian ice bought on Houston Street during the hottest day of the summer; take a whiff of Acapulco gold while sitting in an Iowa boarding house; hear Woody Guthrie singing his children to sleep. And feel your body arching and straining at the peak moment of the best love-making you've ever made. When you've got all that soaked into your body and mind, forget it. Just laugh that wonderful delight you felt when you first saw a hummingbird darting about in your mother's flower-box when you were two years old. That's what "Saint Louis Tickle" is about.

The silence when I hit that final C-seventh just about like to throw me into a vat of STP. So I started "San Francisco." These dudes couldn't have heard it; it's my own private thing. I never played it at the Alley Cat. But they knew where it was at: the bass took over the drone on the E, leaving me free to wander around the high strings; the tabla threw off a ripple of happy beats then settled down to the wistful rhythm of a train clipping off the miles; and The Axe wandered over the Bay Bridge, shot around the esses of Lombard Street, tinkled around Chinatown, stepped in and out of the topless joints, and settled down over the Haight just long enough to inhale and start the trip again.

When it was over, I sat exhausted in my chair. Sweat dripped all over me and pooled in my boots. Every muscle in my body was happily tired.

I could hear the guy talking and someone answering back. It was only vaguely that I realized the answers were coming from battered old radio at my elbow.

"Charley, how would you like an all-expenses-paid trip to romantic islands?"

"What?"

"Tell you what I'm gonna do. I've got an ironclad contract here with no hidden clauses or small print. Our combo is crying for properly trained men." Slowly the meaning seeped into my head. "Are you with us or ag'in us?"

"I'm with you, I think." I mean, what the hell? That's where the action is these days. And these guys . . . well, we meshed. I mean, we really cooked.

"Fine!" He pumped my hand. "Let's go meet Alexander's Ragtime Band. I'd like to introduce you to the boys, Charley."

I followed him to the basement and met the rest of the band:

Bass was a bloated creature about four feet high, looking something like a blowfish about to explode. He created his music by changing the shape of his mouth and blowing through resultant resonant cavity.

The tabla looked like a water pipe with four little bowls and a tube studded with clarinet keys. The drumheads were stretched across the bowls and the creature who played it had four skinny hands with which he manipulated the keys and the tuning pins of the separate bowls.

A child's jungle-gym surrounded a large spider, the smooth skin of his carriage a brilliant blue. He jumped around the cage, sometimes strumming The Axe and sometimes blowing through holes unevenly spaced in the rods.

"Well, are you gonna groove with our combo?" asked the human.

Me, and these three freaks on a stage together, when I wouldn't even play with regular human beings? Who are you kidding, Fred Harmon? I asked myself. You, white as newly-laid plaster with your two-hundred-dollar Martin guitar, playing the songs of Leadbelly and Big Joe Williams, Mississippi-delta plantation blues. Where do you get off at drawing the line between what's human and what ain't?

The bass sung softly, whispering of the vastness between stars; the tabla tried to tell me about planets spinning around innumerable suns; the spider skittered around The Axe, playing songs of galaxies and nebulae, unimaginable skies, and girls with soft green fur.

I took out my guitar and added the cities, mountains, and rivers of Earth, while our agent began charting out the concert tour.

Two

With that settled, I began thinking about it would be like. Can you imagine the effect of these dudes on The Village? We'd be booked solid for months! And on top of everything else, they played music that was out of this world! That's when it hit me: they really were out of this world!

"We'd better start off easy, Clyde," I said to our manager, "because the State Department's going to want to know where these guys are from, mighty quick."

"The State Department?"

"Sure. Look, I'm not one of these sci-fi nuts but it's plain even to me that they're not from this Earth. Even under acid, I could never dream up anything like these dudes. Where did you find them, anyway?"

"Bass comes from a planet of eggheads. They grok all the languages of the Universe. Why, that cat can make just about any noise you want to hear. And our tabla player, the one who looks like a monkey?" I nodded. "From the very hub of the galaxy. Pioneers. Pilots. Star travelers. No trouble at all. Not like Bass, who wished only to stay home."

"And The Axe? The Spider?"

"He truly comes from a planet of musicians. People who devote their entire lives to the growing of trees from which his instrument is made, who painstakingly make only a few of them each year. He is not a great musician, not for his people, but there are not many of them out in the world."

"And how the hell did you get to all these places?"

"The same way you will, Charley. For now we have one of the most unique groups on the Grand Tour: a Spider and a human being. So few humans can play instruments today."

"My feelings exactly. Three-chord idiots, most of them."

He smiled. "Not that way, Charley. You see, there are many humanoid races throughout this universe. Many agents but damn few musicians. The Earth is a gold mine and we're going to take advantage of it before someone else does."

"You mean we're not going back to The Village?"

"We're going out on The Grand Galactic Tour. I'm gonna make a star out of you, baby."

"What if I don't want to come along?"

"Not make the scene? What kind of scam is that, Charley?"

"Well, look, this is my home. I got friends here, parents, maybe someday a lady and a home. Bread. Suburbia. The whole bit."

"Look, tell you what, Charley. One year. That's all I ask. You can come back. No one's gonna pull the slave-trade under-the-shell on you."

One year. Shoot, man, the whole universe waiting to hear me. "You wouldn't be putting me on, would you?"

"Now would I lie to you?"

And he crossed his heart again.

)OOO(

So the next night I stood out under the stars with our agent, a nice Earth-legal contract in my pocket, notarized by the local drugstore pharmacist, and a copy in the mail to my sister in Escondido,

California, because, after all, "we've got to follow the native customs, Charley."

The Air Force must've been having fits as this flying saucer with blinking lights like the old Electric Circus on a Friday night comes swooping down. Bass, Monkey, and Spider all come swarming up out of the basement with their baggage and instruments all nicely packed. (Spider took The Axe down entirely by himself. "Better not touch it," our agent said. "You know how artists are.") In about a minute, we're all inside and off we go, humming like a power line outside Toledo.

"Can I take a look outside?" I asked. "Can I see the cockpit of this thing?"

"Sure. I'll give you the five-bit guided tour."

I followed him up a walkway through a door that irised open for us and likewised behind us. And there was the Earth spread out in front of me.

"Only one pilot?" I asked.

"A World War One Ace," my guide replied. "Snoopy and the Red Baren." He gabbled something at the pilot in a high-speed tape-rewinding voice and the pilot turned around. "Fred, this is our pilot and electronics expert, Aefya."

Zonk! Five-foot-five of blue fur with ears like that Mr. Spock on the TV show, very mammalian in the right places, and eyes like honey and strawberries.

"Howdy, ma'am." I stuttered like a cowpuncher in Matt Dillon's Dodge City. It sounded absolutely inane to me even then, but I was completely at a loss for words. In any language.

She gibbered back at me in the same out-of-control-Ampex style as our agent.

"Doesn't she speak English?" I asked him.

"No. Only Bass and I have mastered the native idiom. Neither Spider nor Monkey have the vocal chords to speak your language. We'll have to teach you our Lingua Galactica, Charley."

"But . . . but she is female?" I stuttered, indicating our pilot, who was now concentrating on the controls.

"Most delightfully so."

I felt a twinge of unreasonable jealousy.

)OOO(

You'd think a civilization that was able to travel from star to star would come up with a painless way of teaching you a new language, but it took me three weeks before I was able to stumble around in Lingua Galactica, as Charley had called it.

Look, before I continue, let me lay a few facts on you. I called our agent Charley because I had to call him something and that seemed to be one of the favorite words in his vocabulary. Bass, Monkey, and Spider you can figure out for yourselves. Sure, they had names of their own, but I always thought of them that way and that's the way I'll call them for now. And the name of our group? Well, literally translated, it was something like Charley's Harmonic, Atonal, and Twelve-Tone Musical Group with Axe, Tabla, Bass, and Guitar (Genuinely Imported From The Savage Planet Earth). So I called it The Interstellar Ragtime All-American Jazz Band, which sort of put the whole thing into one bag.

And there was Aefya. It was great when I was able to say "Hello" to her in Lingua Galactica and she answered "Hi." Of course then I could talk with Monkey too and even Spider could understand me, although he couldn't answer because Spiders don't have the vocal chords for the Lingua Galactica. It was some time before I could understand his leg scratchings, but I won't bore you with the details.

Anyway, what I'm trying to put across is that the names don't have anything to do with their real names. I had to, like, symbolize them with names that have some kind of meaning to me.

Like Hackensack. That was the planet where we had our first concert. Now it wasn't call Hackensack, of course, but it had the same relationship to the main musical life of the universe as Hackensack has to The Village. But, hell, man, you've got to start somewhere.

Three

Charley and Aefya were playing some kind of complicated card game when we decided to quit rehearsing for a while.

"How'd it go?" he asked, as we flopped ourselves into the different positions of relaxation for our species.

"Not bad." Monkey flexed his multi-jointed fingers. "But Fred's got a problem with that machine of his."

Charley raised an eyebrow. "Serious?"

"I don't know," I answered. "I mean, it's a standard problem on Earth, so there's a standard solution. But here, well . . ." I shrugged my shoulders.

"Cut the mystery and spill it."

"Strings, man. I need new strings." Charley was puzzled. "I should put a new set of strings on this thing every week. The old ones stretch, lose their tension, get crud on them. They lose their tone after a couple of weeks. I brought one set of new strings with me. I've been saving them for the past few weeks so I'd have fresh strings for our first concert. But we're going to have to come up with some kind of solution, babe. I've got to get new strings somewhere."

He nodded. "I don't think there's any real problem there. In fact, it makes me think of something else that could be a problem some day."

"What's that?"

"Suppose something happens to your guitar? You lose it or something."

That hurt. I mean, he was right, of course, but that Martin of mine and I had been through a lot together. Across the country several times. I mean, I'm not materialistic or anything, but that guitar held my soul. But he was right. Back on Earth it would be no sweat replacing it. That is, if could raise the money. But here, in the rest of the universe, it was unique. Even The Axe was not unique, though there were damn few of them and they were more beautiful than any guitar could ever be.

"Well, in that case," I said, "I guess we'd have to go back to Earth."

"You underestimate us, Fred. When we land on Hackensack, I'll show you what we'll do. Meanwhile, take good care of that guitar of yours."

)OOO(

Hackensack was one of the most crowded places I've ever been in my life. There were no subways, slideways, or busses. There were cabs but they cost far too much for the members of a beginning musical sensation. So Monkey, Charley, and I walked the streets of Hackensack. That is to say, we bounced from body to body, like halfbacks ricocheting down a football field. It didn't help that I was carrying my guitar. That got me plenty of dirty looks as I bruised people's shins. Sometimes, when we got separated, I wondered how I'd ever find them again. Bass, Spider, and Aefya had enough sense to stay in the ship.

At last, Charley steered me into a small shop shoehorned between tall old-English-style skyscrapers with gables, gingerbread, and the whole bit. The silence of that little shop after the gabble outside was like a pitcher of beer after a hard day pounding the Manhattan streets.

"Can I help you?" The proprietor, salesman, or whatever-he-was stood about four feet high with a pair of torpid eyes in the right places, a sharp warty nose, and a wide mouth. His hands (two) were webbed and his feet (also two) were flat.

"Yes," Charley said. "Is Woret in?"

"He's busy right now. Surely I can help you."

"Tell him Charley's here. Tell him I've got a new group that will set this galaxy spinning at twice the rate it's going now."

Old Flat-foot gave him a sour look and stalked into a room in the back of the store. There were a few squeals and grunts and he came running back out.

"Charley!" he screamed. "You old horse thief! What's this about a new group?" His double (or maybe the original?) walked slowly out after him, looking somewhat crestfallen, despite the fact that he had no crest.

"Take a look. Woret, I'd like you to meet Fred Harmon." I put my hand out to shake hands with him but he was already prancing around me like a buyer examining new horseflash.

"What kind of scam is this, Charley? He's nothing but a humanoid. Where's he from? Frisco? Bar Harbor? Tierra del Fuego?" (I told you I was going to make up my own names.)

"Earth." Charley used the English word.

"Earth? I never heard of it."

"Of course not. It's not a League planet. Primitives. Savages. Totally uncivilized and untamed. Sorry, Fred." He turned to me and I shrugged. Hell, after all, he was right, wasn't he? "And get this, Woret. He plays an instrument. He's a musician." Old Flat-foot looked skeptical. "Go on, Fred, show him. Play something."

"What's all this got to do with new strings?" I asked.

"Woret will make them for us."

So I took out my Martin, sat down on a display case, and nearly fell over as Old Flat-foot's assistant rushed up angrily and tried to pull me off. Old Flat-foot gave him a strategic kick, however, and made an imperious motion for me to begin.

I looked at Charley, undecided. Should I play an instrumental or sing? Charley stared back at me. "Go ahead, kid." Monkey shrugged when I looked at him. With all four shoulders, no less. He was getting pretty good at it.

Oh, well. I played an E-chord to make sure it was in tune and Old Flat-foot's assistant jumped up and started gibbering. Flat-foot swatted him across the mouth. I jiggered around with the tuning pegs while trying to make up my mind.

"That's enough, Fred," Monkey said. "Give it to 'em straight. Play that solo number we've been rehearsing."

So that was it. Mississippi John's "My Creole Belle." Bass, who's a linguistic genius like the rest of his people, had translated it into Lingua Galactica and had done a damn fine job. In fact, I liked his words better than the original.

So plunk! Goes the C-chord, thumb and middle-finger alternating with the ring finger, down to the F with a nice bass. "My darling baby, My Creole Belle." Old Flat-foot's assistant hunched on the floor, his webbed hands over his eyes, head shaking from side to side as if he didn't believe what was happening. Meanwhile Woret himself was looking at Charley with a new look in his sluggish eyes, one of surprise mixed with shrewd business dollar signs. Charley and Monkey were busy looking smug.

I finished up and Woret looked at me with new respect. "I've got to admit, Charley, you've really got something this time. But what do you intend to do with it? And how to I fit in?"

"Look at that instrument of his." Woret came over and looked my Martin over from fret to bridge without touching it. "It's one of a kind." I started to protest. "Not on his planet, of course, but elsewhere in the galaxy. If anything happens to it, we're sunk." Woret nodded. "Do you think you can make one like it?"

Woret's mouth stretched from ear to ear. "I do not call myself The Master Instrument Maker of the Galaxy for nothing, my friend."

"No. You charge an arm and both legs. How long would it take you? And how much will it cost us?"

"I think I'll settle for both legs, no arms." He stood thoughtfully for a moment. "I would have to examine the instrument more closely to give you an accurate estimate of both time and cost." He stretched out a hand for the guitar.

I looked at Charley. "Go ahead, Fred. He knows his business."

Woret held the instrument gently, almost lovingly, which made me feel good. He ran his fingers gently over the strings. At the dischord that quivered in the air, he looked at me. "How did you do it?"

"It's in standard tuning. I don't use a lot of open tunings."

He shook his head. "I do not comprehend. It will take me several hours to examine this instrument. It will be very interesting for me but I don't think you would care to watch it."

"Why don't you show Fred the town?" Charley said to Monkey. "I'll stay here and reminisce with Woret and try to negotiate the price. I'll bring your guitar back to the ship when he's through, okay?"

What the hell could I say? I knew that Charley would take good care of the guitar. After all, I was his meat and potatoes. Nonetheless, it just wasn't the same.

"Don't forget the strings," I said weakly.

)OOO(

"What I don't understand," I said, sipping another of Charley's equivalents of bourbon, "is why they all look the same. I mean, sure, there's differences. Like you." I stroked Aefya's soft furry arm. "But everybody, or damn near everybody, has two arms, two legs, the whole shebang of eyes, nose, and mouth, and all in the right places. There's so few like Spider or Bass. I don't get it. I thought the whole universe would be filled up with weird beasties, like eight-armed praying mantises and octopuses and bug-eyed monsters and the whole bit."

"I don't really understand either," she said, "but there's something about the biped form and the mammalian animal that seems to lead toward intelligence. Something like ninety percent of intelligent life forms are biped and mammalian."

"I'm not complaining," I said, stroking her arm again.

"I'm not either." She squirmed her tail around and started to lean back. "If we were evenly divided between insects and mammals, for example, it would be difficult to develop a Lingua Galactica that both could speak. We're really lucky to have Bass with us. He's capable of speaking any known intelligent language. And he learns very fast."

"I wish I did."

"You do. And so do I."

Before I could follow up that line, I heard the lower hatch open. "That must be Charley," I said.

"Have you two been behaving yourselves?" he asked as he came into the room.

"That's a silly question," Aefya said.

"That's a formal, civilized question that requires no reply. Except by people with guilty consciences." Before Aefya could protest, he turned to me. "There's your guitar." He set the case down on the floor. "There are three sets of new strings inside the case. Let me know how they work." I nodded. "And the new guitar, case and all, will be ready in about six days. It'll cost about four hundred dollars." (I translate, of course.) "You realize you'll have to pay for it."

"But I don't have any money."

"You will. Your share of our first concert is one hundred dollars. And there'll be lots more if you cats are the sensation I'm thinking you'll be."

"Okay. It's your show."

"Right. Come on, Aefya."

Damn!

Four

On a good night at The Alley Cat, I played to thirty, thirty-five people. And many nights I played to only a handful or even one. And that's rough, believe me, when you've got to be a performer for one person. It's like a professor giving a two-hour lecture in front of a single student.

Of course, that wasn't my problem this night. I wouldn't have to say a word, although I'd be doing some singing. There was an emcee and Bass was our official spokesman. There were three or four other groups that would precede and follow us.

I guess what I'm trying to say is, nobody came to see us. They came to see the main attraction, the big stars.

But they came. Thousands of them, a confetti-colored wave of, well, humanity. Call it something else if you want but you know what I mean.

"Take it easy, Fred," Monkey said to me. "Come on back to the dressing room and let Aefya plug you in."

"Plug me in?"

"Yeah. Charley's recording this. Can you imagine what this performance will be worth if we make it to the top?" Monkey was really high. He was tasting green for the first time in his life maybe and he was flying.

Me? It wasn't real. Besides, I was just too damned scared. That wasn't thirty high school and college weekend hippies out there. These were dudes from all over the universe who had heard everything there was to hear. What could I offer them? What could any of Earth's music offer them?

I'm no Segovia and, even if I were, I could never play music like

Spider played on The Axe. And he wasn't even a virtuoso!

"Strip down," Aefya said.

"What?"

"Take off your clothes. I can't wire you if you've got your clothes on."

I stripped down to my shorts and she started placing little wires on my body, behind my ears, up my nose, and the corners of my eyes, under the armpits, all over my body.

"Now take those off."

Well, this was what I wanted, wasn't it? Sort of? No, it wasn't. But I took my shorts off anyway, and she continued putting wires on me. Everywhere.

"Careful there, big boy. This isn't the time for that."

"I can't help it. You've got very gentle hands."

And she kissed me. That didn't help either.

"Okay. You can put your clothes back on."

)OOO(

There they were, thousands of them. And they didn't like the previous group. Not at all. The air was filled with all kinds of soft squishy things and the group was covered with multi-colored splotches.

I'd heard of audiences like that but that was the first time I'd ever seen once in action. And smelled one.

"And now a new group, featuring a unique entertainer, The Interstellar Ragtime All-American Jazz Band!"

The Axe was already on stage, Spider in place, and Bass was sitting in a tub of the water of his native planet. Monkey walked out at the front of the stage while I walked out at the back, trying to be inconspicuous. Nonetheless there was a ripple of interest of something that went through the audience. Apparently word had spread from Woret's shop.

"What we've got to do," Charley had said, "is ease them over to our side. So we'll start with something simple, something they're used to, but something good."

"We'll feature The Axe," Bass had suggested, "and let Fred play simple rhythms and harmony."

"Right. With The Axe, it's hard to go wrong. But we want to drive them out of their skulls."

"Make them lose their cool," Bass said in English.

"So we'll slowly work up to Fred's solo."

We started with a composition by Spider that began with an intro by Bass and Monkey. Then The Axe came in and finally the guitar, strumming slowly, rhythmically, using a few barred chords but nothing fancy. Another ripple of whatever passed through the audience when I began playing.

When it was over, the audience was quiet. I didn't know whether that was good or bad but at least things weren't flying. I looked at Monkey. He held up all four hands, each with a pair of fingers crossed.

And we swung into the next number.

)OOO(

"Why don't they do something?" I whispered to Monkey. "Why are they so quiet?"

Monkey gave me the Ballantine sign and said, "Cool it, Fred. We've got them in the palms of our hands. Can't you smell it?" And he was right. Sometimes you can feel it, like after you've sung a sad song, like Malvina Reynolds' "The Little Boy Salutes" on November 22nd. There's a silence, a dead silence, but you know it's a silence that nobody wants to break, a mood that would be destroyed by applause. And sometimes it seems to last for minutes. That was the kind of silence that now hung over the audience. Even coughs and seat movements were nearly absent.

We had come to "Creole Belle." Fred Harmon and no one else. No Monkey, no Spider, no Bass. Just one spotlight, centered on yours truly.

"We'd like to introduce Fredharmon, a truly talented human, who will perform the next number by himself, unaccompanied," Bass announc3ed. This time the silence was broken by a confused, expectant hum, the combination of thousands of whispers in hundreds of languages. "He will perform a song from his native planet, called 'Creole Belle,' which we have translated into Lingua Galactica."

"We?" I whispered to him. "You should take credit for it."

"We're a team, Fred baby. Remember that."

There was the same silence when I finished "Creole Belle," so we swung into our last number, which we had hoped would be anticlimactic. This time when we finished, the lights flashed blue a couple of times as we stepped back and the audience erupted! All the noise that we hadn't heard throughout our set suddenly came flying up at us. Yells, screams, shouts--it was hard to tell what kind of noises they were making. I looked at Monkey.

"They like us, baby!" he shouted. "They like us."

"Listen," Bass said, taking me by the arm and motioning toward the audience.

I listened. And I heard. From hundreds of throats, some of which were never meant to speak English: "Fredharmon! Fredharmon!"

"Go ahead." Bass and Monkey pushed me forward and once more I was alone in the spotlight. Dumbfounded.

At a coffee house all I'd do would be to say, "Thank you," and that'd be it. But, hell, this was different. "Do something," Bass hissed at me in English. I felt silly as hell, but I bowed, like a goddamn Paganini or Segovia. From the waist. Hands at my side.

The PA system announced in Charley's voice, "Fredharmon is performing a custom of his native planet, wherein the performer expresses his thanks to the audience."

And damned if half of them didn't get up and bow back!

Five

Charley, of course, was jubilant when we came off the stage after doing "San Francisco" as an encore. "We've done it, baby," he chortled. "We're on our way up. Nothing can stop us now. The news of this concert will flash across the galaxy in nothing flat."

"How'd the recording go, Aefya?" Monkey asked.

She grinned. "Great. You were all so nervous it's a wonder that you didn't make more mistakes than you did. Native Boy here really came across nervous. And you should've felt him at the

end. Shivers running up and down his spine."

We went to our dressing room and just flopped into chairs or their equivalents. Charley disappeared, no doubt to bug some PR man. Aefya began unwiring each of us. This time I didn't react at all when it was my turn.

"Poor baby's utterly exhausted," she said as she finished.

"I bet I sweated off ten pounds out there," I said.

"And I can tell where most of it came from."

I swatted at her but she ducked. By that time, Charley was back, fluttering about like the proverbial mother hen. "Get your clothes on, Fred. Come on, you guys. Hurry up. We've got some guys out there who want to write a story about you and take some pictures. We're on our way up. Boy, are we on our way up!"

I put my Martin in its case and followed the rest of the group out. What a snake dance that was--Charley at the front, dwarfed by the spindly-legged Spider, Monkey and Bass doing their monkey- and fish-dances behind Spider, then me, and finally Aefya. You would think I'd have learned not to let her get behind me by now, but I was too excited. So, just as I entered the room, she goosed me.

There were no flash bulbs but, outside of that, it resembled a presidential conference. Pushing, shoving, shouting. Instruments held high. (Cameras? Microphones? I didn't know. Probably both.) And a chubby little flat-foot hustling us to a roped-off area.

"Where did you find him, Charley?"

"Fredharmon, what do you think of Hackensack?"

"Do you think any humanoid could learn to play an instrument?"

Finally the chubby flat-foot managed to obtain some semblance of order and the real questioning began. Charley tried to alternate the answers, so that the whole thing didn't center around me all the time. We covered Charley's discovery of me and gave a brief description of Earth, although it was plain Charley didn't want anyone to know exactly where it was located.

"Do you think anyone could learn to play that instrument?" someone asked.

"Well, not anyone," I answered. "But it's not difficult. Here, wait, I'll show you." I ducked under the rope and headed for the dressing room.

"Wait a minute!" Charley yelled.

"I'll be right back. Don't worry. I can find my way."

)OOO(

I darted down the hallway before anybody could follow me. Actually, I was anxious to get back to the dressing room. It really bothers me to be away from my guitar for long. The thought of someone stealing it really bugs me. And, hell, I can imagine one of the other groups taking it. You know, professional jealousy and all that crap.

And damned if Aefya hadn't left the door open. I half-expected to find the guitar gone when I entered the room.

But it was there. In the hands of a lizard-like creature who had broken two of the strings and had his hand poked into the sound hole.

"What the hell do you think you're doing?" I yelled.

He jerked up his head and squeaked. I stalked over to him and grabbed the guitar out of his hand. And somebody hit me across the shoulders.

I guess he was trying for some kind of karate blow but either he missed or I was built differently from what he was familiar with. He didn't knock me out but he knocked me into the lizard. I was up first, the neck of the guitar in my hand. I turned around as I got up so I could see who the second thug was.

It was a gorilla. Literally. I won't go into the differences. It was a gorilla and he was walking toward me like a grade B western bad guy walking down the main street of Dodge City for a gunfight in the O.K. Corral.

I grabbed the guitar with both hands, without thinking, and swung like Babe Ruth going for the fences. The gorilla didn't even duck and, when the strings and my arm stopped vibrating, he was sitting there on the floor, blood on the side of his head. That got me. The blood. I guess I expected to be green or blue or something. But it was red. Bright red.

He started to get up and I brought the guitar down over his head. You know, like I was swinging an axe. He just sat there, head through the body of my lovely irreplaceable Martin, one string still intact and looped over his head. Then he collapsed.

That's when Aefya walked in and started screaming.

)OOO(

"You don't know where this lizard went?" the flat-foot police lieutenant asked.

I shook my head. "He must have split while I was taking on that gorilla."

"And you know nothing about this?" He held up a little white bag.

"No," I answered for the fifteenth time. It was the flat-foot version of heroin. The cops found it on the inside of the body of my guitar after they had separated it from the gorilla.

"It's obvious what happened, lieutenant," Charley said. "Some smugglers figured out that this would be a good way to smuggle dope to New Haven." (That was the next planet on our tour.) "Who would ever think an ignorant savage . . . excuse me, Fred . . . who would think an ignorant savage would even think of smuggling, even he knew what to smuggle? Fortunately, Fred walked in while they were busy putting the dope in his guitar."

"Well, I can't find any reason for holding you."

"It's certainly obvious that we're not deliberately involved in this, or the whole incident would never have taken place."

"What I mean is that I can't have you held on Hackensack until this is cleared up. Especially after that concert you gave. New Haven can't wait to see you. But contact the police there as soon as you land."

"Certainly."

"By the way, I enjoyed the concert enormously. It's a pleasure and an honor to meet you all, although I'm sorry I had to meet you under these circumstances. I hope to see your next concert here."

"I'll see to it that you get complimentary tickets," Charley said.

)OOO(

"What are you so glum about?" he asked me as we left the now empty theatre for our spaceship. "We could have been here weeks and lost all our momentum."

"But my guitar, man. It's ruined."

"Didn't Charley tell you?" Aefya said. "That was the substitute guitar. The one Woret made for you."

"You mean my Martin's okay? Where is it?"

"Monkey took it back to the ship," Charley said. "Don't worry. Everything's okay. I'll have to order another one from Woret but that's no sweat. I'll take the loss myself. I won't dock you for breaking the first one across that guy's head."

At that moment, I was so happy I would gladly have paid for both substitutes.

"I like to see you smile," Aefya said, taking my arm with one hand and Charley's with the other. "Now let's get back to the ship. I want you to feel this recording."

Six

Aefya placed a helmet over my head and told me to relax. I sat back in the chair, not really very relaxed, while she played with the controls of the electric switchboard that the helmet was attached to.

"Say, this thing can't electrocute me, can it?"

"Relax, Native Boy. There's no more electricity running through your had than there is in the wires to a loudspeaker system." I didn't know whether that was frightening or comforting. "We wouldn't take a chance on frying our fair-haired wonder, would we?" That, at least, was comforting. "Are you ready?"

"Ring-alevio," I said.

"What?"

"Better now than never. Roll them dice."

She disappeared. Everything disappeared. The entire universe disappeared. I was in a gray limbo, or was it gray? It was nothing. I had no arms, no legs, no eyes, no body, no head. I was just a conscious existence.

And I was on the stage again, my Martin cradled nervously in my hands. There was that confetti-colored audience again; my palms were sweating; sounds were filtered through the distant sea of blood rushing in my ears. Bass and Monkey started the intro, Spider slipped The Axe into the melody, and my hands were moving across the guitar, up to a G-seventh then back to a first position C, and I couldn't stop them. I tried to, after I had recovered, but I was completely out of control, just a spectator along for a ride in my own body.

It was gray again.

And then I had four hands, rippling over the drum heads of Monkey's tabla and ceaselessly playing with the tuning pins, the clarinet keys. I took a deep breath and blew into the mouthpiece. Colors were strange somehow; things didn't seem quite right but I couldn't place my finger on exactly what was wrong. Not a single one of my twelve fingers (three on each hand plus an opposable thumb). I wanted to sweat, but I couldn't. I felt like my heart should be racing out of control but I was perfectly calm. Physically. Mentally, I was scared shitless.

And the world turned gray again.

"Are you all right?" Aefya was looking at me worriedly.

"What the hell? Yeah. I guess so." My pulse was racing a mile a minute and all things I hadn't been able to feel physically a few seconds earlier were racing through my body like a speed freak who hadn't had a needle in two days.

"You had me scared there. Your blood pressure went way up."

"I bet it did."

"I never thought anyone could react so violently to a recording."

"Sorry, babe. But you should have warned me what was going to happen."

"It just never occurred to me." She shook her head. "I didn't realize that you didn't know how a recording worked. Oh, Fred. If anything had happened to you . . . " And she fell in to my arms.

"I know. You'd be out the recording sensation of the century."

She looked up and said, "I never even thought of that." We stopped using our mouths for audible conversation at that point.

"Well," I said, after we had both regained our breath, "how about letting me listen to, or feel, or whatever it is iyou do, to the rest of the tape?"

"Are you sure that's wise?"

"I know what to expect now."

Well, it wasn't as easy as all that. When you consider what being in Monkey's body did to me, you can imagine it was like as Bass or Spider, even when I was expecting it. And you'll have to imagine it, because I sure as hell can't describe it to you.

But I'll tell you one thing: I don't like recordings. They may be okay for audience-type people, but they're not for me. There's something very frustrating about not being able to control what's going on.

I guess what I'm trying to say is that I'm just not cut out to be an audient.

Seven

Spider chittered angrily as I screwed up again, flatting out the entire sequence.

"Let's take a break," Charley said. "I don't think we're going to accomplish anything today, the way Fred's playing. Maybe he needs a good rest. Okay, man?" He looked at me and I nodded.

"Sure."

"What's the matter?" Monkey asked as Charley left the practice room.

Bass prepared to slide down the chute that led to his room. "He's just under a strain, that's all. Hell, who wouldn't be? I'd be shook if someone tried to bust my musical instrument." He laughed and disappeared down the chute.

"Just don't think about it, Fred. Think about something pleasant. Like Aefya."

I watched him leave. Spider had already gone, leaving me alone in the practice room with our instruments. My guitar was still in my hands and I strummed it idly. Every chord seemed to be sad and haunting, poignant. A-minor, B-flat, C-major, D-major. A barred chord, a seventh, what? I counted frets: B-flat-seventh.

Think about something pleasant. Think about Aefya.

That two-bit guitar I'd busted over the gorilla's head? Frightening at the moment, sure, but kind of funny in retrospect. In fact, I was rather proud of myself and I had a great story to tell when I got home.

If I ever got home.

The bit with the dope kind of bothered me. That's the Big Leagues and I don't want to get mixed up with it. Not even accidentally.

B-flat-seventh. A-flat-seventh. B-minor. F-seventh.

Think about something pleasant. Think about Aefya.

Aefya and Charley sweating and groaning, pressed tightly to each other. Hell, I've never been possessive. I mean, a chick is a chick is a chick. But I wanted Aefya and I didn't want to share her. I guess my Puritan forebears were beginning to come to the fore.

But I liked Charley, damn it. I didn't want to screw him too.

A-minor, B-flat, C-major, D-major.

"That's pretty. What is it?"

"Nothing. I was just fooling around."

She sat down next to me. "It was kind of sad, though. Don't you know anything happy?"

"I guess I'm just not very happy today."

"Charley told me you were making all kinds of mistakes today. But don't worry. You'll get over it."

"Did Charley ask you to come in here?"

"No. I just thought . . . " Whatever it was, the thought dwindled off, and we sat in silence for several long seconds.

Finally I got up and put my guitar away as Aefya watched me silently. Then I kissed her on the cheek, you know, brotherly-like. "I'm going to get some sleep. Maybe I can sleep it off."

Of course I couldn't.

)○○○(

New Haven was a lot more pleasant than Hackensack. Like Bass's home, it was a university planet. Although there was a lot of industry, the planet still had a rural, pleasant, slow-motion air to it. There were wide boulevards and streets, spacious greens, long fields filled with flowers and grazing animals, lots of shade provided by broad leafy trees. And everywhere you went, the streets were filled with students. I've seen a lot of students as I've bummed across the country, and they weren't any different on New Haven.

All right, so maybe I can't come up with original names. But it fit.

Call it Cambridge, if that makes you feel any better.

This, of course, was all in the future when we landed. What was immediate was the large group of students waiting for us. I looked at Charley, a bit scared. He wasn't, not at all. He smiled at me and said, "Here. Pop this," and jammed a seashell into my ear.

". . . with their new sensation, Fredharmon, a musical humanoid from a planet at the far edge of the galaxy. Not only did Fredharmon create a musical sensation at The Interstellar Ragtime All-American Band's first concert but he also singlehandedly apprehended a member of a dope smuggling ring . . . "

It went on and on in that vein interminably.

We were on our way up. And I remembered two old sayings: "What goes up must come down" and "The bigger they are, the harder they fall." But that's something else.

꘠OOO꘡

I felt sorry for the big guys. The concert had been signed before we made our splash in Hackensack, so we were still No. 2 in the billing. But when we came on stage, we had to wait nearly five minutes for the tumult to die down before we could finally begin playing.

And all the trouble we had had during rehearsal disappeared. It was that night in the farmhouse on Earth all over again. We pulled the same type of sequence on New Haven that we did on Hackensack but this time it wasn't to accustom the audience to Earth-type music but rather to play out the string, build up the suspense. We played about two-thirds of the songs we had played on Hackensack and about a third new stuff. Besides "Creole Belle" in Lingua Galactica, I played and sang "Saint James Infirmary" in English. Nobody understood a word of it, of course, but they all dug it anyway. I had Bass and Monkey behind me on it, while Spider took a break.

The reception was even wilder, if possible, and I was beginning to feel like a sneak thief. I mean, I couldn't begin to approach Bass, Monkey, or Spider as a musician, yet I was getting all the attention just because I was different. It didn't seem fair.

As we came off the stage, Charley said, "Next time we'll head the bill."

꘠OOO꘡

We fought our way through the crowd at the stage door, leaving behind thumb- and finger-prints, as well as pieces of clothing, mostly mine. When we got back to the ship, we found Woret's latest copy of my guitar had arrived.

"Where to now?" Monkey asked, busy drinking a bulb of Monkey-nectar.

"We stay here for a few days, hopping from college to college. I've already been assured that we'll be at the top of the bill." Charley turned to me. "And we'll make enough that you can pay off what you owe on your guitar and have some left over."

)OOO(

I flopped down on my bed and stared at the ceiling, which was a collage of folksingers that Charley had had made specially for me. It featured a browned photo of Woody Guthrie at the center.

As soon as I lay down, the bed continued its latest lesson on Lingua Galactica. I switched it off and flipped around the various recordings Charley had included: classical galactic music, featuring three Axes in contrapuntal harmony; the latest newscast from New Haven ("Continuing their fabulous success, The Interstellar Ragtime All-American Jazz Band took Admin City by storm . . . "); several other galactic groups; Lightnin' Hopkins.

I settled back and stared at Woody while Lightnin' sang his "Santa Fe Blues."

"What's wrong, Fred?"

"Don't you ever knock before entering?"

"It's more than that dope problem, isn't it?" Aefya reached out and stroked my cheek.

"Don't." I pushed her hand away.

"Why not?"

"Because. Because I want you too damn much, that's why."

She laughed. "What's wrong with that?"

"Because I want to own you, that's why. I don't want to share you with anyone. With Charley. With no one."

That got to her. She smiled weakly. "Native tabus, huh?"

"Call it that, if you want."

"But there's nothing between Charley and me. It's just . . . just a matter of convenience. And being near each other. We don't own each other."

"But I don't want to break things up. If the band falls apart, what happens to me?"

"You would still be a sensation, Fred."

"Big deal. A little pet monkey that does tricks. At least, with the group, I belong. I'm part of everything. And when all the furor of me being a pet monkey dies down, maybe we'll still have something. I can't walk out on the others like that, let them down. This is their big chance."

"Maybe your trouble is just that you've been too long without a woman. And here I am, always around you, so you fall in love with me."

"Sure." I didn't believe a word of it.

"Come on. I've got an idea."

We walked through the elm- or whatever-lined literate streets of Admin City. No one gave us a second look and why should they? We looked a lot less weird than some of the other geeks walking around.

She stopped in front of a fine old brick building. "Here." She stuffed some money in my hand. "Go on in and have a good time."

)OOO(

She was waiting for me when I came out two hours later.

"Well, how was it?"

"Great. Wonderful. Thanks, Aefya."

She had been five-foot-five with blue fur and pointed ears. She was completely mammalian where she should have been and had eyes like honey and strawberries. She was most delightfully female and very talented. I tried to pretend she was Aefya.

But she wasn't.

Eight

I decided to try out Woret's latest guitar. I had never had a chance to use his first one as anything more than a club. He had done a beautiful job--I wondered if I would have been able to tell one guitar from the other if he hadn't replaced the "Martin" on the headstock of my guitar with a group of symbols that I suppose spelled his name.

I was tempted to look inside for drugs but that was silly. For one thing, the balance of the guitar would have been affected and I'd have noticed. At least, I think I would have.

After fooling around with it for about fifteen minutes, I set it down on the bed and examined the case. Woret had taken it back while he worked on the second guitar and sent the guitar to us inside the case.

He had done just as nice a job there. It was a good solid hardshell case with a plush purple velvet lining. I tried the key to my original Martin case. It worked on this lock too.

I opened the pick-box. It was empty, of course. I started to put the guitar to bed when it struck me. I took the guitar out and opened the pick-box again. I was right. It seemed somehow shallower. I stuck my little finger in it; it went all the way down to the first joint. I slipped my finger down the side of the pick-box. It went down past the next knuckle almost to the base of the finger.

I carefully closed the case, leaving the guitar on the bed, and sat there, wondering what to do. You're just being melodramatic, I said to myself. Maybe Woret made a mistake in the case at that point and covered it up by raising the floor of the pick-box a little.

But I had to find out. So I left my room and went to the kitchen. Aefya was busy preparing dinner for us. "Are you feeling better?" she asked.

"Fine. Have you got a sharp thin knife in there?"

"What? Oh, no, Fred, you can't!" She dropped a box of something and ran into my arms, pinning me against a counter.

"I can't what?"

She pulled away, looking at me warily. "What do you want the knife for?"

"I want to pry something open."

"Here." She pulled something out of the counter. "I'll come with you. What do you want to pry open?"

"My guitar case."

"What in the world for?"

Suddenly I realized she might be one of them. Aefya could be a smuggler. That hadn't even occurred to me. In fact, maybe the whole band was in on this, everyone but me.

"Never mind," I said. "I'll look silly if I'm wrong."

She sat down on the bed and watched quietly as I pried open the pick-box. The space underneath was filled with a greenish powder.

"What is it?" she asked.

"I would guess it's some kind of narcotic."

"I'm afraid you're right, Fred." Charley was standing in the doorway holding a weapon in his hand. He came into the room and closed the door behind him. "Now kindly put the cover back on"

I did as I was told. "I suppose you'll have to kill us now."

"Really, Fred, do you think I'm the homicidal type? Besides, I like you. I really do." He did look pretty shook up about the whole business. "No, this screws up a lot of things but I don't want to kill you. We'll have to go back to Earth and drop you off there. There's nothing you could do to us then."

"What about Aefya?"

"Aefya won't say anything, will you?" He looked at her steadily and I wondered again if she were part of the gang. "Because if she does, someone will get back to Earth and see that you are killed. And you don't want that, do you, Aefya?"

"Couldn't you leave me on Earth with Fred?"

Charley shook his head. "There are laws against that sort of thing. Sorry, lovebirds."

"What do you mean, lovebirds?" I asked.

"You really are blind, aren't you, Fred? Everybody else here knows how she feels about you."

"Aefya?" was all I could say.

She nodded dumbly.

"Now if you will get over on the bed with Aefya, I'll be taking this thing from you."

"What then?" I asked, doing as he said, leaving behind me on the floor that sharp glittering knife. Well, what the hell, I couldn't have killed Charley anyway.

"Then we take off for Earth, with you two locked here in this cabin until we get to Earth."

"What about Monkey and the others? Are they in on it?"

"They know nothing about it. I'll just tell them that the police told me we had to return you to Earth. Disturbing the native population and all that crap." As he bent over to close the case and pick it up, my hand touched the guitar on the bed.

It was really a shame to use such a beautiful instrument to club someone over the head. Especially someone as nice Charley. But his head wasn't as hard as the gorilla's. He was out of action on the first swing.

Nine

The four of us sat around in the lounge the next day, trying to figure out what to do.

"We've got to stick together," Monkey insisted. "We can't let go of the roller coaster now, just when things are going great."

Spider scratched his agreement.

"But we need an agent," I said. "We need someone to replace Charley."

"That's no problem," Bass said. "We've already had offers from fifty different people. We're hot, and everybody wants a finger in the pie."

"The problem is, who?" Monkey asked. "We don't want just anybody. We don't want someone who'll ride along for a while, take what he can get out of it, and then disappear.

"What we want," Bass said, "is someone who cares about us."

"What we need is a nursemaid," I muttered.

The door to the lounge opened and Aefya came in. She had disappeared after we had breakfast in bed together, which happened after . . . well, never mind. My possessiveness problem had been licked, or conquered, or whatever, at least for the time being.

Spider started chittering urgently and Bass told him to slow down.

"Where have you been?" I asked as Aefya settled into my lap and started curling my hair in her fingers.

"Oh, into town, checking on things."

"Things? What kind of things?"

"Yes!" Bass yelled suddenly. "That's the answer! Did you understand that?"

I looked at him; Aefya looked at him; Monkey looked at him. "I caught some of it," Monkey said, "but I'm not at all sure what Spider was getting at."

"Aefya," Bass said, "how would you like to be our agent?"

"Me?"

"Sure. You've been Charley's right hand now for years. You know everything he does about the circuit, maybe more. What do you say? Will you give it a try?"

Monkey urged her to accept the idea and Spider chattered eagerly.

"What about you, Nature Boy? What do you think of that idea?"

"Me?" I grinned. "I think it's great. I'm all for it."

"Will you marry me?"

"Marry you?" I yelped. "But . . . but, well, damn it, Aefya, we can't even have kids."

"Yes, we can."

"How do you know?"

"I went to see a geneticist this morning. He took samples from me . . ."

"Fine. Sure. So you can have kids."

"And I brought him samples of your sperm."

"How did you . . . ?" That would have been the silliest question of the year.

"And he says that, with some minor genetic alterations, we can have children."

A line from an old children's folk song, "Mr. Froggie Went A-Courting," ran through my head: "There'll be no tadpoles covered with fur."

And if I didn't marry Aefya, well, hell, that would probably be the end of The Interstellar Ragtime All-American Jazz Band.

"Okay, you win," I said. "On one condition."

"Which is?"

"The first stop on our next tour is Earth."

The Potomac River Ice-Breaker was in for a surprise.

The Timedipper Who Stayed

Only a few startled squirrels and a couple of mourning doves witnessed Orimanie Rix-Dollar's appearance in a wooded section of a small town south of Baltimore, Maryland. A tiny bit of sparkle, like Venus in a daytime sky, moved down from its perch on a limb of one of the trees and positioned itself close to the ground before dilating into an oval through which Orimanie stepped. As soon as she was clear, the oval diminished to the sparkling bit and repositioned itself on the tree limb again, looking like a tiny piece of tinfoil lodged there.

Orimanie was a moderately attractive woman in a pair of slightly-worn jeans and a light plaid shirt, unexceptional in any way except that she had stepped out of thin air. She looked around to make sure no one had seen her arrival, then checked her bag to see that everything that should be in it was there, although she had done the same thing several times in the hour before her arrival. Then she walked out of the wooded area to the town's street, no longer Orimanie Rix-Dollars but now Ramone Nixon.

She bought a newspaper from the dispenser outside a diner, and read the paper swiftly but thoroughly as she rode the commuter train into Baltimore, making mental notes of some of the stories. She acted as though she had done these things a dozen times or more, as indeed she had. But the previous times had been in a mock-up at the Time Institute. She looked casually around her, but inside was a turmoil of fear and expectation – fear of acting incorrectly and drawing attention to herself, expectation of the research that lay ahead of her.

No mock-up could begin to approach the beehive of people coming and going at the Baltimore station; no virtual experience could fully prepare her for the sounds and smells – the vehicle fumes were stronger than those she had experienced far in the future, but she found them exhilarating and exotic. The noise of horns and engines, the sudden squeal of brakes as a cab pulled out in front of another seemed louder than the ones she had heard at the Time Institute. She stopped to experience it all before following the directions that seemed to be engraved in her mind.

She went to the Pratt Library to find out which of her subjects were already dead, which still alive. As expected, some of them had died many years earlier, although only one belonged to the previous century. Several were not mentioned at all, which meant that they had still to make their mark, if indeed they had even been born yet.

Although Robert Bianca, her favorite author, was not yet mentioned in any of the Authors' Who's Whos, she found one novel of his in the catalogue. Bianca was the man who had predicted the domed cities and their downfall with surprising accuracy. It was eerie reading his novels and finding many of the institutions and life styles he had predicted had indeed come to pass. It was true he hadn't foreseen the Black-and-White War and the way it would affect the domed cities, forcing the North American continent into an isolation that would last far longer than Bianca had predicted. Still, he had made an astonishing number of correct predictions.

She left the library early enough to set up five-hundred-dollar accounts in several banks. There was a moment of panic when one of the tellers looked at one of the bills with suspicion then drew a pen across it and accepted the bill. Later she would invest some of the money in stocks suggested by the Time Institute.

After taking a room at a hotel, she went back out into the cool evening, watching people rush past her on incomprehensible errands, observing the bums who wandered about aimlessly on the streets, mumbling to well-dressed passersby, the constant come-and-go of traffic, the strange mixture of shabbily-dressed youngsters and well-dressed older people.

Harborplace glowed with neon lights in a dozen colors. No amount of training could possibly prepare her for the sounds and sights, the breeze with its impossibly intermingled odors, the taste of genuine meat with sauces prepared by cooks with dozens of years of experience in preparing it. The Institute's attempts at recreating the past for Timedipper training was a pale ghost of the real thing.

Orimanie reveled in the experience, even in the fear that rose inside her, the fear of being discovered (absurd!), of being thought crazy and put in an institution, never able to get back to her own time (a little more likely), of being assaulted and attacked, perhaps even killed (was that as likely as she thought?). The fear itself was part of the experience, as unique a taste as she would find in the multitude of restaurants in Baltimore or anywhere else in this world of her past.

She spent the next week in and out of libraries and bookstores, trying to track down those authors who had not been listed in the reference books. Eventually she came to a used-bookstore that specialized in science fiction. She immersed herself in names and titles, many of which had never heard before, occasionally coming across a name she recognized. She found a lost title, which she kept for purchase and eventual return to her own time. Two shelves below it she found *Crystalline Eyes*, Robert Bianca's first book, one that didn't deal with the domed cities.

She picked it up and cradled it as if it was a living thing and brought it to the cash register with her other book.

"You ever read anything else by Bob?" the clerk asked, a bear of a man with a shaggy beard and rimless glasses.

"Bob?"

"Bob Bianca. The guy who wrote *Crystalline Eyes*."

"Oh. He has other books out? Do you have them?"

"Not yet. *Masques* will be out next week, but he's had short stories in all the magazines and anthologies."

"You know him? I mean, you called him Bob, not Robert."

"Sure. He comes to Baltimore every now and then for a meeting of the science fiction club, or the Balticon. That's the Baltimore Science Fiction Convention. Mostly, though, he just stays at home and writes."

"He lives here?" She couldn't believe her good fortune. She knew that Robert Bianca had lived somewhere on the East Coast of the United States; that he actually lived *here* and that she had met someone who actually knew him was luck too incredible to believe.

"No. He lives out in the boonies in Pennsylvania just over the state line, a little town called Clarks Landing."

)OOO(

It wasn't difficult to find Robert Bianca's phone number. He had a pleasant voice on the phone but, after she explained that she was a college student doing a thesis on science fiction, didn't sound particularly pleased that she wanted to see him. Nonetheless, he agreed to let her visit.

Getting to Clarks Landing wasn't as easy as getting his phone number, however. She had to take a bus that stopped at every little fork in the road. They had no trouble recognizing each other when she stepped off the bus: she was the only passenger to get off at Clarks Landing and he was the only person waiting for the bus.

"Miss Nixon?" he asked unnecessarily as the bus moved away.

"Yes. I can't tell you how pleased I am to finally meet you, Mr. Bianca."

"Bob, please." And she, of course, became Ramone. "Is that all you brought with you?" She had a small flat briefcase, a pad and pencil for taking notes, while the small holocamera inside the briefcase's handle silently recorded everything it saw and heard. "Didn't you bring any luggage?"

"Oh, no. I was planning to take the bus back this evening."

Bob Bianca smiled, an impish smile that seemed to make light of Orimanie's folly. "I'm afraid the bus won't pass through here again until tomorrow morning."

Orimanie's hand flew to her mouth. "Oh. I hadn't realized."

"That's all right. We've got plenty of room."

"I don't want to cause you any trouble. I can stay at a hotel."

Bob Bianca raised an eyebrow. "In Clarks Landing? Come on. It's just a short walk to the house."

His voice had a strange nasal twang to it that Orimanie found very pleasant and reassuring, a bit like the old country philosophers she had seen on pieces of film remaining from the Twentieth Century. He was nearly two meters in height, with a quirky smile, and sandy brown hair which nearly covered his jughandle ears, a bit clumsy and ill at ease, but very open and likeable, not at all like the elderly gentleman of the arts in the photographs remaining of him in her time.

"I hope you won't mind. One of my friends is staying here over the weekend. He writes science fiction too."

"What's his name?" Could it be possible that she would meet two famous writers in one day?

"Frank Harrigan. Have you read any of his stories?"

"No. No, I can't say that I've even heard of him." She tried to keep the disappointment out of her voice but she was afraid that it showed anyway.

"Well, don't tell *him* that." Bob Bianca chuckled reassuringly.

It was a little over a two-block walk down a shady street with a few patches of tar broken loose, well-worn but not quite shabby yet. The house itself fit the street, with gables and curlicues of gingerbread, especially over the porch, which covered the front of the house and flowed over to half of one of the sides. The white paint was already graying but not yet peeling. It had seen better days but it wouldn't take a great deal of work to make it quite respectable again, the kind of house that was just as bit too much for one person to keep up – as one thing would be repaired or cleaned, another would need attention.

Bob Bianca's wife, Peggy, was a trim, efficient woman, with

pointed features that were softened by her friendliness and liveliness while heightened by the sharp intelligence that glowed behind her eyes.

"And this is Frank Harrigan."

Frank was noticeably older than the Biancas, a bit on the chubby side, with a high forehead. His shy demeanor immediately made Orimanie feel awkward in empathy with him.

"Ramone Nixon." Bianca finished the introduction. "I hope you're not any relation to Richard."

"Richard?"

"Richard Nixon. The former president."

"Oh. Oh, no. I don't think so." She wished now she had paid more attention to the political history sessions but her interests lay elsewhere. It was obvious that neither Bob Bianca or Frank Harrigan thought much of Richard Nixon.

"Ramone's doing a thesis on science fiction writers."

"Oh." Frank Harrigan obviously thought he should say something but he didn't know what.

"Not just science fiction writers," Ramone said. "It's a group of selected writers."

"I'm not sure I understand."

"Well, it's rather hard to explain." How had she gotten herself into this? "It's a group of seemingly unrelated writers that I'm trying to show really are related, if you know what I mean." With each word, she seemed to make things worse and worse, she seemed to make herself seem sillier and sillier. How could she explain what Robert Bianca had in common with Ernest Hemingway and Jack Kerouac, except that they were all writers whose works had survived for more than five hundred years?

But Bob Bianca smiled his quirky smile. "I think maybe I do. I've got a Masters in English myself."

Orimanie was saved from putting her foot further into her mouth when Peggy Bianca announced that dinner was ready, that Ramone must be very hungry from her trip on the bus, and that they could discuss literature later.

)OOOC

Despite the poor beginning, things went well. Her strange statements were soon forgotten and they talked about Bob Bianca's books, the small amounts of money he had made from them, and the book he was working on now. Frank Harrigan and Peggy listened politely, occasionally interjecting comments, interrupted frequently by the Biancas' two preschool children, until they were carted off to bed. While Bob read his children a story and Peggy excused herself to do some sewing, Orimanie was left alone with Frank Harrigan.

"I'm sorry," she said, "but I don't think I've read any of your books."

"No one has. I haven't published any."

"Well, I haven't read any of your stories either, I'm afraid."

"Not many people have."

She had yet to break through that reserve, the wall he put up between himself and others. Occasionally she had caught a glimpse of humor in interchanges between him and Bob Bianca but he rarely talked directly to Orimanie or even to Peggy, unsure and awkward. There was no good reason for her to want to break through that wall except that she might discover an unknown master.

"You write science fiction too?"

"Mostly. That's all I've published. I've written a lot of mainstream but that's a tough market to crack."

"And you haven't written any books?"

"One. It's making the rounds. I'm afraid it really isn't very good."

"Well, you never know," she said weakly. "They say that writers are the last people to judge their own works."

"This one's not very good. Even *I* know that."

"Then why did you write it?"

"I didn't *intend* for it to be a bad book. It just came out that way. Anyway, I've read a lot of other books, especially science fiction, that were worse."

"Then why can't you sell it?"

"It doesn't have a happy ending, the protagonist is a teenager, and... I've done a dozen things wrong, that don't fit the formulas, and it isn't written well enough to overcome those problems."

Bob came back to the room. "Well, I guess that takes care of them for a while. You know how kids are. They get all excited whenever we have company."

)OOOC

Orimanie spent the night in the Biancas' guest room while Frank Harrigan slept on the living room couch. The next day, instead of taking the bus to Atlanta, Frank drove her back in his sports car.

Instead of taking the superhighway, Orimanie found herself traveling along twisting rural Maryland highways, so different from the bus trip to Clarks Landing. The pounding weariness of the bus ride was transformed into an exciting spin through the country. The sports car was low to the ground, and she could feel the pull of centrifugal force on her as the car accelerated around the curves, whipping her hair around like writhing snakes. On the straightaways, her nose was filled with the smells of the country.

There were those of her acquaintances in the future who would have panicked at the deluge of raw new sensations, who would have fled back to the warm safety of their own time. But they would never have even considered being a Timedipper in the first place.

"I like this!" she shouted over the roar of the air rushing past.

"Ever ridden in a sports car before?" Frank glanced over at her briefly then returned his gaze to the road.

"No."

"I've been driving them for nearly fifteen years now. I love them."

Now in his element, confident and relaxed, his hand casually draped over the steering wheel, nudging it just enough to take the curves smoothly without accelerating, he was a different person from the shy, insecure, uncertain man she had met in Clarks Landing.

"Did you ever... did you ever race cars?"

"No." He shook his head. "Never really had the chance, never knew the right people. It's probably just as well; I doubt if I'd ever have been a very good driver. I'm too chicken."

"I think you'd be very good."

He grinned. "Thanks. But keep your seat belt buckled."

)〇〇〇〇(

The spin through the countryside was over far too soon as they came into suburban Baltimore. It was that Frank obvious felt as unhappy about the change as Orimanie did. The sparkle went out of his eyes and drove carefully, a bit on edge.

"I hate high-speed highways," he said. "I'd much rather drive on country highways."

"I like it better, too. At least when you're driving."

He reddened a little but said nothing.

They reached the Baltimore Beltway. "Where do you want me to take you?"

It was the question she'd been dreading. What kind of story could she make up that wouldn't make him suspicious? She was supposed to be a student at Towson State but, since she had expected to return to Baltimore by bus, she had left her suitcase and belongings in a locker at the bus station.

"You can let me off at the bus station. I left some things there. I thought I was going to be taking the bus back."

"Where do you live? I can drive you there after you pick up your things."

"Oh, no. I don't want to put you out of your way. You've been more than kind enough already."

"Oh, for crying out loud, Ramone, it's all right. I love driving. You know that. And you're pleasant to be with. I'll take you anywhere you want."

"I... please, Frank. I'll just take the bus home from the bus station." She turned away, unable to bear the look of hurt that crossed his face.

"You're sure?"

"Please, Frank." They drove in silence, all the joy of the country ride destroyed, and past, Frank trying unsuccessfully to hide his hurt while Ramone tried to think of some way she could assuage the pain she had caused.

"Frank?" The puppy-hope of his face was painful to see as Orimanie got out of the car. "I'd like to read some of your stories some time. Could you give me your phone number and I'll call you later this week?"

The tone of his voice was light but the disappointment remained in his eyes. "Sure." He gave her his phone number and they said goodbye.

)OOO(

Undoubtedly Frank Harrigan thought he would never hear from Ramone Nixon again but she called two days later and asked him to meet her at a street near Towson University. When he drove up, she was waiting for him on the porch of a boarding house where she had taken a room.

"Have you had dinner yet?" he asked. "I know an excellent Mexican restaurant out on Belair Road."

"Mexican? I... I don't think I've ever had Mexican food before."

"If you'd rather go someplace else ..."

"No, no. Please. I'd like to try it."

"If you're sure..."

"I'm sure. Did you bring your stories?"

The food was quite hot and spicy, and Orimanie reveled in still another novel experience, different from the diners and middle-class restaurants at which she had been eating so far. She enjoyed the meal, though not as much as Frank Harrigan obviously did. Then they went to a movie and, with just a little encouragement from Orimanie, he kissed her good night.

They went to a Greek restaurant and a French restaurant, a play and a rock concert, which Orimanie justified to herself as research, ignoring the fact that she wasn't seeking out the other authors she was supposed to be interviewing and meeting.

She was impressed and enchanted by his stories. Some of them were trifles, about children who used matter transmitters to fill parking meters with peanut butter and jellybeans, but others were poignant pieces about people who tried to communicate, people who were lovers and had to separate, not with fights and acrimony, but with tenderness and sorrow. There were no villains in his stories, no black-hearted stepfathers, or vicious killers, only people trapped by their characters and inabilities, by the binds of society and culture. It was incredible to Orimanie that a writer of such depth and understanding would not live beyond his own time. Could it be that he would die young, before he could attain the fame that should be is? The possibility worried Orimanie.

If Frank Harrigan was hesitant and shy in personal relationships, he was just the opposite in the physical world: if he saw a road he hadn't traveled, he had to return and find out where it went; if he saw an interesting-looking restaurant, he had to try it. His apartment was a third-floor walk-up in a graceful old house. The rooms were a jumble of belongings: books piled on the floor, manuscripts stacked around a typewriter in one room, magazines and newspapers and records and tapes in a jumble of piles in another.

"It's really fairly orderly," he said in apology. "I can find just about anything I want. But I'm afraid I'm not really very neat. I just keep moving the piles around."

It was then only a matter of time before she moved out of her rooming house to live with him. This provided a new set of problems. She could no longer pretend to be a student and it brought about a tearful admission in which she claimed that the whole thing had been a ruse so that she could meet Bob Bianca, one of her favorite writers.

"You won't tell him, will you?"

"Not for a while. But he'll have to find out sooner or later."

Then she had to explain that she wasn't working, that she was supporting herself from the inheritance she had received when her parents had died two years earlier (Frank made the proper sounds of consolation – awkwardly, of course – and the deception made her feel even worse), and that she had no close relatives or friends. Oh, the string of lies she told, her fingers mentally crossed.

And how could she justify to herself her dereliction from duty? She wasn't merely "researching some more," she was spending her time with an unknown and unimportant writer, hoping that she could somehow prevent the tragedy that undoubtedly was due to happen to him that would prevent him from becoming the major writer he should be. She read his unpublished novel and, yes, he was right – it wasn't as good as it could be; it lacked the poignancy of his short stories. But it had its moments and it could be improved.

She learned of his life, of the woman he had loved briefly, whose paths had touched and then diverged with the same sadness, the same feeling of *kismet* that throbbed in his stories.

She learned of the close friends who now lived hundreds and thousands of miles away, the pain of how many goodbyes with no one to blame, no one to curse but the unforgiving gods.

"I'll never leave you, Frank." Even knowing that it was untrue, that she would eventually have to return to her own time, she couldn't keep herself from saying it, hoping there was some way she makes it be true...

His smile was wan, full of remembered pain. "Perhaps. But maybe *I'll* leave you. I've done it before."

"You can't leave me. I'll follow you, wherever you go."

And there was that grin, that impish grin that came at sudden and unexpected moments. "Even to the men's room?"

)OOO(

When she finally "confessed" her duplicity to Bob Bianca at a science fiction convention, he wasn't angry at all. "I'm rather flattered," he said. "And a lot of good came out of it, didn't it? Otherwise you and Frank wouldn't have met."

But if Bob Bianca was pleased with the situation and Orimanie Rix-Dollars was confused about it, caught between her loyalty to her mission and her love for Frank, Frank Harrigan felt that he was caught on the horns of a dilemma.

"Looks like things are going pretty good for you," Bianca said to him.

"I don't know." Frank shook his head slowly.

"What's the matter? You two seem to get along quite well."

"It's not that. It's just that she's... well, she's a bit strange."

"She doesn't seem strange to me."

"You have to be with her a while to see it. Remember when we first met her and she didn't seem to know who Richard Nixon was?"

"That's nothing. I wish *I* didn't know who Richard Nixon was."

"That's it. That's exactly it. There's no way anybody who's lived in the United States in the past twenty years or so could *not* know who Richard Nixon was. And there's dozens of little things like that – Jimmy Carter, Elvis Presley, the Beatles. The Beatles, for God's sake. How could anyone not know who the Beatles were even, if they didn't like rock'n'roll, even if they didn't know their names?"

"Have you said anything to her about it?"

"No. How can you tell someone that you think they're crazy, really crazy? She says she has no relatives, no friends, that her parents were killed in an automobile accident two years ago and she's been living on the money they left her."

"Maybe she was in the accident too and has some kind of amnesia."

"She refuses to talk about her past, where she's from or anything else."

"It's probably pretty painful for her, Frank."

"Sometimes I think..."

Bob Bianca waited patiently.

"Sometimes I think she's spent most of her life in a... an institution or something, and that's why she's so ignorant of the most common things."

"Frank."

Frank, who had been looking at his hands and everywhere but at Bob Bianca, finally looked at him.

"You love her, don't you?"

Frank nodded.

"She's a good person, isn't she?"

"Yes. I think so."

"Then does it really matter what she was, what happened to her? You need her and... what maybe more important, she may need you.

Very much." He put a gentle hand on Frank's shoulder. "There's an awful lot I don't know or understand about Peggy. Someone once said that men and women are different species; sometimes I think he was right."

)OOO(

By now you've probably guessed the rest of the story. Orimanie Rix-Dollars never went back to her own time. Frank Harrigan managed to sell several novels and they bought some land near Clarks Landing, where he managed to make a respectable, if not sizeable, living from his science fiction books. They were good stories, even exciting ones, but they lacked the poignancy of his earlier work.

He also wrote stories for children, stories that were full of his quirky humor, and those sales didn't hurt their bank account either. She discussed with Bob Bianca his ideas about the future with its domed cities. The tragedy that would strike Frank Harrigan before his great and memorable works never struck. But, then again, he never wrote any more such painful stories, either. There was very little room left in him for pain.

)OOO(

They say that nothing comes for free. Perhaps. I only know that once in a while the price is a joyful one to pay. Would Frank Harrigan have traded the love of Ramone Nixon for literary greatness and immortality?

Would you?

THE FUTURE

Ask Lafferty

Have you ever had someone come up to you and call you by
another name?

    Insisting he was right?

    And you knew somehow he was?

        Not once

                but hundreds of times.

And always by the same name.

Is there someone walking around with your nose?

Have they confiscated your eyes?

    Stolen your lips?

    Counterfeited your eyes?

    Hijacked your hair?

Or are you someone else?

There is a legend about a double race
   who lead two lives
      never knowing they have two names.

Ask Lafferty.
  He knows about them.
  He'll tell you.

So in the night
 I hear a whistle over the back-alley fence
    and I slide down to the sheets
 to a rendezvous with other immortals
   who rule the world
       secretly
 or with a five-foot basketball team
   before returning to bed
  remembering it all as a dream
        if at all.

Driving down a country road
    wondering
  How did I get here?
  Whose car is this?
  Where am I going?
Then I find myself in a farmhouse
  under a bombed-out dam
       with puddles of water
     footsteps leading to the mud
      and a glow in the stars.

Policemen
> obsequious

Lawyers
> sycophants

Mayors
> bowing

Presidents
> kowtowing

Suddenly they look up
> as if seeing me for the first time

and chase me
> charge me with
>> trespassing
>>
>> vagrancy
>>
>> loitering
>>
>> public nuisance
>
> and resisting arrest.

I look in the mirror:
> eyes that have seen the Great Wall building
> hair ruffled in an African breeze
> nose that has smelled Cleopatra's perfume
> lips that have kissed Marie Antoinette's
> ears that have heard Beethoven make mistakes
> hands that have handled Pyramid stone.

There is a double race
> a twin people.

A Simple Twist of Fate

How often is history changed by a simple twist of fate? Not chance, mind you, but fate: "That which is destined or decreed; appointed lot." Is there anything which is chance, pure chance, and nothing more?

There is a woman. She calls herself Sharon Williams. A simple name. Common enough to bring her no attention, but not as common as Smith or Jones or Brown as to be suspicious. It is not, of course, her real name, her given name, but that does not concern us. She is a researcher, piling up data and conclusions in old New Orleans, the Vieux Carre, the French Quarter. It is exciting, for this is her first trip alone. Although she had been well trained, there is nothing as fearful and exhilarating as that first solo trip. It is an important test for her in many ways.

In her handbag is a small harmonica, a common, ordinary harmonica, but its importance to her is extraordinary. It is the key to her return to the future. For Sharon Williams is a Timedipper.

She walks along the waterfront docks, by the Jax brewery, the smell of fermented yeast in the air. She walks down Bourbon Street, down by the arcade, hearing Dixieland music and the bump-grind of the striptease shows. In a small bar, a slender man with long hair is singing the blues. Another longhaired young man asks her for spare change and she gives him a dime, a thin piece of silver-coated copper with the visage of Franklin Delano Roosevelt imprinted on it, quaint, feeling slightly greasy under her fingers.

Down at the French Market, the odors of rotting fruits and vegetables mingle with the salty smell of fish, and the combination is heady. Tomorrow she'll begin her research; now she just wants to breathe in the air of the past, listening to the clatter of horse's hooves and the tourist carriages on Bourbon Street; the rumble of the wheels of the carriages on the cobblestones of the street; the muted hush of traffic around the French Quarter; the occasional horn. The Timedippers look indulgently on all this, accepting it. They know; they've been there too.

Finally she goes into the Morning Call, one of the little shops near the waterfront, for one of their donuts – beignets, they call them –

and chicory coffee. It's crowded, as it usually is. She winds up sitting next to a handsome-looking black man with a thick but well-trimmed beard. He looks almost satanic when he glares at her as she sits down next to him. None of this bothers her – in her world, crowded conditions are common, and nearly everyone has some Negro blood in them. She shows it more than most, with her café-au-lait color, her thick lips, and her dark hair.

She shakes powdered sugar from the battered tin can onto her beignet.

"Watch it!" the man says with a harsh but resonant voice. "Don't you know how to use that thing?"

"I'm sorry," she says, a bit rattled by his brusqueness.

He brushes the sugar off his dark pants, leaving a light gray streak. "Here." He sprinkles the sugar deftly onto her beignet and hands it back.

"I'm sorry." She bits into the hot donut. It is almost too hot for her. "I'm new here," she says.

"Tourist." The word is almost a swear word.

"Yes. I guess you could say that." She drinks from the thick, chicory-tasting coffee, not quite bitter. It tastes good, full of new tastes to her mouth.

"Where are you from?" he asks, the bitterness and the brusqueness of his manner only slightly blunted.

"Oh," she says, laughing, "a long, long way away from here. Farther away than you could possibly imagine."

"Africa?"

She shakes her head.

"I'd like to go to Africa," he says. "That's where our people came from originally, you know."

"But that's so far in the past, it doesn't matter," she says.

"Some people don't think so," he says darkly. But there is something in those haunted dark eyes that flashes out at her, a touch of intelligence and compassion, the bitterness of a man who has seen too much of the dark side of life, who has been disillusioned one too many times, frightened and hiding that fright beneath a veneer of cynicism.

So she reaches out her hand and lays it on his dark arm, the mocha color of her hand looking almost white against his skin. "Would you like to show me around the Quarter?" she asks. It is a natural thing to her, a part of the excitement. She has nothing to fear, for she's been trained to take care of herself, and, indeed, has had to do so twice in the past. But she is a good judge of character as well and knows that this man, despite his bitterness, is to be trusted.

He looks at her from those deep wells of bitterness and disenchantment, judging her, making his own conclusions, distrustful, but yet, oh so vulnerable.

"Why should I?" he asks.

"Why not? Have you got anything better to do?"

Again that long pause while he sizes her up. "You trust me?" he asks at last.

"Certainly. You're a good man. I can tell."

And he laughs, a loud bitter histrionic laugh that makes the other patrons of The Morning Call turn to look, to see who this madman is, laughing that loonybin laugh.

"All right," he says, and the smile on his face, even touched with bitterness as it is, is genuine enough to make it all worthwhile. "You win, lady. I got nothing better to do. I got no job. You can't get a job in this town unless you're a Steppinfetchit, an Uncle Tom. And Brian Salerno may be many things that aren't much good, but an Uncle Tom isn't one of them."

"Is that your name? Brian Salerno?"

He nods. "A strange name for a man like me, isn't it? Not what you'd expected perhaps. Something like Joe Williams or Tony Brown would be appropriate. Or maybe Muhammad M'bangi? No, Brian Salerno it is, for the time being. But someday I'll have a name that fits my heritage. And your name, lady?"

"Sharon Williams. I'll make it worth your while, Brian."

"I'm sure you will," he says in a voice that stops a few millimeters short of being menacing. "I'm sure you will."

So Brian Salerno shows Sharon Williams the sights of New Orleans, old and new. They stop for a drink at Lafitte's Blacksmith Shoppe, supposedly the actual building where the pirate had a business. They visit the Witches' Workshop, with its old powders and papers full of incantations. Next door they have a beer at the Seven Seas, the current hangout of the young people. As the evening sky grows dark, they sit together in Jackson Square, under the Saint Louis Cathedral. He takes her to a strip show and she buys him dinner at Antoine's. Then he drives her through the Negro shantytown.

"Segregation is over, they say. Equal opportunity. Look around, Sharon. Is *this* equality?"

"But surely there are white people who live like this as well?"

"Yeah, a few," he admits grudgingly. "But not many. And they've got a better chance to get out of it. How much chance do these poor kids have?"

"What about you?"

"Me?"

"Yes. Do you live here?"

Brian laughs that half-bitter, half-triumphant laugh of his. "Me? No. I'm one of the lucky ones. Come. I'll show you."

Brian's apartment is a two-room affair in the quarter, with shutters on the outside. It is a bit on the messy side, but the furniture is solid and the walls are clean.

"You seem to be doing all right," she says as he goes into the tiny kitchen to prepare some coffee for them. "Is this yours?" She goes over to small oil painting propped up against a lamp.

"Yeah," he says gruffly.

"It's quite good." It shows a black man hanging from a tree, while men in white robes kick a woman and her young children out of their way as they are leaving the scene.

"I call it 'Strange Fruit.' That's a Billie Holliday song, you know. Quite daring for its time. Hell, even for today. But do you think anyone cares? No one gives a damn. They don't want that kind of thing. They're running scared, the whole pack of them, and they don't want any part of it."

"I'm not sure what you mean."

He put a cup of coffee in front of her. "I had a showing last year. Two days later, someone broke into the studio and slashed every canvas to shreds. And I got several hate notes warning me to stop painting. Here's one of them."

He pulls a rumpled piece of paper out of a pile of books; in letters cut out from magazines and newspapers, it reads, "Better know your place, or it'll be swinging from a tree."

Sharon looks at it, appalled, and yet delighted, for it is further verification that she is living in the past, when conflicts and prejudices still exist so strongly.

"I thought this was all over," she says at last.

"That's what they all say. But they don't have to live with it. If you stick in your place, you don't run up against it."

"But surely this is only a few people." She protests. "Some hangovers from the past."

"It's all of them, lady," he says viciously. "Oh, I know what they say out front, pretending they're oh-so-liberal and oh-so-unbigoted, but I know what they say when they think they can't be heard. But they're scared of us too, and they've got good reason to be. You can push a people just so far. One of these days we'll rise up and wipe those bigots off the map."

"I... I find this hard to believe."

"Yeah, I know," he sneers. "They treat you so nice to your face, maybe want to be your lover, get a little dark meat. But they don't want to marry you, do they? You have no idea what they say behind your back."

"I'm sure you're wrong." She *knows* he is wrong; the history books all show that he is, that the merging of the races has already begun, that those who had slashed his canvasses were just anachronisms. The Black-and-White War would prove that, with American blacks fighting side by side with their white brothers against the African dictator Mkono la Simba.

"A lot you know," he says.

"Where are the rest of your paintings?" she asks brightly, trying to change the subject.

"That's the only one I've done since the showing," he says. "I'm through painting. No one wants to see what I have to show them; no one wants to see the truth."

"That's not true!"

"Do *you*? Do you want to see the truth?" He shoves the painting in front of her face. "Can you stand it?"

"But that's only part of the truth, Brian, only a small part."

"Sure. Then there's the lies and deceit that the white people pass among themselves, from the president of the United States on down. Well, they've stepped on Brian Salerno one time too many. I lost my job, today, Sharon. That's why you found me in the Morning Call. They didn't say why, just a 'cutback in personnel.' I was the only one fired; the rest were just laid off. But they don't want me back. And do you know why?"

Sharon shakes her head dumbly.

"Because I'm a trouble-maker, that's why. Because they learned about my past, that I had held that showing, that I'd been kicked out of college because of my involvement with causes, and so now I'm working as a lousy stock boy and I can't even do that, even that's too good for a black trouble-maker!"

"Brian!"

"But I'm ready for them, Sharon. One day they'll come looking for me and I'll be ready for them." He pulls out a wicked-looking knife with a blade that seems about nine inches long. "And there's a pistol in the bedroom."

Sharon can't believe it. This is supposed to be a hiatus in the days of violence, between the racial times of the early Twentieth Century and the war that would come at the end of the century when Mkono la Simba united the African continent and slaughtered whites in a bloodbath that rivaled Hitler's campaign against the Jews.

"Put that away," she says. "You're frightening me."

"But you're good for me, I can tell. I don't know why you talked to me in the Morning Call, why you didn't slap me and walk away, but you're what I need. I don't expect you to make any decisions right now. All I ask is a chance, you see? A chance to prove myself."

"I don't know what you're talking about."

He takes her hands in his. "I like you, Sharon. A lot. You're the first person who's treated me as a human being in a long time. Just say you'll give me a fighting chance."

"I like you too, Brian, I do. I think you're awfully mixed up but I think you're a good person under all that bitterness."

Brian begins to walk around the room, gesturing as he talks, overcome with eagerness and energy. "Damn! This is great. You're just what I needed. A sign, an omen. It's all going to work out. It's all going to work out."

"I'm just going to be here for a few days, Brian. I'll be leaving in a week."

"That's all right. That's all right. A week is all I ask. Just a week."

She smiles at his eagerness, almost childlike, glad to see it replacing the bitterness. Perhaps in one short week, she can do something about that bitterness. "But I really will be leaving in a few days. I want you to understand that."

"Sure, sure."

)OOO(

Several hours later they lie on their backs, staring at the ceiling in the dark, their bodies touching in a dozen places, feeling sated and relaxed. Someplace far off, a saxophone plays and the music drifts through the window.

"There's so much to tell you, Sharon. My dreams, my plans."

"I'm sure you'll do well, Brian. I'm sure everything's going to work out for you." For the past couple of hours, a little imp has been nagging at her brain. The name Brian Salerno has set off a trigger. It *is* going to work out for him. She knows it, for his name isn't a complete unknown to her. Apparently he will become a quite famous painter for, if she had heard his name, however briefly, it must have become quite well known. She is not an art historian and can name only half a dozen artists.

"One of these days, Sharon, one of these days... we'll all be united. Africa will belong to the blacks, to whom it originally belonged. We'll drive out the whites and create our own country, a truly black African united country."

Sharon lies beside him, willing her body not to become as tense as she feels. She feels a tingle to her bones. The pieces fall into place: Brian Salerno will not become a famous painter.

"What will you call yourself?" she hears herself ask. "Surely the Africans won't unite under a man who calls himself Brian Salerno."

"I've thought of that. I'll use a Swahili name, or Zulu. I'm thinking of Mkono la Simba. It means arm of the lion in Swahili. I like it."

For a long time after Brian Salerno falls asleep, Sharon Williams lies awake, afraid to move, feeling unclean in every pore. She slowly gets out of bed, stopping whenever she hears Brian move. She gathers her clothes together, picks up her handbag, unlocks the door, and flees.

Brian Salerno, Mkono la Simba, the man who will go down in history with Adolf Hitler and Attila the Hun as one of the greatest mass murderers, not only of the innocent white people who would be caught in Africa when he gains control, but also of tens of thousands of his own people, who will fight against him and all that he represents, and who eventually will plunge the world into the infamous Black-and-White War which will only be ended by an atomic bomb on his capital on the banks of Lake Tanganyika.

And she had slept with him! She had felt sorry for him! She races down the streets of New Orleans, still bright and alive with nightlife. She throws a handful of coins into the cup of a beggar but that cannot assuage her guilt. Nothing can. Blindly, she takes a trolley car to the end of the line and leaves the city at last, walking to a small patch of woods with a deserted knoll that won't be bulldozed down for a housing development for another three years.

Once there, the panic still driving within her, she takes the harmonica out of her handbag and blows five notes in an unusual pattern. For a moment nothing happens, then the air in front of her seems to shimmer and a voice says in a language that is not English or Hottentot or Zulu or Swahili: "So soon?" She steps into the shimmering air and disappears, never to return.

)OOO(

When Brian Salerno wakes up, the room is bare. He is angry and bitter at first but sweeps that aside, trying to convince himself that she has gone out for some reason that has nothing to do with him. Feeling an emptiness inside, he pushes the window open. He can't stand another disappointment, one more slap in the face. She has left no note, however, and when she hasn't returned by noon, he goes out in search of her, the anger growing inside.

He stalks through the French Quarter like a beast of prey, stopping in every bar and bistro to glare at the patrons until he is certain that she's not among them. He asks all the bartenders and waiters if they have seen her, if they remember anyone like her, but no one does. He spends five dollars in dimes calling hotels and motels for a Sharon Williams, only to find that she is registered in none.

At last he walks down by the waterfront, by the Jax Brewery, and sits down in the Morning Call, with the forlorn and angry hope that she will have enough sense to meet him there, if indeed she is still in New Orleans and wants to see him again. And the blackness smolders inside him like dark flame. He'll show her; damn it, a man can take just so much and then he has to turn. The bitterness and disappointment transmutes itself into an anger that will not be appeased, not until he's had his revenge. He'll show them all; he'll show them all.

)OOO(

How deep is the wound that never heals? How many times must a man try before he ceases to try? A simple twist of fate sent Carl Weiss to Huey Long in 1935, Oswald to Dallas and John F. Kennedy in 1963, and Arthur Bremer to George Wallace in 1972. There would be no bullet for Brian Salerno; his adopted name would go down with Hitler, the marauding Mongols of Attila, with Stalin and with Caligula. And all because of a simple twist of fate.

But you already know that song.

The Key

They worked in a dingy basement near Dupont Circle in Washington. Once they had been respected scientists but now they were just another handful of gray people in a city full of gray people, gray-haired and white-bearded. They were trying to change the world and sometimes it seemed as if everybody who had lived in the past fifteen years was a key. But they narrowed it down to a hundred fairly easily and then painstakingly down to ten. Finally they chose one key out of the ten but their criteria were so ill-defined that they might just as well have chosen of the ten at random.

)OOO(

It was quitting time. The streets of Washington were filled with people rushing to their homes, driven more by the fear of being caught outside when curfew fell than by the bitter October wind that sent leaves scuttling across the city streets. Dean Cabot was one of them, scurrying from his dishwashing job to his tiny cubbyhole of a room several blocks away from Dupont Circle. Like everyone else, he was dressed in drab colors, in blacks and dark grays and dark blues and dull browns, not like the many-colored and many-patterned shirts and blouses people had worn when he was a young man, only fifteen years earlier. But these days no one wanted to draw attention to themselves. A policeman scowled at him and he moved more briskly, past the newsstand with its headline blaring about the latest proclamation of the president-for-life. And somewhere buried inside, Dean knew, was a brief item about the resignation of the latest vice-president. There were be nothing of the about the rumors of strife and riots and Seattle and St. Louis.

It had been so different when he was younger, when he and Gail had been together. Then there had been hopes and dreams of a newer and better America. But all those hopes had been dashed, for Dean at least, when Gail had died in a car wreck. That's when America had turned sour, or so it had seemed to Dean.

As he walked along, his gaze downcast along with his mood, a glint of metal in the gutter caught his eye and he stopped. Looking around furtively, he scooped up the piece of metal, wondering as he did so what had made him stop for something so insignificant; then he stepped back into the rhythm of the incessant stream of homeward-bound people.

It was only a key but, even as he realized this, Dean's heart seemed to take a little leap in his chest. It was just like the key to the outside door of the rowhouse where he had shared a top-floor apartment with Gail fifteen years ago. A number was stamped on it: 1416. Once again Dean felt a little jolt—that had been the address of their rowhouse. Could this key belong to one of the current occupants of that house? Unlikely: there were many 1416s in Washington. But would their keys have the same shape? Some maybe, perhaps some in that same area, sharing the same landlord. Nonetheless, when he crossed the street where he and Gail had lived, Dean turned down it after an instant of thought, toward that brief nest of love and security, knowing how silly it was.

He stood before the house. Like the people of today, it too was drab, a dull brown building with nothing to distinguish it from its neighbors. Even the buildings didn't want to draw attention to themselves these days.

When Dean and Gail had lived there, the door had been a brilliant red, flowers and stained-glass hangings filled the windows, and music poured out whenever the weather was warm enough to open the windows.

Dean smoothed down his thinning hair. Even that had changed; back then he had had a stubborn cowlick that he constantly had to brush out of his eyes. Now he had a widow's peak that kept receding and never again would he have to push hair out of his eyes.

He stood hesitantly before the door then pressed the button for the third-floor apartment. A wave of dizziness passed over him and he leaned against the building while he caught his breath. These waves had overcome him frequently in the past several months and he knew he should see a doctor, but who could a doctor these days? If it wasn't anything serious, then there was no sense. And if it was, then he would soon be with Gail, if only in blessed oblivion.

He looked at the crimson door in front of him and blinked. That wasn't right. It shouldn't be red now—it couldn't be. But the red door refused to go away. Dean brushed his cowlick back; there was something wrong with that too, but he couldn't think of what. He stared at his hand, trying to remember.

The door swung open and Mr. Brannum, his landlord, who lived in the small apartment on the first floor, was standing there. "Come in, boy. Are you going to stand there all day.?"

"No... no." Dean stepped into the tiny vestibule, still confused. From the stairwell to his left, the sounds of "Monday, Monday" drifted down from the second-floor apartment. The girls who had lived there had played it incessantly until Dean had hated the song. Now, though, whenever he heard it, it brought him back to when he and Gail had been together, with all those bittersweet memories.

"Are you all right, son?"

"Sure... sure. Just dizzy." He wanted to ask if Mr. Brannum still owned the building but that was a silly question. Who was living on the third floor now?

"Well, you just go upstairs and lie down for a while. I've got to get to work now." The older man, seemingly unchanged by the passage of time, closed the door behind him. Dean wondered if Mr. Brannum still had the part-time job he had worked fifteen years ago to augment his rental income.

Slowly, fearfully, Dean mounted the stairs. There was definitely something wrong here. "Monday, Monday" grew louder. Dean looked at the key in his hand. Gisela was standing on the landing outside her apartment. She too hadn't aged a bit. She was still the gum-chewing, chubby twenty-year-old she had been... but that was wrong too. There was no way she could still look the same. Dean's heart took another extra leap in his chest and he felt his muscles grow tight with fearful tension.

"Hey, Dean, what are you doin' home so soon?"

"Uh, nothing. Just a little dizzy spell."

"Maybe you been smoking' too much weed."

Dean grinned. The expression felt forced and phony. "No, I'm sure it's nothing. Just a touch of the flu."

"Gail's sure gonna be surprised to see you home this time of day."

"Gail?" *Is she alive?* Dean wanted to say but instead he said, "Is she home?"

"You must be really mixed up. She's only got morning classes today, right?"

"Oh. Right." Dean started up the stairway to the third floor, feeling even more apprehensive and frightened. What day of the week was it? What time of year? It didn't feel like October. And exactly why was he frightened? What was he frightened of?

"See you later, Dean." Gisela went back into her apartment.

Frightened. Could these people be the same ones from fifteen years ago or they really different? Who was in that third-floor apartment? Was it really *his* Gail or another Gail? If this was fifteen years earlier, was another Dean Cabot working in the tiny bookstore off Dupont Circle? What would happen when *he* got home from work? All these questions flashed through his mind while he trudged up the stairs. Dean felt dizzy again, trying to contemplate all the possibilities.

He stood before the door to the third-floor apartment, hesitant. The sound of a Beatles record drifted through the door. Finally he knocked. Familiar footsteps approached and then Gail's voice: "Who is it?"

He felt weak. "It's me." He had to clear his throat. "Me. Dean."

"Well, come on in, for Christ's sake?" The door swung open and there she was, a robe over her petite figure, her mouth in an irritated pout. "Why the hell didn't you just come on in?"

"I... I lost my key."

"Not again! And what are you doing home so early?"

"I felt sick. Dizzy."

The irritation left her face. She reached out to him. "Come in. Come in." She placed her hand on his forehead. "You do seem a little bit warm. I'll make you some tea and soup."

"I'm all right. I just need... I just need to sit down."

He walked into the front room—it was just the way he remembered it: the ratty old couch that had come with the apartment, which Gail had tried to cover with the exotic Indian cloth that sold cheaply in the head shops. Her guitar was leaning against the tiny bookcases in the wall and the worn old rug was partially covered with a small phony oriental rug they had picked up in W.T. Grant's.

He sat down on the couch, remembering a day he had come early from work, feeling dizzy and out of sorts, pushing her aside when he had tried to be solicitous.

"You sure you don't want anything to eat?"

"I'm all right, I told you!"

She stood there looking down at him. "Well, I'm not going to spend all afternoon playing nursemaid to you. I've got work to do."

"Then do it!"

"I've got to get that psych paper done this afternoon and it needs a lot of polishing."

"For Christ's sake, Gail, you're acing that course. You don't have to do anything the rest of the semester. I don't know why you had to take a Saturday morning class anyway."

The tightness was back in her mouth. "I'm going to grad school next year and I'm going to the best damn college I can get into. I don't want to fuck that up."

It was an old argument. "What's wrong with George Washington University?"

"You can't get all your degrees from the same university. It doesn't look good. You need diversity."

"Christ, you sound like a politician. So go to American U. They've got a good poly sci program."

"I'm tired of Washington. I've spent my whole life here." She had grown up in Alexandria, the daughter of a now-retired lifetime government employee. "I want to see the rest of the country."

"Just another year!"

"And what are *you* going to do? Spend the rest of your life working in some goddamn book store?"

"No! I just need time to figure things out."

"I thought you would come around but, Christ, you've been in this funk for half your life!"

"Two years! Christ, I came home to get a little peace and quiet and what do I get? An argument!" He got up and headed for the door.

"Where are you going?"

"For a walk!"

"Great! Go on! Get out of my life!"

He slammed the door behind him and stomped down the stairs. It seemed as if they were arguing all the time now. Was it his fault that he had no ambition? He had been sailing along with a high B in nuclear engineering when the draft lottery had been held and he had come up with number three-sixty-five. Since he had been in school primarily to escape the draft, he dropped out. A year later he had met Gail and they had hit it off. But now she wanted to go to grad school and leave him behind.

He stepped out into the street. It wasn't October; it felt like early summer. Why did he think it was October? Of course it was summer; it was June. And why had he left Gail alone in the apartment? Something terrible could happen to her. But what? It seemed as if he knew but it stayed there at the edge of his mind. To hell with her. He started walking toward Dupont Circle.

Why couldn't she understand? It made no sense to go back to

school if you didn't want to. That was just a waste of time and money. But he loved her so. The thought of losing her hurt so bad, as if someone were mangling his body, pressing the life out of him with unyielding metal. He had never felt this way before, so lost, so alone, so destitute, as if he had already lived the rest of his lifetime without her.

The newsman alongside the People's Drugstore at the corner of P and 20th caught his eye. He realized that it wasn't the man who usually sold papers there, but an older man with a long white beard. The man looked at him intensely as he held up the latest issue of the *Washington Post*. The headlines were about the SALT treaty and a Russian visit to Hanoi, and there was a picture of the President embracing the Mexican president. Something about the newspaper disturbed Dean. He moved closer to see the date: June 17, 1972. But that was the day that... Impossible memories flooded into his mind.

"Why don't you take a paper home to your lady, son?" the old man said but, before he finished, he was speaking to no one. Dean had turned and started racing back toward his apartment.

She was already at the second-floor landing when he got home, her suitcases in her hands.

"Where are you going?" he demanded.

"Home. I'll spend the rest of the semester with my parents."

"Don't go yet," he said desperately. "One more day! Please, that's all I ask."

"I've given you enough chances already, Dean. Get out of my way." She started down the stairway but Dean refused to move, blocking her exit. "Get out of my way!" she repeated.

"I won't let you go," he insisted. "It's dangerous out there."

"Don't give me any of that male bullshit. Honestly, Dean! I thought you were above *that*!"

"That's not what I mean."

She tried to push her way past him and suddenly they were in a twisted mass of arms and legs and suitcases crumpled in a heap at the bottom of the stairs.

"Damn you, Dean!"

"Are you all right?"

"I think I've twisted my ankle."

"Let's see." She got up and limped around the foyer a couple of times. "Well, that's that," he said. "You certainly can't drive with your ankle in that shape."

"Yes, I can."

"Be sensible, Gail. You've got to go upstairs and put an ice pack on it. Then, if it doesn't swell, I'll let you go home if you want. But if you don't do something immediately..."

"Damn you, Dean!" She started limping up the staircase. "Bring my suitcases back up, will you?"

"Sure." He couldn't keep from grinning broadly.

"And wipe that shit-eating grin off your face. As soon as I'm sure this thing is okay, I'm leaving."

"Okay. I won't stop you then."

She looked back at him with a puzzled expression. "Do you *want* me to leave?"

"No. But keeping you here against your will isn't going to do me any good, is it?" She shook her head, more in exasperation than in agreement, and started back up the stairway. "But I warn you, Gail, I'll follow you wherever you go."

"Fine. As long as you're going to school at the same time."

"Maybe I will." He deposited the suitcases in the living room while Gail limped into the kitchen to get some ice. "I'll go out and get some Chinese food, okay? We can talk about it over dinner."

"I'm leaving, Dean."

"Sure. Right after dinner."

He raced down the stairs to the Oriental restaurant around the corner, where he ordered beef and snow peas to go. While they were getting it ready, he went to the liquor store next door and bought a bottle of Lancer's. Then he hurried back to the apartment, noting with relief that her car was still there. But when he reached the door and was fumbling for his key, he was struck by another wave of dizziness. He stood there, the key in his hand, feeling suddenly chilly, when the door opened.

"You found it?" a man with a white beard said. "Thank you." He held out his hand and, without thinking, Dean put the key in it. What had happened to the Oriental dinner and the wine? And why did he have a jacket on in June?

"Don't you think you'd better go home to your wife?" the man said.

"My wife." Dean turned and started down the stairs.

"Thank you, Dean," the man said. Dean turned, but he door was already closing on that white-bearded face.

He started walking toward the Metro then stopped. Metro? There had been no subway when he and Gail had lived together... or in that other world that now seemed like a dream, a world where the president had barricaded himself in the White House for fifteen years, a world where the United States was deeply divided, fragmenting more and more with each passing year. *This* world... Dean inhaled the October air deeply, as disconnected memories flooded his mind. The people didn't seem any happier but they didn't seem as harried, as frightened. There was a businessman with a vividly colored tie, a young man with long hair, a brightly painted bus. No, this may not be the best of all possible worlds but it was a damn sight better than the one Dean had left... how long ago? Minutes? Seconds? Fifteen years?

But why? What had happened? Gail must be the clue, the key to it all. Because in this world she was alive, waiting for him with their two young children. In this world she had gotten her doctorate and was now an advisor for a political think-thank in Washington. And Dean? Well, he had settled for a bachelor's in engineering and was doing well. But he wasn't the key; it was Gail. Somehow the fact of her existence had changed the world.

It had to be her—the guy who had been driving the other car had been just a night watchman in some apartment complex called Watergate.

Younger Than Springtime

He had tried to save himself. "You've got to be less impulsive. You've got to think things through more carefully."

"Thanks. I'll think about it, old man."

A quarter dropped into his hand and then he watched himself walk away. "Wait." He tried to follow himself but couldn't keep up and soon lost himself in the people on the sidewalk. Soon she would be laughing with himself about the encounter.

He looked down at the coin in his hand. It wasn't a quarter. It was a Susan B. Anthony dollar. He had never realized that.

"I bet you never even considered that he wouldn't listen to you."

The voice cut through him but when he turned around, she wasn't there. Instead an old woman was looking at him.

"It didn't work for me either," she said, "but I didn't really expect it to."

The well-remembered voice sent familiar emotions through him. "I never... I never thought that *you* would be here."

"Never crossed your mind, right? Still as impulsive as ever."

"No, not quite. It's hard to be impulsive when you've got a trick knee that could go on you at any moment without warning. But why *are* you here?"

"Perhaps I'm a little bit more impulsive than I used to be. I tried to tell myself not to be so anal retentive."

"I never called you that."

"But you thought it." Her smile was as quirky and comfortable as ever. "I didn't listen to me fifty years ago and I didn't listen to me now."

"You never told me that..."

"It happened just after we met. I almost told you when you told me about... that old man who had stopped you on the square but..." She paused.

"You were too anal retentive." He tried to smile away the bite of the words. "But why are you here now? I mean, it was months ago when we... they met."

"We can't go back. I thought you knew that. We're here for the remainder of our lives."

"It just wasn't important. I didn't even think about it."

"Impulsive." She smiled again. "So, as long as I had to stay, I thought I'd come here and watch the encounter we had laughed so much about. That old man seemed to know so much about us. I didn't plan to say anything to you. That was... an impulse."

"So you're not as anal retentive as you used to be."

"And you're not as impulsive, perhaps. Age has a tendency to smooth things over, doesn't it?"

"Except for the pains." He sighed. "Do you have a place to stay?"

"I do. I've been here for several months. Do *you*?"

"No. I wasn't... I wasn't thinking."

She looked at him for a long moment. "Come along then. This time the treat's on me."

)OOO(

Her room was a simple one, just a few blocks away from the square. He couldn't help thinking that it was also just a few blocks away from where their younger selves lived. She sat down on the bed.

"I guess we sleep together again. There's no place else."

"That's all right. I can find a place of my own. I don't want to be any trouble."

"It's no trouble." She cupped his wrinkled face in her wrinkled hands.

)OOO(

Her breasts now sagged with age but he could still see the firm full ones he had known when they were young. He touched them as though they were more precious than the rarest of gems. When they tired of talking about what had happened in the years since their parting, they finally went to bed, where they was surprised to find themselves capable, both emotionally and physically, of desires that they had thought were years behind them.

They made love with greater tenderness and more passion than their younger selves were doing at that very moment, fifty years in their past.

The Gogfather

The gogfather was a huge, slug-like beast that lounged in a corner of its sumptuously-furnished apartment high in the tallest building of the largest city on Manhattan. The gogs were all his children, slimy lizard-like creatures, one of whom I'd met before under conditions I'd rather forget about. And I was (and still am) Fred Harmon, an itinerant guitar-picker who'd been picked up by a flying saucer and was now the musical sensation of the galaxy.

Confused? Not nearly as confused as I felt at that moment. Confused and scared. More scared than confused. I kept hoping that it was all a product of my mind, that I'd scored some bad acid and that any moment now it would all wear off and I'd find myself in a cornfield in Iowa, which was the worst fate I'd ever thought about back when I was still on good old Earth. But I knew that wasn't going to happen.

Let me lay a few facts on you before I continue—when I said we were on Manhattan, I didn't mean the island in New York State on good old planet Earth. I've gotten into the habit of dubbing the various planets we've landed on according to the characteristics they have in common with places I'm familiar with—New Haven, Iowa, Hackensack. Some of the names in their native language, if you want to call it that, I couldn't even speak. So Manhattan was not an island but an entire planet—an island in space if that makes you feel any better. It didn't make *me* feel any better. I was already beginning to realize that I should have called it Corsica instead.

"Fredharmon?" the slug said. It didn't just lounge in the corner—it filled the entire space, a loathsome white grub that grew loathsomer with each minute I spent in that room. I expected a rotting garbage stench to come from it but actually there was a pleasant aroma in the room. That didn't make things any easier for me, however.

"Y-y-yes," I stammered. I didn't speak in English, of course; I'd already been force fed the Lingua Galactica and spoke it like a native.

"I am the gogfather. Step closer." The slug leaned forward. I would have thought it was impossible for it to move at all. Actually it would be more accurate to say it *rippled* forward. "Ah, yes. You *are* a humanoid, indeed."

"That's what my mother told me," I said with more aplomb than I felt.

A slender appendage—an arm, a branch, a tendril, *something*—came out of the grub and waved aimlessly around the room. "These are my children, the gogs. *All* the gogs are my children."

"Uh, pleased to meet you all. You must have quite a family." I remembered the one I'd seen on Hackensack, the one I'd caught with its mitt in my guitar, who had taken it on the lam when I'd clobbered its companion gorilla with my guitar, which they had been stuffing with drugs. "Uh, about that incident on Hackensack..."

The tentacle waved again. "It is no matter. We have more important things to talk about."

"Great! Well, if you guys got more important things to talk about, I don't want to get in the way." I turned around to leave but one of the lizards threw me back.

"You are a musician?" the gogfather said as if I hadn't attempted to make a break for it.

"Well, yeah, I guess you could say that." Compared to the skills of my alien partners in the band I called The Interstellar Ragtime All-American Jazz Band, I was strictly Johnny One-Note but for some reason other humanoids have no musical talent whatsoever so I was something of a sensation.

"And you come from... Dirt?" He used the Lingua Galactica word.

"Earth," I said in English.

"Uruth," he repeated. A tentacle whipped out and grabbed one of the gogs by the throat and dragged it closer to the gogfather. "You hear? Uruth. Not... dirt." Another tentacle came out of the sluggish mass and whipped the lizard across the face several times. "Remember. I have lots of children. I get hungry at times."

"I will... I will remember, gogfather." The lizard backed away quickly, bowing profusely, as the grub let it go.

"Good." The gogfather seemed to turn back to me, although it made no movement other than to tuck away those tentacles. I vowed to myself that I would get nowhere near them if I had any choice in the matter. I suspected that my preferences would make little difference, however. "Where is this Uruth?"

"Uh, out there." I waved my hand in the direction of the stars. "Thataway."

A tentacle whipped out and one of the lizards pushed me into its range. It burned as it wrapped around my throat. "I need more precise information, Fredharmon."

"Uggle, wuggle, goo, goo," I said, and the tentacle released its pressure a bit. "Urgh." I reached up to massage my throat. "Uh, look, gogfather, I'm not a n astronomer. I'm just a musician who got picked up off my home planet and flown here and there all over the universe. I don't even know the names of the stars. All I know is the Big Dipper."

"The Pig Dippurrr?" I'd said it in English.

"A... a star formation, a whatyoucallit, a constellation."

"Tell me about your home planet, your stellar system."

"My stellar system? Oh, you mean the solar system. Well, let's see. There's nine planets and Earth is the third one from the sun. Then there's Mars, Venus, uh, Jupiter, Saturn..."

"I am not interested in your names for them. They mean nothing to me. What color is your star?"

"Yellow."

"Nine planets. Describe them, please. Which are gas giants and which are habitable?"

"I don't know that kind of stuff. One of them has a ring, Saturn, if that helps any."

"A ring." If ever a slug could sound disgusted, this one did. "Do you know how many planets in the universe have rings?"

"Uh, four?"

"This one is useless. Throw him out... wait!" I let go of my breath. For a moment there, I'd thought he was going to let me go. "Hold on to him. Let's talk to some of the other members of his group."

So I wound up several rooms away from the gogfather's headquarters, in a broom closet or its equivalent. It was dark, barely large enough for me to stand up and turn around in. It wasn't exactly comfortable but it could've been worse. But I had lots of time to worry about myself and my friends.

The band consists of me and three aliens: Bass, a fishlike creature who uses the cavity of his body to produce one part of our rhythm section; Monkey, a four-armed creature who plays a tabla-like instrument with four tunable drum heads; and Spider, who plays The Axe—a large jungle-gym-like structure that produces the sweetest music this side of the Pig Dippurrr... or anywhere else, for that matter.

When they had picked me up, there were two other members in our troupe. Our agent was a very human-looking guy whom I called Charley. He had put the group together and "recruited" me from

Earth but now he was in the slammer in New Haven, for his part with the drug smuggling ring that been using our instruments to carry dope from one part of the universe to another.

So our new manager was the pilot of our "flying saucer," a delightful blue-furred lady of very humanoid characteristics, Aefya, with whom I was sharing the rest of my life. Check that: I was sharing the rest of my life with a broom closet in the possession of the gogfather, who controlled the drug business, the music business, and god knows what else in the universe, and who now wanted to find the planet that was full of humanoids who were musically talented.

I explored my broom closet, looking for a way out. If I stood up in the center of it I could take one step in any direction and bump my nose into a wall. I could stand up to my full height and not touch the ceiling. When I raised my hands, I bumped into the ceiling. There didn't seem to be anything sharing the closet with me. I began feeling my way around the closet, trying to find an electrical socket, a secret passageway, anything. I couldn't find anything, not even the door by which I had entered. By this time, I was sweating, claustrophobic terror gripping my throat so that I could hardly breathe. Was, in fact, my air running out? Was I going to suffocate? Was I going to die in an alien closet a thousand light years from Earth? I slumped down to the floor of the closet, depressed, beaten, the lowest I've ever been in my life.

And, believe me, I've been low. I've hitchhiked on the Great Plains with a wind so bitter I seriously thought of breaking up my precious Martin guitar for firewood. I've played in coffeehouses in Iowa and Kansas when the waitress, the owner, and me outnumbered the audience. I've been kicked out on the street without notice, just because what I played wasn't the current "in" thing. I thought I knew what it was to be low, to be down, but they were all manic moments compared to what I felt now. I've sung the blues but, as Peter LaFarge put it, "You don't know the blues till you've been out in the rain without a raincoat." Or inside a closet with no exit.

So I slumped down to the floor of the closet and, as my rump thumped the floor, the wall of the closet gave way and I tumbled to the floor outside, my eyes blinded by their sudden unexpected trip into the light. I started to get eagerly to my feet, to make my escape... and I was helped up, not very gently, by a couple of lizards who took me to their father. Believe me, if he had been *my* father, I'd have committed patricide. Or at least disowned my family.

He wasn't alone; Aefya was with him. She smiled at me but,

instead of her usual dazzling smile, it was a wan echo of the real thing. Her blue fur seemed drab and her ears drooped and the honey in her honey-and-strawberry eyes had turned to glop.

This was where the hero (me) is supposed to say something like, "Unhand that woman, you grub," and gallop off into the sunset with her. I felt like my mouth was full of soggy grits and my legs had the strength of a dead B-string. What could I say to this woman (yes, woman) whom I loved? I couldn't do a thing for her. Was she to be tortured and raped by lizards in front of my eyes? I knew I was going to fail her and there was nothing I could do about it. For a moment, I wondered about the other members of the band—were they all now lying dead now in pools of their own blood or whatever it was that coursed through their veins. But that thought quickly went out of my head as I contemplated what lay ahead for Aefya and me.

Her face seemed the echo the same thoughts that passed through my mind and I suspected my face was just as pale as hers. "Well?" the gogfather said. "Do you believe me now?"

"I don't know what the hell you're..." I started to say but Aefya interrupted me.

"It's not him," she said, shaking her head. "You've got the wrong humanoid." Her voice was shaky.

There was a rumble from inside the grub. "You think you can fool me, you poor little *tairona*? Everything in your poor excuse for a body says otherwise. Even your voice trembles at the lie."

"Poor excuse for a body?" I yelped. Aefa? That lovely soft body with which I'd lain so many times, that had eagerly given up its secrets to me. "Look who's talking." I struggled against the gog that was holding me. "If I had a body like yours, I'd commit suicide to put myself out of misery."

The gogfather was unperturbed. "Well, then, if this is not the humanoid to whom you are bonded, *tairona*, you won't mind if anything happens to him."

"I can't help you," she said, trembling. "It was Charley who had all the coordinates."

"Ah, but you were the pilot. You had to plot the course and make the jumps."

"But that's all back in our computer. I don't remember them. And Charley had them erased so that no one could find the planet and undermine our success."

"I know that. I've already had your computer checked."

Not quite sure what was going on, I watched them like a spectator at a ping-pong match. I had thought they were going to torture Aefya in front of my eyes but instead the gogfather was ignoring me and cross-examining Aefya instead.

He turned to me and the lizards who were holding me. "Well," he said, "since we've got the wrong humanoid after all, there's no sense in keeping him." Were they going to let me go, after all? It didn't make any sense. "Throw him out the window."

What?

One lizard grabbed my legs while another gripped me under the armpits and they started giving me the old heave-ho, just like we used to do in high school, one-and-a-two-and-a-...

"Wait!" Aefya screamed. "I'll tell you."

... three! And I was sailing through the air.

"No, you idiots!" the gogfather roared. "I was trying to frighten her. Can't you get anything right?"

I hit the plastic of the window and it sagged under my weight. I was suspended over the street countless stories below. I hate to tell you what I did then but, when people talk about being scared shitless, they don't know the half of it. Still, I was suspended there in the air for a moment and I thought that maybe the plastic wouldn't give way under my weight, maybe it would snap back and fling me back into the room on top of those lizards, and...

"But, gogfather, you said..."

"I know what I..."

The plastic gave way and I fell.

)OOO(

Don't tell me about your whole life passing before your eyes. My first thought was, "Shit, Fred, you've really done it this time." Then I thought of all the things I've wanted to do and had never done—not exactly *thought* of all of them, but regretted not having done them. That still left me quite a lot of time to scream as I pinwheeled through the air, wondering what kind of a splash I'd make on the street and if I'd feel anything at all, wishing I could pass out.

Then something grabbed me, slowed my fall, stopped it, and I was hanging frantically onto some spindly arms, grabbing onto anything I could.

"Take it easy, Fred. You're okay now. Let me do all the work. Stop it or you'll bring us down with you too." Somehow that reached me and I went limp, letting Monkey drag me in with his four arms. I opened my eyes to see him hanging onto Spider, who was slowly crawling up the side of the building with those incredible legs of his.

"We've got to stop meeting like this," I said weakly, and Spider made that chittering of his that corresponds to laughter. I guess he'd never heard that one before. I just hoped he didn't laugh so hard we fell off the building. "What the hell are you guys doing here like this? Not that I'm complaining, mind you."

"After you disappeared, we found out the gogfather had you and we knew he wouldn't quit until he found out where Earth was, and so... we kept an eye on each other and, when Aefya was abducted, we followed her." Monkey told me all this, since Spider belongs to one of the few species incapable of speaking Lingua Galactica and I still can barely understand Spiderese. "Now tell me everything that happened to you."

As I told him everything, from the time the lizards had grabbed me on the streets of Manhattan/Corsica and rushed me off to this building to Aefya's appearance and my sudden disposal, Spider continued his slow climb up the wall. I looked down once and was glad that I hadn't had lunch in a long time. I didn't look down again.

"Where's Bass?" I asked when I was through with my tale.

"He's back at the ship." Monkey held up a communicator. "We're keeping in touch with him through this."

There was, of course, no way that Bass could join us. He had to stay close to the nutrient bath from his own planet.

I thought we'd never reach the window from which I had made my unexpected exit. Strong as he is, and agile as he is inside The Axe, Spider had to move ponderously up the side of that building. I had visions of the surprise on the gogfather's face when Monkey, Spider, and I leapt through that open window.

Monkey had had enough sense to bring some weapons with him, though I hadn't the slightest idea where he'd gotten them and I had no idea how to use them.

"Did you call the police?" I asked.

Spider laughed again.

"On this planet?" Monkey asked. "Do you know who the police *are*, on this planet?"

At last we reached the window where I had been so rudely ejected. It had taken me only a few seconds to reach Monkey and Spider on my descent, but it must have taken us another fifteen minutes to regain that height.

The room was empty.

)○○○(

My heart fell. How could we possibly find Aefya now? She could be anywhere in this city of lizards, if indeed she wasn't already on her way out of it. We climbed in through the window and I began looking half-heartedly around the room. In the next room was a lavatory, with lizard-sized sinks, lizard and slug plumbing, and seven taps, each dispensing a different fluid.

I turned on the tap that said "hydrogen hydroxide" in Lingua Galactica (I had quickly learned that meant "water"), stripped off my pants and shorts, and washed them out in one of the sinks. It left quite a mess but it was the least I could do for the gogfather. It also left me with soggy underwear but that was an improvement over the condition they had been in.

We searched that room with everything but a fine-toothed comb and we'd have used one of those if I'd had one with me. It was useless. There wasn't a sign of where they had gone. We went downstairs and asked the clerk, a lizardly fellow who claimed quite loudly to know nothing. He had seen nothing and furthermore there was no such thing as a gogfather—it was a vicious rumor passed by the enemies of Manhattan/Corsica to discredit his world. Besides which...

He was still screaming and yelling when we left the building. "I don't think they're in the building," I said, probably unnecessarily. We were surrounded by lizards and a few other strange creatures, but mostly lizards—not a gogfather in sight, and I felt quite nervous, expecting to be yanked off the streets again. "What do we do now?" I asked.

"What *can* we do?" Monkey asked. "We go back to the ship."

"Don't you guys have some kind of superscientific gadgets with which you can trace her?"

"Don't be asinine, Fred."

So we wound up back at our spacecraft, commiserating with our fourth member, Bass, who sat disconsolately in his dish of bathwater. I wasn't the only one touched by the loss of Aefya—she was the heart of our operation, our manager, our pilot, or director of roadies and technicians. That was she was also my lover only gave me one more woe than my comrades. I hardly noticed the extra load—Aefya was our friend.

"Better lay off that stuff," Bass said to me as I took another pull on a bottle. When Charley had picked me up off Earth, he also laid in a couple of cases of primo whiskey. "We've got a concert to do tonight."

"Concert?" I found the word a bit difficult to pronounce. My tongue kept getting caught in my eyeteeth and I couldn't see what I was saying. "What concert? How can we put on a concert tonight without Aefya?"

"We've got a contract to perform, with or without Aefya, and the gogfather isn't going to let us out of it that easy."

"I don't care who... the gogfather?" Suddenly I was sober as a judge. (Cancel that: I've had enough experience with judges in my itinerant life to know the falsity of *that* particular cliché.)

"Calm down, Fred. You think there's only one gogfather on this planet?"

"But... Oh, yeah. I guess so." I slumped back down in my seat then got struck with an inspiration. A small one, but it was better than nothing. "But maybe he knows the other one and he can release Aefya for us. Tell him we can't perform without Aefya's help."

My three bandmates looked at each other then Monkey shrugged his shoulders. He had learned that particular mannerism from me and it was rather impressive when he did it. "It's certainly worth a try."

So a few minutes later there was the image of another slug projected in the corner of our control room, the control room of a flying saucer than none of us could fly. The slug looked just like the gogfather I was already too familiar with. I could see no difference—I guess when you've seen one gogfather, you've seen them all.

Monkey explained our problem but the gogfather, let me call him Gogfather Number Two, was unimpressed. "Does your manager perform with you?"

"No, but she..."

"She manages. And you will manage without her. I have technicians to take care of that end of the performance. You have a contract."

"How would you like another contract?" I asked.

The gogfather's eyes swiveled over to me. "What are you talking about?"

"This other gogfather, the one who kidnapped me and Aefya: how would you like to take out another contract on him?"

"I will take care of him. Do not worry. We have a long-standing misunderstanding and I will see that he is taken care of."

"Listen," I said anxiously, "whatever you do, make sure nothing happens to Aefya."

"I will do what I have to do," he said coldly. "And you will do what *you* have to do. You will be at the auditorium this evening and you will perform."

"And if we don't?"

"I will do what I have to do." Without another word, he broke the connection.

I looked at Monkey, Spider, and Bass. "What are we going to do?" I asked.

"We will do what we have to do," Bass said in a precise imitation of the gogfather.

I could've killed him right then and there.

)OOO(

The atmosphere before our concert was like no other I've ever experienced. At the first one, we had been nervous but excited and, as our reputation grew, we grew more blasé. After all, it was just a job—more glamorous than most, perhaps, but just a job. At least, that's what I kept telling myself. But, always, just before we'd go onstage, there would be that moment of doubt and excitement—this was what I'd always wanted back when I was a two-bit folksinger on the dying coffee-house circuit on Earth but it went way beyond my wildest dreams back then. And so there was always that fear that this was it, this would be the concert that would break the bubble and I'd go plummeting back to the bottom—and surely the bottom in the Galaxy was far deeper than the bottom on Earth, just as the top was so much higher.

And I knew that Monkey and Bass and Spider felt the same way. They'd been scrambling too long for that gold ring not to enjoy it and fear its loss when they had finally obtained their meal ticket to the Big Time... me! That I wasn't half the musician that any of them were was beside the point (although Monkey kept telling me I was selling myself short): without me, they were just another group, quite good but nothing exceptional.

"It's not just you, " Bass said. "It's also your music. You've got a whole heritage of music that's been separated from that of the rest of the universe and so it's new, exciting, and everyone wants to hear it."

So we were all still excited and nervous, none of us used to being the Toasts of the Universe, all of us having long ago assumed we would never make it.

But not tonight. Nervous? Maybe a little, but not about our performance. We were worried about Aefya. Excited? Hardly. Depressed? Most definitely. Every little thing reminded us that Aefya was in the tendrils of the Gogfather. It wasn't Aefya who came by to wire us for the night's recording; it was an anonymous faceless lizard (!) technician.

There were lizards everywhere—running the sound, the lights, the box office. Even the warm-up group was a bunch of lizards. They would form the large part of the audience, as well. Did each of them have a gogfather? I hadn't thought of that before. How many gogfathers were there? I gained the impression that each gogfather had a lot of lizard children. And what about the gogmother? What did *she* look like? I really didn't want to think about that very much. Nonetheless, I asked Monkey about it.

"I don't know," he answered. "I've never heard anyone talk about the gogmother. Maybe she's got a different name. Or maybe they're all one sex. Or ten. I don't know."

"Well, the gogfather... the one that kidnapped me and Aefya... said that all the lizards were his children. How many of them *are* there?"

"Thousands. Each gogfather has thousands, maybe millions of children, for all I know. They eat most of them and those that grow up to be lizards fight among themselves until one of them can metamorphose into a gogfather and start having little gogs and start the process all over."

"And the gogfathers fight among themselves too?"

"That's the way it works. It's a gog-eat-gog world."

The lizard warm-up group finished and the gogfather promoter motioned us over to his motorized lounge. "You are going to perform, yes?'

"Yes," Monkey said.

The promoter looked at me. "And you, Fredharmon?"

"We've got a contract."

"That you do. Normally I do not come down to see these displays personally. I do it this time for two reasons: one, I have heard much about you and I wish to see this humanoid play music; two, I want to make sure you perform the letter of your contract. You do what you agree to do and the gogfather will treat you well. If not..." A tendril made a slicing motion in the air.

"Don't worry," I said. "We'll do what we have to do. You see if you can find Aefya."

"Be ready in twenty minutes, after the intermission." He wheeled away from us, surrounded by his gog-children.

I looked at Monkey, Bass, and Spider, then let out a heavy sigh. "Shit," I said in English. They didn't need a translation.

☽○○○☾

As I had expected, there were a lot of lizards in the audience, but there were quite a few other aliens there as well. Down in the first row, an octopoid perched on a stool, taking a hit from his respirator every now and then. A couple of rows behind him, there was something that looked like a cross between a rooster and a horse, with two bunny ears and a vicious-looking beak surrounded by a circle of six or seven bright yellow eyes, one of which turned red when I stepped out into the stage lights.

There was the usual nauseating introduction and then, without any further ado, we started to perform one of the current Galaxy-wide hits. That was part of our strategy—we would run through a number of songs that were familiar to everybody (even me, by now), with me mostly playing rhythm guitar, every now and then stepping out for a brief solo. It built the tension, everybody waiting for the moment when I was in the spotlight and we were playing songs from Earth, from good old delta and Chicago blues (which had been my bag back in the coffee-house days) right up to the Beatles and the Rolling Stones and beyond. I hadn't paid a hell of a lot of attention to what was going on in pop music when I had been an Earth musician, but Charlie had laid in quite a collection of records, cassettes, CDs, and even some 8-tracks, and we had assimilated quite a lot of it, although there was still a hell of a lot left to learn.

I won't say it was our most inspired concert. Hell, we just couldn't get into it. But Monkey, Bass, and Spider are all professionals, and I'd bounced around enough that I could fake it fairly well. Besides, we all enjoyed jamming together, and even the loss of Aefya couldn't quite take that completely away.

So we played, Bass changing the shape of his mouth and creating strange rhythms through the instrument of his own body; Monkey running his four skinny hands over the keys and tuning pins of the bowls of his tabla-like instrument; Spider skittering around The Axe, a gigantic jungle-gym maze that he strummed with those massive legs of his or played like a wind instrument on the holes unevenly spaced in the rods. And Fred Harmon tried to hold up his end by strumming on his very mundane and prosaic Martin guitar. It was (need I say it?) unearthly music.

We managed to get through the happy songs without too much trouble and we played the sad ones with an extra dash of sadness and loneliness and, when it came my turn for the spotlight, I played the blues with more feeling than I'd ever played them before.

We finished off with an Alice Cooper song that we'd translated into Lingua Galactica. The Alice Cooper group had just reached its peak when I'd been drafted by Charley, and I often wondered where music could go after that—I mean, after all that grease-paint and makeup, the heavy metal chords, and all that show biz, what was there left to do in that direction? I had sneered at them when I was on Earth, but we had all the records they had made up to that point and there was some good music inside all that dreck. So we played "No More Mr. Nice Guy," which came from the last album of theirs that we had, and I had to wonder what that Galactic audience made of it.

But they liked it and I was feeling properly mean as we left the stage. The audience was kicking up a storm, doing the things that denoted applause for them, the lizards thumping their tails against the floor, the octopi hooting, the whatzits clacking their hooves together, and so on.

"No encore," I said as we came off the stage. I wasn't in the mood for anything except getting drunk.

"You will play an encore," the gogfather said.

We played an encore.

It was the Beatles' "Octopus's Garden," which I've always thought kind of appropriate; even Bass liked it. The octopus down in the front row went crazy. I looked off into the right wing of the stage: the gogfather was scowling at us. I wondered why—we had done everything we had contracted to do. I looked off to the stage's left wing: there was the gogfather scowling at us. I looked back to my right... the gogfather was still there. I looked left again... there was something in the gogfather's tendrils.

I didn't need Mario Puzo to tell me what was about to happen.

"Down!" I yelled to Monkey, who was stage front with me, then I grabbed floor. There was a sizzling sound over my head and a piece of stage near the promoter-gogfather went flying off into the audience. Several lizards scrambled for it, looking for some memento of our performance, I guess.

Monkey and I crawled on our bellies toward the back of the stage, where Bass was trying to submerge himself in the tub of water he played/sang from. Spider seemed to be unconcerned by the sudden display of fireworks. "Keep playing," he chattered in Spiderese.

Meanwhile, the front of the stage was crisscrossed by rays of light and numerous odd-shaped projectiles that went back and forth from stage left to stage right. Soon the audience joined in with their own missives, which pelted Spider, Monkey, Bass, and me as we struggled vainly to play from the rear of the stage while trying to keep out of the range of the battle between the gogfathers.

A stray shot from Gogfather Number One struck the floor near the octopus in the front row, bathing him in a shower of sparks. He just grinned (I swear it!) and uttered the Lingua Galactica equivalent of "Far out!" I wondered just what was in that respirator he kept inhaling.

We finally finished off "Octopus's Garden" at the same that the battle ended. There was a moment of silence then the audience erupted in applause and noise—I guess they'd never seen anything like it before. I know *I* hadn't.

But I didn't wait to take a bow; I raced off to stage left. It was foolish; I might be running into one of those laser rays or whatever they were, but at that moment I was more worried about Aefya than I was about myself.

The air was filled with the smell of burnt lizard flesh and the body of the gogfather was surrounded by that of his children. The lizard technicians were all huddled over in a corner, not wanting to have anything to do with the whole mess.

"Fred!" Aefya picked herself up from the floor on the other side of the mass of dead lizards and started toward me.

One of the lizards began to twitch. "Look out, Aefya," I yelled and my tender, soft, loving, blue-furred Aefya calmly picked up one of the weapons that were lying casually about on the stage floor and drilled the gog through its lizardly head. Then she was in my arms, hugging me tightly.

We were interrupted by the touch of a spiderly arm upon my shoulder. "Fred," Monkey said, "we'd better get out of here before someone comes and starts asking embarrassing questions."

"And not even say goodbye to the gogfather?" I said giddily.

"Come on, Fred," Aefya said. "This is no time for jokes."

I wasn't even sure which gogfather was where, which one was dead or if both of them were. But Aefya was right—it didn't matter: the main thing was to get the hell out of there, as quickly as possible.

It wasn't easy—pandemonium reigned in the audience. There was a mass of lizards and others out there, including our octopoid friend. I think they were friendly but I also think they wanted souvenirs. There was a high ululating note in the air—it wasn't exactly like a cop car's siren on Earth, but I recognized it anyway. I'd heard it before.

Our choices didn't look good—to be torn apart for souvenirs or to face the gogfather's police. We looked at each other—it was obvious the others didn't know what to do, but I'd been in similar situations several times back on good old Earth.

"Let's go," I said.

"Where?" Aefya asked as they followed me.

"Down."

We found a stairway that led down into the bowels of the building, Bass's precious water sloshing out as Monkey and Aefya carried him down to where greasy machinery lurked in stark inadequate lighting.

"What now?" Aefya asked.

"There should be an exit here somewhere, a passageway, something."

It took us a little while to find it, but it was perfect. Behind a big piece of machinery that looked like a furnace with a huge piston going up to the ceiling, a narrow passageway full of greasy leaky pipes, barely wide enough for Spider and his folded-up Axe, stretched out for quite a distance, occasionally passing machinery-filled rooms.

"Do you know where we're going, Fred?" Aefya asked.

"I bet there's a whole series of these underground tunnels, honeycombing the entire city. This is perfect."

"Sure," Bass said. "God knows where we'll end up."

We came to an intersection. Six tunnels all came together.

"What do we do now?" Aefya asked.

"Pick one at random," I said.

"Wait a minute." Monkey was peering at the cryptic markings on the pipes and walls. "I think we've struck it."

"Struck what?" I said. "Oil?"

He pointed to one of the markings. "This way to the spaceport," he said.

It was easier said than done. We got lost a couple of times and it was one hell of a walk, especially carrying Bass and our instruments. Several times we heard other voices but no one came near us and, about two hours after the end of our concert, we surfaced in the basement of the spaceport's administration building.

From that point on, it was Fat City. Half an hour later, we had left Corsica/Manhattan behind us and were on our way to our next concert. I took a hot shower and crashed on the luxurious gelatin bed that had once been Charley's and now belonged to Aefya and me. About half an hour later, Aefya, having turned the ship over to the computer, snuggled up next to me.

"Don't ever do that to me again," she said. "Don't get separated from us. You don't know your way around yet."

I rubbed her back, trying to get the tension out. "What's our next stop?"

"Would you believe Greenwich Village?"

She didn't mean a section of New York City; she meant a planet whose relationship to the general culture of the Galaxy was the same as Greenwich Village's to America.

"I'll believe it when you're talking about the good old Greenwich Village I used to know—the San Remo Café, the Village Vanguard, Washington Square..."

"Someday, Fred. As soon as possible."

I didn't say anything. I was too tired. I fell asleep to dream of lizards and gogfathers patrolling the streets of Earth.

THE DISTANT FUTURE

Hark, Hark, the Quark

Hark, hark, the quark!
The quintessential quark.
So quick it leaves no trace,
   no picosecond spark to mark its place
           in subatomic space.

Hark, hark, the quark!
The quick-reacting quark.
Ere gigavolts can shake
   the nanocosmic quark apart, 'twill make
           charmonium and never break.

Like Neapolitan, it has three flavors.
What? No spumoni?
O, let us talk of physicists and rings,
Of pion, muons, bosons, gluons,
Of tokamaks and other things,
And such bologna
That the theorists dearly love and savor.

Hark, hark, the quark!
The quasi-real quark.
With charm to soothe atomic breast,
   in existential dark its spark our quest,
          we find no way, no final test.

There's No One Left to Paint the Sky

Peter Allison left yesterday. He said he wouldn't but I knew he would. He used to go down to City Hall to play with the dials on the transmitter, running his hand idly around it, just like the others did.

Now I'm all alone. The last man on Earth.

It doesn't seem right. All the crowd is gone; Antoine's is empty. No more raucous laughter; no more of LaFarge's roaring out for beer; no more lung-racking coughs thanks to the eternal haze of cigarette smoke; no more sudden arguments and ineffective fist-fights. They're all gone.

All the silly vanities that used to annoy me; how I miss them. I have only my own now.

I wander through Antoine's, hearing ghost-laughter, stopping for a long drag at a bottle of absinthe without having Henri (whose real name was Fred) dun me for silver. There are still a lot of full and half-full bottles left, although Henri left over a month ago. By then, only Peter, Dylan, and I were left. Dylan's real name was Patrick.

Why do I say "was"? As far as I know, they're still full of life and juice, drinking absinthe or mescal or some celestial equivalent on some planet revolving 'round Altair, smoking joints under the light of Capella, arguing in the darkness of interstellar space. Yes, I guess they're alive, but they are gone from my life forever, so they might as well be dead.

Or am I the one who is dead?

Igor came back a couple of weeks ago, glowing with accounts of his travels and adventures. Igor was his real name.

"What have you written lately?" I asked him.

"Oh, my mind is a swirl of melodies and harmonies, vast symphonies and etudes. You've got to come out with us, Edward. There are instruments and music you've never thought of. Rhythms and tonalities. The music of the stars, Edward, the real music of the spheres!"

"But how much of it have you put down on paper?"

"Oh, none of it yet, but I will. I will."

That's what they all say. And who knows? Maybe they will. But I haven't heard of anyone who has yet.

"Well, that sounds great for a musician," I said, "but I can't see anything in it for a poet."

"But you *will*, Edward. It's not just the music that gets to you but the poetry as well, the vast artistry of God. It all gets into you and you become bigger, more at one with humanity."

"'More at one with humanity.' I like that phrase."

"You see, here on Earth I was just a composer. Just part of an artist. But when you go out to the stars, when you visit other planets and universes, your artistry expands to include all the arts. Not just music or poetry or writing or painting, but all of them. I'm not just a composer any more, Edward. I'm a painter and a poet and a singer and a musician. I can play any instrument that was ever made!"

"You've tried, I suppose?"

"That's not the point, Edward. I *know* now, where before I only thought I knew or hoped I knew."

He didn't stay long.

I especially miss Peter Allison though. Not only was he the last to go, but he was the most talented of us all. He didn't take much with him, just a suitcase full of clothes.

"I probably won't need these either, Ed, but just to be on the safe side..."

He left all his paintings behind, the ones hanging in Antoine's, the ones in his studio, even the unfinished ones. He left them all behind.

I wonder, when I look at those glorious sunsets and sunrises of his, whether anyone will ever paint another. And something will be gone from the universe. No one could ever paint the sky like Peter: so real you could watch the clouds change from horseheads to faery-castles, so deep a blue that it seemed a hundred miles away, stars that glittered and twinkled like celestial cities. No one could paint like Peter.

He was the best of us. And now he's gone. He walked down to City Hall, played with the dial on the transmitter for a few moments then carefully set it and stepped through.

It's very lonely here now. Without Peter. Without Dylan. Without Henri.

If you're a minor poet, maybe you find the idea of Milky Way wrappers around our galaxy poetic. Or a Pepsi-Cola bottling plant under the light of Denebola. Man can go wherever he wants now. There are poets, painters, sculptors, musicians, composers, writers, dancers, actors, and plain ordinary people scattered throughout the universe.

I don't know where the transmitters came from. No one I knew did. One day they just appeared, free, for everyone and anyone to use. Some said they were a Communist plot, or a capitalist plot, or the invention of some mad evil genius, or some kind of General Motors advertising gimmick. Peter Allison claimed they were left in the night by alien creatures who want Earth for themselves. Dylan said they were left by fairies.

It didn't matter. People used them anyway. They all left, everyone, at first in twos, then in droves, then by the millions: the poor, the rich, the honest, the criminal. Everybody went out into the universe leaving me alone to tend the store. I mean everybody! Literally. Hindi, European, priest, rabbit, mad motherfucking idiots, every bloody soul that lived on the earth.

It wasn't a matter of leaving the sick and the maimed behind: they took them too. They moved entire hospitals to other planets. Something about the climate, or the atmosphere, or the gravity.

The congenital idiots, the institutionally insane, those who were in continuous coma; these they took along with them to Altair IV or the seas of a dead planet in the far arm of the galaxy or to wherever their whims or urges took them.

They moved entire buildings; they moved whole prisons full of people. Condemned prisoners got one last look at the universe and reprieved, suddenly shared that vision with the rest of humanity.

How can you kill a man who has seen the Beauty of the Void and shared it with you?

You realize that these are not my words: these are the words of those few who went out there and came back, the artists and friends who became missionaries of the Universal Voidal Beauty.

"Come with us, Ed. We're going back. The Earth is too confining. You don't know. How can you turn your back on it till you've done it?"

And who's left to do the work, to paint the paintings, to write the music, the prose, the poetry? Who's left to till the fields, to man the foundries, to crush the grapes? Oh, there's more than enough left here for one man to live out a life of ease: wines and whiskeys, lobsters and caviar, or just plain hamburgers, beans, and beer; all frozen and canned for instant use now or fifty years from now.

But sometimes I walk down to the transmitter at City Hall and I run my hands over the dials, turning them, knowing that, as I do, its beam crosses and recrosses the beams from London, from Mars, from Alpha Centauri, from Vega, from Sirius. And where those beams cross, Man walks.

And I turn away, frightened.

His Hour Upon the Stage

Stuart sat in the pool of light, motionless. Then the tape recorder began again with the final lines of *Krapp's Last Tape*. I irised down to a pinspot on Stuart's face, held it for a second, then shuttered the spotlight out and kicked off the last dimmer.

The sound of my applause echoed in the empty theatre as I brought the stage lights up with my foot. Stuart stepped out to the edge of the apron and bowed. I brought the lights down again and pushed a large red button. The curtains began to move slowly and majestically across the stage. I backed the carbon rods in the spotlight away from each other until the arc was broken, turned off the spot, and brought the house lights up.

By this time the curtains had closed so I turned on the work lights backstage. Then I walked out of the balcony, down the stairs to the main lobby, through the house, and backstage. There's a door off the balcony that leads directly backstage but I enjoy the trip through the theatre.

Stuart was taking off his makeup. "How'd it look?" he asked.

"Not too good. You're losing your edge. I think we ought to quit doing surrealism and go back to the classics for a while."

"Fine with me. Hand me the cold cream, will you?" He started rubbing the cold cream in his face and hair, taking out the makeup and the white dye. "How about doing *Macbeth* next?"

"Sure. We haven't done Shakespeare in months."

"Or how about *Othello*?" He turned to me. "I've always loved your Iago."

"*My* Iago." I sat down on one of the benches. Stuart nodded. "Who'll run the lights if I do Iago? You?"

"You could teach me."

"All right. Tomorrow night. I'll be here at seven."

"I can't do it," he mumbled. "Angie's expecting company tomorrow night." Then he turned to me again, quickly, savagely. "But we don't need light changes for Shakespeare. Just put them on one setting and we can do it together again, Tim."

It was an old argument, one we'd been through thousands of times since I had retired from the stage ten years earlier.

"It wouldn't be the same, Stuart, and you know it. If we're going to do these things, we ought to do them the best way possible."

"Maybe it's time we stopped then."

I felt as if my heart was doing cartwheels like the jester in *Once Upon a Mattress* but I managed to keep a calm exterior. "If that's the way you feel, Stuart, then certainly there's no need to keep going."

"No, that's all right," he muttered. "I want to keep going, Tim, you know that. For all we know, we may be the last actors doing live theatre in the world."

"Or in America, anyway," I said.

"But sometimes it all seems so futile." He turned to face me. "It's been so long since you've been on stage, Tim. And our days in this theatre are numbered. This is the only place Metropolitan has left that isn't being used. They'll be into it and converting it to a TV studio in a few weeks."

"That's an old rumor."

"But this time it's true, and you know it. This is your last chance to go back on the stage."

"There are other cities."

"Your last chance, Tim," he repeated quietly.

"I'll think about it." We both knew I wouldn't.

)OOO(

I took the chair, table, and tape recorder that we had used for *Krapp's Last Tape* off the stage and rolled the Shakespeare platforms into place. Then I went back to the light booth I had jury-rigged on the balcony and set the dimmers for *Macbeth*.

Finally I eased myself into the crawlspace above the suspended ceiling and began resetting the ante-pros. It was tedious, re-aiming and refocusing the ellipsoidals and fresnels to the tape marks on the stage, but I'd gone through it innumerable times before.

For nearly four years, after the rest of America's live theatre had stumbled to rest, Stuart and I had been putting on performances in the deserted theatre. At first we did them for a dedicated little audience. As the audience drifted away, we did fewer shows. But we still tried to do at least two a week.

I don't know why we kept on. I guess we each thought it was what the other wanted. We were perhaps the last performers of legitimate theatre. When we quit, thousands of years of theatre tradition would come to an end.

"Tim, are you up there?"

I looked down at the stage. Stuart, a tiny figure in a ridiculous opera cape, was shouting up at me. I hollered back at him.

"Is there anything I can do to help you?" he asked.

"Sure. Walk down right a little, will you? To the red tape mark."

He did and I focused a Leko on his face.

"Okay, now go over to stage left. Back a little bit. Hold it right there."

I scrambled across the catwalk until I came to the Leko that was supposed to be focused on that area. After changing gels, I refocused it on Stuart and shuttered it so that the light cut off a little below his shoulders.

"Okay. Thanks, Stuart. You can go on home."

"Right. See you Friday."

He made a flying leap off the apron, over the orchestra pit, and almost tumbled into the first row of seats. One of these days, he's going to break his neck with that silly jump.

When I was finished with the ante-pros, I went back to the light board, turned off the lights I had been working on, and set the stage lights. Then I dragged the stepladder onto the stage and began working on the first and second pipe.

I should've re-gelled the ground rows but it was nearly midnight and I was beginning to get tired. Hell, I could do them tomorrow.

So I opened all the circuit breakers and went off to my cot in the ticket office.

)OOOC

The next morning I went to Studio L, where we were taping a new drama for Metropolitan. Paul Denesha, the boss of my light crew, gave me the disc for my computer.

I'd like to have thrown it in a trash can. I haven't been running lights as long as Paul or most of the guys at Metropolitan but I feel that light crews ought to do more than just punch buttons on a computer. There's no soul to it, no art, just as those clowns people watch on the box aren't actors any more, just extensions of the director and the editing room.

But the light crews are even worse. They're nothing but a bunch of featherbedders. There are three on my crew: Paul, myself, and Artie Wright, an old-timer who'll be retiring in a few years. Five years ago there were four; in twenty or thirty years there'll be just one guy feeding the disc or whatever into the computer and punching the

ADVANCE button.

In some office miles away, a computer programmer who's never even seen a light board in his life, much less run one, figures out the cues and sequences for the show. Then he keys them into a disc which Paul picks up. It's really pathetic. If it weren't for the Electricians' Union, we'd all be out of a job.

"Quiet on the set." The floor manager's voice came through the headphones.

"Let's have preset one." I pressed the ADVANCE button and the computer read the instruction on the disc, setting the lights for the opening sequence.

〉OOO〈

Between cues and while the director talked to the actors, the crew members talked over the phones.

"I hear they're going to convert St. Mark's into a tape studio in a couple of weeks," one of the stagehands said.

"Ah, that's an old rumor," I replied.

"It's true this time," one of the sound men said. "They're going to tear into it a week from Monday."

"Where'd you get your information?" I asked.

"Up at the front office. My daughter's one of the secretaries. She saw the letter to the agency herself."

"What're they gonna use it for?" Artie Wright asked.

"Commercials. It's too small for anything else."

"That means they'll need another light crew," Paul said. "Why don't you try to get crew chief for it, Tim?"

"I'd rather stick with you. What about you, Artie? You've got the seniority."

"I'm thinking about it. I don't know if the extra work's the extra few dollars."

"Maybe you should start acting again, Tim," Paul said.

"Those days are gone," I replied.

"You were one hell of a Falstaff."

"It's been nearly fifteen years. I've probably lost it all by now."

"Quiet on the phones," the floor manager said. "We're going to retake it from light cue ten, sound cue nine-A."

I keyed in a 10 and punched the ADVANCE button. The lights flickered rapidly through the sequence until they were set for the scene we were about to re-record.

⟩○○○⟨

In the afternoon we recorded a bunch of commercials. Stuart was in two of them and I waited for him after we were finished.

"They're really going to tear into St. Mark's," I said.

"I know. I told you."

"Stuart?"

"Yeah?"

"I fell lousy about this, but..."

"Don't tell me. I can guess. You want to play every night until they tear St. Mark's down."

I nodded.

"It's not a bad idea, Tim," he said softly. "Sort of a last farewell to the legitimate stage by its last real actors."

"We could do a panorama of the best plays of all time. There's a lot we'll have to skip, but I'd like to try."

"Sure. Sounds great. We could start tomorrow night. Have you got the stage all set for *Macbeth*?"

"I can have it ready by tonight."

"I'm sorry, Tim. I don't think Angie would appreciate that. But we'll start tomorrow, for sure."

"And after *Macbeth*, we'll do *Faustus*. We ought to do a whole panorama of the theatre, from Greek tragedy up to the modern day."

"Right. We can figure out what we'll do after *Macbeth*."

⟩○○○⟨

I went back to St. Mark's and walked around the theatre, touching the plush-covered seats, trying to print the proscenium's whitewashed gargoyles indelibly on my memory. In a few weeks, remodeling crews would come in, tear out the seats, and make the balcony into a control room.

After ten years of stumbling and four years of one drawn-out dying gasp, the legitimate theatre was finally coming to its death and there wasn't a damn thing Stuart or I could do about it. Except to go out in one last flicker of glory.

After dinner I reset the big board for *Macbeth*. Since I couldn't lug it up to my lighting booth, all I did was give it one setting, which I turned off and on with a toggle switch in the balcony. I took the props out of the prop closet the next night and set them on the tables in the wings. Stuart would take care of his costume changes himself.

It had been a long day with Paul Denesha and Artie Wright but I was eager for the beginning of our last run. As I walked up to the light booth, I noticed that Stuart had already signed in on the callboard.

I ran through the light changes, making sure all the lights were working, gels hadn't slipped, and everything was focused properly. I had to stop twice, once to re-gel a Fresnel in the first pipe that had bleached out and once to re-aim one of the ante-pros.

By that time it was nearly eight o'clock. I went down to the dressing room. Stuart was lounging around in witch's makeup and Macbeth costume. His wife Angela was with him.

"Hi, Tim," she said as I entered. "Long time, no see."

"You haven't been here for a while," I said. "You ought to come down more often. Your husband's quite an actor, if you remember."

"Oh, I vaguely remember some critics once saying he was the heir apparent to Tim Schroeder."

"Well, he's got the throne all to himself now."

"I noticed you put the props out."

"I always do."

"Mind if I help tonight?"

"Of course not. Glad to have another old trouper with us." Angela had been working makeup when she and Stuart met. "Curtain in half an hour."

"Tim?"

Here it came. I could feel my stomach starting to tighten up already. "Yes?"

"When are you going back on the stage again?"

"We've gone through that a dozen times before, Angie."

"But it's different now." Her voice was almost a whisper. "This is the end, Tim. This is your last chance."

"No," I said breezily, though I didn't feel breezy at all. "If nothing else, I can always do commercials for Metropolitan."

"You're still going to stick by that silly vow of yours to stay off the stage?"

"It's not silly to me." If only she knew how much I wanted to go back, in more ways than one.

"You won't break it? Not even for Stuart?"

I forced a smile. "That's a low blow, Angie. But no. Not even for Stuart."

"I'm sorry," she said. "I didn't mean it that way." She smiled. "You're still the best actor around, Tim."

I wondered what she meant by that. "Thanks. Curtain in half an hour. I'd better get up to my booth." I looked at Stuart. "Break a leg."

I went back to the light booth, closed the curtain, and sat back to relax, going over the script for *South Pacific*.

About fifteen minutes later, Angie called me over the headphones. "Hey, Tim, are you there? Can you hear me?"

"Loud and clear, Angie. Curtain in ten minutes."

"Right."

Five minutes later, I called into the headset, "Places."

"Places," she answered.

I flicked the houselights a couple of times, ran the second pipe up to half, and killed the work lights backstage. Then I took another minute to finish off the first act of *South Pacific*, brought the houselights to half, killed the second pipe, and ran up the preset for the witches' scene.

Ordinarily there would be anywhere from two to seven people on a light crew; a couple of spotlights and up to five running the light boards. Plus a stage manager to call the cues. I had to run two light boards with six dimmers each, a spot, and assorted switches but, after four years, I could run them with my feet almost as well as I could with my hands.

Of course, with only one actor, we didn't run very many full plays anyway. *Krapp's Last Tape*, of course, but not much else. For *Macbeth*, Stuart would only do some of the long speeches, mostly Macbeth's, but he couldn't forego the witches' scene entirely nor the gatekeeper's.

Now you may think Stuart as a witch is silly but actually it is theatre tradition to have at least one of the witches a male.

"When shall we three meet again

In thunder, lightning, or in rain?"

Stuart's face glowed greenly in the black light focused on his fluorescent makeup. A putty nose and shaggy eyebrows completed his witch's makeup, and a long cloak covered the Macbeth costume.

He skipped from place to place in the witches' speeches, weaving several speeches into one.

"A drum, a drum!

Macbeth doth come."

I faded out all the gray areas slowly until the focus was on Stuart alone, standing behind a platform on stage right.

"Peace! The charm's wound up."

Blackout.

The two Macbeth monologues at the end of Scene 3 were next. I threw the breakers on the top board and preset the dimmers. "Ready, Tim," Angela whispered into the headset.

I threw the switch. The sudden flood of light caught Stuart a little too far downstage.

"Two truths are told," he said, moving unobtrusively into the focal area, "as happy prologues to the swelling act of the imperial theme."

As the performance progressed, I could see that Stuart was benefiting from the change of plays. He could no longer rely on a simple light pattern and small movements; he had to think and be on his toes. I thought seriously of deliberately missing a cue to see how he would respond but decided that would be too cheap.

Now Duncan was dead, murdered in his sleep. Macbeth wandered around the stage, wide-eyed and frightened:

"Whence is that knocking?

How isn't with me, when every noise appalls me?" I brought the dimmers down with my feet, clapping at the same time.

When I stopped clapping, the applause didn't stop. We had an audience! Scattered throughout the house, they must have sneaked in during the blackouts.

I smiled. Our audience was coming back for our last performances. We might even have a full house for closing night!

It was a long blackout between the scene just finished and the next, for Stuart had to get into makeup and costume for the drunken porter, but I was still standing in the booth, bemused and jubilant, when Angie whispered, "Ready" into the headset.

I raced the settings and overshot on the antepros so that I had to inch them down to the proper setting. I had missed the second pipe entirely and had to easy that in slowly. Since I also had to cue in the knocks from the recording, by the time I had the settings right, Stuart was nearly finished with the speech.

"But this place is too cold for hell. I devil-porter it no further..."

I peered into the gloom of the house but I could see nothing. The stage lighting was too dim to penetrate any further than the second row.

"Anon, anon! I pray you, remember the porter."

This time I had the settings completed well in advance of Stuart's return to Macbeth costume and makeup. I let the audience take care of the applause.

"Ready, Tim."

)OOO(

"To-morrow, and to-morrow, and to-morrow,
Creeps in this petty pace from day to day..."
We were nearing the last scene. I had been able to make a rough count of our audience during the brighter sequences and estimated that we had about twenty-five people.
"Out, out, brief candle!
Life's but a walking shadow; a poor player
That struts and frets his hour upon the stage
And then is heard no more. It is a tale
Told by an idiot, full of sound and fury,
Signifying nothing."
Blackout.
In the final scene, Stuart wove together Macbeth's speeches as he fought and argued with Macduff, pacing across the stage and fighting an imaginary adversary until he came to the last line:
"... lay on, Macduff;
And dammed be him that first cries, 'Hold, enough!'"
I blacked out the stage lights, leaving Stuart in the halo of the spot for a moment. The audience began to applaud, Stuart leapt out of the light into darkness, and I turned off the spotlight.
At curtain call, Stuart stood on the brightly lit stage, bowing. He looked up at me for a moment and smiled. It wasn't a triumphant grin or anything like that, just a gentle, fleeting, comradely smile.
Then there was darkness again, and the curtain was closing.
"What do you think of our audience?" he asked over the headphones.
"Great. Did you invite them?"
"I didn't have to, Tim. Everybody knows about us."
"You make it sound like we're having an affair," I growled.
"You know what I mean."
"Anyway, someone had to tell them we were performing tonight."
I could almost hear Stuart blush over the phones. "Well, okay," he admitted. "I did tell a few people. But not all of those," he hastened to add.
"What's all that noise in the background?"
"What do you think? We're having a party. Come on down."

I hung up the headset and turned off all the switches, double-checking and triple checking that everything was in order. I'm not usually that careful but I needed something to occupy my hands while I thought.

In a way, of course, I looked forward to the backstage party. It would be like old times again: a short opening night party backstage before we all adjourned to someone's apartment or a restaurant to wait for the reviews. There would be a folding table spread with punch in little paper cups, bite-size cookies, and tiny sandwiches with the crusts removed.

But I'd have to face so many people that I hadn't seen in years, fending off those old always-asked questions.

"Well, are you going downstairs or not?"

I turned. It couldn't be true, of course. The same face, those same delicate hands, the same beautifully shaped legs... legs that had lain, broken and mangled, under a light pipe.

"Vicki?" It was a whisper, a sigh, barely more than a breath.

She smiled. "Have I changed so much you don't recognize me anymore?"

"No. I just didn't expect to see you here."

She *had* changed, though: wrinkles were forming at the corners of her eyes and mouth; makeup had been judiciously applied to her brow to hide the wrinkles that were starting to form there; her body was filled out somewhat, no longer slightly girlish. She was a woman now; there was none of the girl left in her.

But she hadn't changed nearly as much as I had. I was beginning to develop a paunch despite the work I did at St. Mark's and despite my exercises. I was wearing glasses instead of the contact lenses I had worn as an actor. And I badly needed a shave.

She smiled as though she were reading my mind. "No, I guess you didn't."

"Where have you been? I tried to find you."

She stopped the rush of words with a single fingertip at my lips. "Later. There are other things to do now. Come on."

She led me out of the light booth and we started down the stairs to the dressing room.

"No." I started to protest.

She looked at me, slightly puzzled, perhaps intentionally puzzled. "I thought you wanted the legitimate theatre back, Tim. That's what everyone thinks."

"I can't face all those people," I whispered.

"You have to, Tim. Come on." And she led me like a little child.

)OOO(

Ten years earlier, she had been dancing the dream ballet in *Carousel*. She was alone on the stage when the counterweight broke, sending a light pipe crashing to the stage.

Ignoring the audience, I had rushed out before anyone else could move, trying to lift the pipe off her broken and mangled legs. They had pushed me away and I went to her, took her hand.

"It's all right," I had babbled over and over again. "Don't worry, Vicki. I'm here. It's all right. You'll be okay."

She had looked up at me and smiled, not a sign of pain in her face.

"She'll never dance again," the doctors told me. "Both knee caps are shattered, her left thigh is broken in two places and her right thigh in one. She'll probably be confined to a wheelchair for the rest of her life."

I went in to see her. The shock had worn off and even drugs couldn't keep the pain out of her face. I tried to talk her into marrying me but she refused. "I couldn't saddle you down with an invalid," she said. "I'd be useless to you."

After she left the hospital, she returned to her family in the Midwest. I tried to follow her, tried to keep in touch with her, but she never answered my letters. Finally I gave up, being content to send her a card every now and then.

"I'll never dance again," she said as we reached the orchestra pit of the now-empty auditorium. It was as if she'd been reading my mind. "I'll never dance again," she repeated, "but look."

She lifted her skirt, exposing her legs. They were still trim and well-formed. She turned around slowly, not awkwardly, but without the grace she had once had.

My eyes filled with tears for a moment, but that was enough time for her to come back to my side and kiss me lightly. "Come on, Timmy," she said gently. "We're waiting for you."

)OOO(

A buffet had been laid out in the wings just as in the old days. There were about twenty people there, chatting among the counterweights and pulleys. Some of them were wearing evening gowns and coats and ties.

I pulled back but Vicki pushed me forward.

"Ah, here he is." A heavy man with a bald head came forward. "We were beginning to wonder what and Vicki were up to." It was Ike Rodell, who had directed the three of us in *The Fantasticks* more than ten years earlier.

I mumbled something while the others gave me casual hellos, as if we'd been working together for the past several weeks. Most of the faces were familiar, even after ten years, although I could remember very few names.

Paul Denesha walked up. "I was just telling Ike what a fantastic job you've done with the lights."

"Yes," Ike said. "I still don't believe one man is doing all the work. Are you sure you don't have a computer up there?"

"It's not as hard as it looks," I said. "Not after you've had a little practice."

"Oh, it doesn't look hard at all," Ike said. "It's so smooth it's hardly noticeable. If Paul hadn't been sitting next to me, I would never have noticed the lighting."

"I guess that's a compliment," I said.

"But the performance was something else." Ike shook his head sadly.

"What was the matter with the performance?" I asked. "Stuart's an excellent actor. He did a fine job tonight. No one could have done any better."

Ike held up a hand to quiet me. "No, no, it wasn't Stuart. It was that barbarous way you had to chop Shakespeare up so one man could do it. You need more people, Tim. An entire troupe."

"A troupe of those zombies on the Metropolitan lots?" I asked.

Ike gestured around him. "Look around you, Tim. We haven't all died. Not yet." He sipped from his punch.

"Where were they years ago when I needed them? It's too late now, Ike."

"Is it? Come on." He led me over to where Stuart was busy talking with someone, while Vicki caught up to me with a cup of punch and some sandwiches.

I didn't recognize the man that Stuart was talking to until Ike introduced us. "Tim, I'd like you to meet Mr. Boggs."

I'd never seen him in person before but he was familiar to me from his photographs: D. Clark Boggs, Metropolitan's vice-president in charge of production. What was he doing here?"

"The famous Tim Schroeder," Boggs said. "I was really surprised to learn you were with us."

"The reports of my death have been greatly exaggerated," I mumbled and Boggs laughed politely.

"No, I didn't mean that. I didn't know you were working for Metropolitan until Ike brought it to my attention."

I looked at Ike, raising an eyebrow. Ike interpreted the question accurately. "I'm Clark's assistant in charge of special productions," he said.

"Wait until you hear," Stuart broke in excitedly. "It's a great idea."

The two executives looked at each other for a moment then Boggs said, "Go ahead, Ike. It's your idea."

"It's not really mine; it sort of evolved from all of us: Paul, Stuart, Vicki, everybody." I wasn't sure I wanted to hear it but there didn't seem to be much choice. I was surrounded by those faces, all beaming eagerly. "When we learned that St. Mark's was about to be converted, we knew that the last bastion of live theatre was about to be violated. So I began talking to people and everyone agreed. We got together last night, put the whole thing before Clark, and he agreed to come down tonight to see if Stuart still has the old touch."

"Stop being so damn mysterious, Ike, and tell me what you've got up your sleeve."

"Well, look at it this way, Tim: live theatre—I mean the real live theatre, the stage, Broadway—it's dead. Nobody goes to the theatres any more. They don't even go to the movies. They all stay home watching the TV screen. Right?"

"Right," I said sourly.

"Well, if people won't go to the theatre, we'll bring the theatre to them!" He looked at me triumphantly.

Twenty eager faces watched me while D. Clark Boggs placidly waited for my response.

"You're going to transmit live theatre?" I asked, chopping each word short. The response wasn't quite what they'd expected. There was a nervous rustle and Boggs scowled. "Starring Stuart?"

"What's wrong with that?" Stuart asked indignantly.

"What's wrong with it? Why are you doing soap commercials instead of starring in your own show?" He started to protest but I cut him short. "When was the last time someone offered you a part? It's not that you're not good enough, Stuart. It's that you're too damned good! Those clods out there don't appreciate you." I swept my hand out to indicate the great faceless mass beyond the walls of St. Mark's.

"You've got to give them a chance," Ike said quietly. "You've got to educate them."

"They had their chance! They turned their backs on us ten, fifteen years ago. They told us what they wanted. So give it to them. Don't bother Stuart and me with your hare-brained schemes."

I stalked off. What were they trying to do, anyway? Destroy the last vestige of pride that the legitimate theatre had? Stuart and I had our last shows to do but, no, old Mass Media had to butt its head in and make a mockery of our last rites, our wake, our funeral, our burial.

Couldn't they let us die in peace?

)OOO(

I could hear Vicki behind me but I kept walking, through the house out to the lobby. Then I turned around to face her.

"What are you trying to do?" she asked. She was angry now and she was clipping her words short just I had a few minutes earlier.

"What am *I* trying to do?" I had my anger under control now and there was the edge of sweet reason in my voice. "I didn't ask those ghouls here."

"You ass! We're trying to save the legitimate theatre."

"Well, go right ahead. You don't need me; I don't know why you dragged *me* into this."

"Because you *are* legitimate theatre. To the rest of us, anyway."

"Well, this idea of Ike's... and yours too, isn't it?" She nodded. "It's not going to work, Vikki. You ought to know better. It's not the same thing."

"Tim? Are you going to walk out on us? Are you going to play the martyr and make every last one of those people feel miserable?" There was fire in her eyes now and I was finding it hard not to smile. Christ, it was like old times. "Why don't you just go up and spit in their faces and get it over with? You... you used to be a god, not a spoiled tantrum-throwing brat. We even put up with that grand gesture of yours." She struck a noble pose. "'I'm quitting the stage because of my one true love.' We thought you'd be back. And then we thought we'd do this one last thing for you..."

And then she was in my arms and we were both crying. I heard one of the lobby doors start to open then close again quietly. At least someone in this theatre had some tact left.

"All right," I said quietly. "If it's what you want, I'll do it. I guess there's no harm in it. But you know it's not going to work, don't you?"

"Once I did," she said. "But we've all got so worked up over it, trying to sell it to Mr. Boggs, that we all believe it'll work." We started back to the house. "Timmy, don't throw cold water on it, whatever you do. I mean, for all of us. If Boggs begins to think it won't work, we'll never be able to do it. So what if it's a turkey? The thing to do is to do it. Just this once. We all want it, Timmy; it's not just for you. It's for us too. Do you understand that?"

"Sure, Vicki." I kissed her lightly as we reached the lobby door. "But you really don't need me. We'll never be able to run a TV show with that jury-rig I've got upstairs."

I opened the door for her.

"We don't want you to run lights, Timmy. We want you to act."

)OOO(

I stood there, all the pieces of the puzzle falling into place in my head. I started to back away but it was already too late: Ike Rodell was at my side. "You'll do it, won't you, Tim?" he asked.

"You're crazy." My voice was a husky whisper.

"For us?" Vicki asked. "For me?"

"It'll be the three of us together again," Stuart said. "You, me, and Vicki, like old times."

I looked at Vicki for confirmation. She nodded.

I didn't seem to have any other choice. "Well, if that's the way it's to be, I'd be silly to keep up my retirement, wouldn't I? After all, I quit because Vicki wasn't on the stage any longer."

)OOO(

The next few days were hectic, as I argued with Ike about the script they had chosen. It was a conglomeration of bits and pieces from every possible play they could think of, from *Oedipus* to the last piece done on the legitimate stage, a gawdawful play called *The San Alamos Mesa*.

"You're trying to put thousands of years of theatre into one hour on the idiot box?" I screamed. "You're out of your minds. It can't be done. You've only got three speeches from Shakespeare. Where's *Macbeth* represented, or Falstaff? What about the closing speech from *The Tempest*? That was Shakespeare's last play and you don't have a single word from it. And only one speech by Marlowe. Not one damn thing from *Tamerlane*. One song from Rodgers and Hammerstein, none from Rodgers and Hart, one by Romberg, and, for God's sake, only *one* from Gilbert and Sullivan? It can't be done, Ike; it can't be done."

But little by little we pieced together a script that satisfied Ike Rodell and D. Clark Boggs, even if none of us were too happy with what was left out.

Meanwhile the wrecking crews came in to tear apart the last legitimate theatre still in business. The entire balcony was remodeled into a control booth, all the plush seats and draperies torn out. When they started to take the seats out of the main house, I put my foot down.

"I won't do it," I said. "I'm an actor, not a boob-tube zombie. I need an audience to react to, not a goddamn idiot light on a camera."

"But, Tim," Ike protested, "times have changed."

"Ike, if we're going to do this, we're going to have to do it right. This is a one-shot deal, anyway. After this show they can finish the job tearing St. Mark's apart. But I'm going to play to an audience, not those damn cameras. It's your job to pick out the best camera angles; just keep them away from my nose, that's all."

Ike sighed. "Well, I suppose we can edit the angles later."

"Later?" I screamed. "What do you mean, later? I thought we were doing this live."

"Tim, no one does anything live any more. Everything's recorded now. You know that."

"But this show isn't going to be like 'everything,' Ike. This is going to be different, a harkening back to the days of live theatre."

"Think a minute, Tim. This way, if you make mistakes, we can go back and correct them."

"Jay-zus Christ, Ike, you never worried about retakes in the old days. We were on our own and, if we made mistakes, why, we made mistakes. That was that and somehow someone kept the show going. Listen, Ike, you talked me into this. I didn't come back to the stage to be another boob-tube zombie."

So, in the end, we wound up on that tiny St. Mark's stage with a mishmash of "great quotes from the theatre," two cameras with zoom lenses in the balcony, one in each of the wings, and a house full of network VIPs.

Meanwhile, the promotion department was trying to keep it all under a hat, planning to spring this on the public a day or two before the telecast, so that the other networks wouldn't get wind of it and try to scoop us. Fat chance they had of succeeding: I had hardly walked back to the party with Vicki, Ike, and Stuart before the other networks knew about it and were busy trying to sign up old actors.

Only one of them succeeded however and their show, a half hour synopsis of *Hamlet*, was aired the day before ours. By that time our publicity department was going full guns and their show was a big flop.

"See?" I said to Stuart. "It's over, finis. People don't want to see actors anymore or watch plays that make them think. Tomorrow's going to lay a big fat egg."

"What did they have, Tim? Not a single name actor and most of the bit parts were held by TV actors, who don't know how to handle a live role. Besides, everybody's waiting to see the three of us together again, Tim. We're still big names; it hasn't been that long and a lot of people still remember us."

"Stuart, you've got the brains of a chorus girl."

)OOO(

But willy-nilly, for better or for worse, opening and closing night came upon us all at once; the last rehearsals were over; Ike had his camera angles figured down to the last centimeter; the VIPs in their tails and evening gowns were rustling about in the house, nervous and yet probably comfortable too in old reminiscences. Everywhere in that old theatre the ghosts were out and haunting, sending shivers all over the place without the need for cameras and microphones.

"Now remember, Tim, during the travel song from *The Fantasticks*, you go down to the red cross-mark downstage right while Stu goes stage left. I never know which way either of you will go. Tim, right; Stu, left. Got it?"

"And turn my face three-quarters to the left balcony camera and smile so that my dimples show. Right."

"Mr. Schroeder, will you come out under the lights so we can check your makeup?" someone shouted.

"Coming."

"Break a leg, Tim," Ike said as he went back to the control booth.

I was beginning to get nervous. "This is ridiculous," I said, holding out my shaking hands for Stuart and Vicki to see.

"Butterflies in your stomach?" Stuart asked.

"It feels more like winged elephants."

He nodded. "I know. It's silly, but I feel the same way."

We went out to the wings.

"Bring the house to half," the stage manager said into his headset. "House out. Start the overture."

Beyond the curtain, an orchestra started playing Elizabethan music at the same time that the work lights went off. "Break a leg, Timmy," Vicki whispered in my ear. I held her, kissed her briefly.

"Break a leg, Vicki."

She smiled, aware of how hard it was for me to say that.

Then I was alone on the darkened stage, waiting for the curtain to go up. My knees wanted to collapse; my stomach tried to tie itself in to a slipknot; and I had to clear my throat several times.

In the control room an announcer was giving his spiel while the credits reeled off in front of the closed curtain. There would be no commercials for the next hour: it would be Stuart, Vicki, and me with all the others as supers, others who had once been Broadway stars.

The curtain went up, the music stopped, and I was alone in a circle of light.

"All the world's a stage,

And all the men and women merely players."

I forgot my knees, my stomach, all my aches, and became the infant, the schoolboy, the lover, the soldier, the justice, the old man, and finally the dying man, "sans teeth, sans eyes, sans taste, sans everything."

I was in darkness again and, on the other side of the stage, Stuart was performing a short speech from *The Taming of the Shrew*:

"Your honor's players, hearing your amendment,

Are come to play a pleasant comedy...

... melancholy is the nurse of frenzy:

Therefore they thought it good you hear a play,

And frame your mind to mirth and merriment,

Which bars a thousand harms and lengthens life."

It wasn't in our script but I couldn't help but add Sly's line that ends the prologue:

"Well, we'll see't. Come, madam wife, sit by my side,

And let the world slip: we shall ne'er be younger."

As we raced to the quick-change booths, the orchestra played a medley of musical comedy songs. They were nearly drowned out by the applause.

"Stick to the script," the stage manager warned me. "Don't ad-lib.

We don't have time."

Then I was on stage again. We romped through three thousand years of the theatre, from Aeschylus to Beckett and beyond. The show was a collage of speeches and scenes that jumped from Greek drama complete with masks and chorus up to *West Side Story* and back to Marlowe's *Faustus*. Chronologically it made no sense but there was a glorious thread that somehow wove from one scene to the next.

But it had hardly begun before it was over and I was alone on the stage again, doing Prospero's last speech from *The Tempest*:

"Our revels now are ended, these our actors... were

all spirits and are melted into air, into thin air; and like the baseless fabric of this vision the cloud-capped towers, the gorgeous palaces, the solemn temples, the great globe itself, yea, all which it inherit, shall dissolve and like this insubstantial pageant faded leave not a rack behind: we are stuff as dreams are made on, and our little life is rounded with a sleep."

A brief blackout and we were all on the stage for the curtain call, those red lights on the cameras in the balcony winking at us like half-alive demons.

Then I found myself being pushed forward, alone.

There was a movement in the house. Someone was standing. Another. And another. Now the whole audience was standing. Whistling. Shouting. Boors. The crazy, silly boors.

The lights had winked off and the moment was ours, all ours, shared only by the people in St. Mark's and not carried into millions of living rooms.

Tears were running down my cheeks. I held out my hands for Stuart and Vicki to join me downstage.

Two curtain calls later, I held up my hand as the curtains closed. "No more," I said. "No more."

The stage manager called for houselights but the audience still applauded. We waited but they weren't about to leave. We were shoved back toward the stage and the curtains parted one more time.

I smiled at Stuart and Vicki as the curtains closed again. "We did it," I said. "We went out in style. I don't know how I'll ever thank you."

"Were not going out," Stuart said. "This is just the beginning."

Somehow Ike Rodell was down there with us. He must have flown all the way from the balcony. "We did it, baby, we did it! I hate to say you were wrong, old sourpuss, but you were. America bought it all.

The figures are already in. Eighty-six percent tuned in to see you return, Tim. Eighty-six percent! Why, sometimes there's not eight-six percent watching a TV set, much less a single show."

"I don't believe it," I said. "Somebody made a mistake."

"Metropolitan doesn't make mistakes," Ike said. "They're not in the business of making mistakes."

Then I saw D. Clark Boggs over in a corner of the wings beaming like a brand-new papa and I knew it was true. Somehow, I was wrong and America wanted us back.

)OOO(

So many people had come up to me to shake my hand and tell me what a wonderful performance it was that I had lost count. I also wanted to puke: these were the same people who had turned their backs on the legitimate stage years ago when it had started to falter. But now they had a brand new bandwagon to jump on and I was it.

Somehow I wrested myself free and made my way to the dressing room Things were hectic there too but at least I was among my own people: Stuart, Angie, Vicki, Ike, Paul, the twenty or so people who had planned and put the show together. It was spoiled by the presence of D. Clark Boggs and his flunkies but, what the hell, I guess he had as much right to be here as anyone.

Without D. Clark Boggs, it would all be over now instead of just beginning. Without D. Clark Boggs, perhaps Stuart and I would have been able to finish off our run in St. Mark's in peace and quiet.

"Tim, look at the telegrams!" Stuart waved a handful of yellow paper in my face. "And the phones have been ringing constantly."

"There's a guy in Washington," Ike said. "He's called us twice. Said he owns a theatre there. It's been dark for years but, if we ever want to perform there, it's ours for the asking."

"How about that?" someone else said. "We can become a traveling repertory company."

"Forget that," Boggs said. "Anything he has to offer, Metropolitan can easily top. This is just the start of big things for us, just the start."

Washington. It had been years since I had been in Washington. But there wasn't a chance: not now, not since the show was a success. Metropolitan had us all tied up in half a dozen different legal knots and they weren't going to let us go as long as we were successful. Boggs hadn't said so in as many words but we all knew what he meant.

Vicki came over to hold my hand. She didn't say a word but it was as if she had been reading my mind.

More Metropolitan bass came into the dressing room to share the celebration and hardly anyone noticed when one of Boggs' flunkies entered to whisper something to him. Boggs conferred with one of the other executives, the flunky left, and Boggs called Ike over.

Vicki saw me watching and followed the exchange too. "Timmy, do you think something's wrong?"

"The way Boggs is acting doesn't look good."

It made me happy, though, to see him worried.

Stuart joined us. "Here, have some more champagne." He thrust a glass into my hand. Vicki stopped him as he started to leave.

Ike was elbowing his way through the crowd toward us.

"What is it, Ike?" Vicki asked as soon as he got to our side. "What's wrong?"

"It's nothing. Nothing. Just a mistake."

"I thought Metropolitan didn't make mistakes," I said drily.

Stuart was beginning to realize that something wasn't quite right. "Spill it, Ike. I don't know what's going on but I'd like to find out."

Ike licked his lips. "The ratings."

"What about them?" Stuart asked.

"They dropped. They dropped all the way down to fifteen percent by the end of the show."

The look on Stuart's face and Vicki's swept the triumph out of my eyes. "It's probably a mistake," I said.

But of course it wasn't. The news spread out from us like ripples in a pond and with it a silence that was broken by a nervous and embarrassed undercurrent of whispers. In an hour, there were only twenty or so dejected people sitting around in a dressing room that would soon be dismantled.

D. Clark Boggs wasn't there to share this with us.

"Well, it was good while it lasted," I said. "Thank you. Thank you all. I'd forgotten what it was like. I really had." I got up and helped Vicki to her feet. Everyone sat around, still dejected. "Well, I've got to go back to work tomorrow, I guess." I started to leave but almost got bowled over as Paul Denesha came running in.

"He hasn't changed his mind," he said excitedly. "He hasn't changed his mind!"

"Who?" Stuart asked. "Boggs? That guy's all business; he knows this kind of show is a loser."

"No, not Boggs. The guy in Washington. I just called him."

The dejection of the dressing room suddenly turned into a babble of excited voices then a ragged council-of-war and, when it was over, everybody had agreed to go to Washington.

Everybody. Even Paul Denesha was willing to give up his security blanket with Metropolitan and head the light crew in Washington.

Everybody. Except me.

"But why?" Stuart asked for the seventeenth time. "Why won't you join us? We need you. We need a star."

"Because I'm tired of pretending I'm the last bastion of civilization. This whole production we've just put on has opened my eyes to how blind I've been for the past five years. I'm not going through that again."

"But we need you," Angie said. "We need an established star."

"You have an established star. You've got Stuart. Please, don't let me stop you. I wish you all the luck in the world. But I'm not going through that again."

In the end they left, excited about going to Washington and back to the legitimate stage while a bit depressed because they couldn't convince me to go with them. Vicki was the last to leave.

"I'm going with them, Timmy."

"I'd hoped you would. You should go back to the stage, Vicki. They need every bit of help they can get."

"It's not that I don't love you."

"I understand. I love you too, Vicki, but I'm not going with you. I can't explain why. Not just yet.

Then there were no more words, just two bodies pressed tightly against each other yet already hundreds of miles apart. We walked together, arm in arm, through the dark house, the lobby and out to the street. We kissed one last time then I watched her walk away. At the corner, she stopped, smiled weakly, and waved goodbye.

I walked back through the house. There was no possibility of my running the light board one last time. I could never program the computers in the balcony. The only light left in the theatre was a single naked bulb backstage that cast garish shadows across the stage floor.

I stood in the light, feeling vaguely foolish.

"'What need I be so forward with him that calls not on me?'" I mumbled. "'Well, 'tis no matter; honor pricks me on.'"

As I continued the speech, my voice grew stronger and the feeling of foolishness fell away. I dredged the harbor of my memory for every speech, every line I could recall, all the marvelous speeches of Shakespeare we'd been unable to use, those of Moliere, Ben Jonson, Euripides, Ionesco, even Colley Cibber.

It was silly, I know, but you have to remember that I'm an actor. Even as a lighting technician, I'd been acting, striking dramatic poses, weighing the words as I spoke them, becoming angry when the situation called for anger, placating when the time required it.

And so I made this great, grand, empty gesture because it was unreal and dramatic. The only reality over which I've had any control is the false reality of the theatre. Maybe that puts me one ahead of everyone else.

I stood in the silence on the empty stage of the empty theatre, trying to find one more speech. But I could only find the one I'd been saving for last. I had to give it before I lost my nerve and realized the silly futility of this gesture:

"Now my charms are all o'erthrown,

And what strength I have's mine own..."

As Shakespeare said his farewell to the Elizabethan stage through Prospero's speech, so did I.

"As you from crimes would pardon'd be,

Let your indulgence set me free."

The applause began, starting from a hillside in Greece, continuing through a thousand small medieval towns to the Globe Theatre, on up across the seas to the glittering lights of Twentieth Century Broadway, and ending quietly in a small theatre that was soon to be a TV studio. And it was all in my head.

I gathered up my things from the box office and left, carefully locking the door behind me. At the corner, I stopped to look at St. Mark's one last time.

I should have felt sad, I suppose, but I didn't. I felt lighthearted and carefree, as though I'd been in a turkey that had finally folded after too long a run. The future was uncertain, but it would not be desperate clutching to a dead past.

Nothing Personal

Computers are bastards. It's nothing personal, just a fact. For example, the first central city computer banks were wonderful but... they gave an architect the wrong stress figures for steel; the building collapsed when it was 95% occupied. Sometimes the computer would substitute strychnine for saccharine in a grocery order. Instead of doping the water supply with chlorine, occasionally it would substitute arsenic.

When an earthquake destroyed Topeka, the SAC computer decided it was a nuclear attack and the on-duty tech was 3.00002924 seconds late on the override. The Russian computer didn't like having Vladivostok destroyed. Nor St. Petersburg or Moscow.

I'd better go oil the tape drives. I know a mech can do it but I like to feel useful. Please be careful with my next meal. It took me an hour to separate the ground glass from the scrambled eggs this morning.

I realize it's nothing personal.

THE REALLY DISTANT FUTURE

Carrara

So the morning ran like water
                over the marbled city of dreams
        and in the alleys
            I and my free kind
    wandered back to the empty rooms
                to listen to the lost years' wail
            and to dream
                    our own
        unmarbled dreams.

When the morning sun had turned green
                        in the west
            my woman woke me
                    turning from her other lover
            twice she woke me with her lips
                a token of her love
                a toke and her love.

We entered the quicksilver time of night
        to sell our minds
        to the marbled denizens
                        of the city of dreams
    walking like tourists of time
        of the time
                wherein I and my free kind dwell

Grant Carrington

in the marble cracks
where we mate
to wait
the watered dawn.

Half Past the Dragon

Lie down, my love, and I'll tell you a story.

Of course it's a true story.

No, most true stories don't have happy endings. The true ending of most true stories is death.

Now be quiet, and I'll have a surprise for you when the story is over.

It takes place in deepest interstellar deep space, where gravity is only a whisper, where lithium ions taste like cotton candy. It is only here, far from planetary masses, that space dragons will be found, for the dragons are fragile creatures, wisps of hydrogen and helium, traces of argon and nitrogen. You could pass your hand through one and never feel anything but vacuum. Should a dragon approach a planet, it would be torn to shreds. A painful death. And perhaps a common one for space dragons, for they are curious beasts. Perhaps that's why there are so few of them.

I was the good ship *Kimono* in those days, plying the trade between Babe Ruth and El Nair. In those days, I tasted the stellar winds. Some of us saw them, some heard them, some felt them. Our brains, all that was left of what we were born with, encased in cryogenic cabinets deep in the bowels of our ships, interpreted the data in different and individualistic ways. I greedily gulped the gravy-and-potatoes of hydrogen, the rare roast beef of helium garnished with a sprig of ferric ion. I sipped the fine Chablis of oxygen and for desert I feasted on the baked Alaska of nitrogen. Sometimes I could tell where an argon atom had been born simply by the fragrance of its bouquet.

Oh, I had heard tales of space dragons, yes, and I thought of them as you do now—mere tales by space-drunk ships. I had never seen one, felt one, smelled one, tasted one, heard one.

They are different, Sam Hall told me. (It was this same Sam Hall who was going to write a book, The Synaesthetics of Space.) We all see and experience dragons the same way, No matter how you experience anything else in space, you will see a dragon, smell the brimstone on its breath, feel the ghostly heat of its flame, and hear its roar.

And what does roasted dragon taste like?, I asked, trying to be sarcastic in my youthful ignorance.

Like rotten flesh, he answered.

How did we talk, without mouths? Without sweet mouths like yours, my dear? Yes, made for kissing and caressing. Why, we had radios, of course.

Sleep? Of course we slept. Humans need sleep, whether they are just brain or have all their protoplasmic complement.

The computer was perfectly capable of taking care of all the routine chores, taking off, landing, and so on. In fact, I slept eighty percent of the time.

We were needed for those unforeseen instances. We were always awake at liftoff, orbital insertion, and landing, nominally in control, but in reality with our mental fingers over imaginary buttons. I only remember one time when I had to do something, and that has nothing to do with tonight's tale.

Okay, I'll tell you tomorrow night. Move over a little, will you? There, that's much better.

No, our emergencies always took place in empty interstellar space.

Yes, like space dragons, And wandering planets and renegade alien pirates. Ah, yes, those were exciting days, back before the galaxy was completely tamed. Of course, I didn't think so then. Many were the times I shit in my pants. That was embarrassing. And dangerous.

No, but my anal sphincter control was attached to the exhaust tubes. I lost a lot of fuel that way, fortunately never enough to keep me from getting to a friendly planet. It was close a couple of times, though.

Yes, I'll tell you about them some other night.

Of course it was embarrassing. Can you imagine what it's like to try to explain to a planetmaster why you're short on fuel?

Now quit asking questions and let me tell you about the dragon. Yes, that does feel good.

It happened on one of my first trips as the *Kimono*. The *Kimono* was a lovely ship. I've worn many ships in my day, but putting on the *Kimono* was like slipping on a familiar old glove.

Ah, *Kimono*! My house, my home, my castle, my very being for so many years.

I'd heard about dragons, yes, but I thought they were just so much space gas, if you know what I mean. Space-yak and space-flak. Well, in a way I was right, of course. They *are* space gas, but not in the way I'd meant it.

There I was, somewhere between the Horsehead Nebula and El Nair, half-asleep, as it were, in that eternal haze-land between sleep and wakefulness that you spend so much time in when you're in space, when there's nothing for you to do but sleep.

What? Oh, yes, there's other things to do. You can play volleyball, handball, football, baseball, basketball, hockey, chess, checkers, squash, ping-pong, or lacrosse; you can read any book you desire (as long as you've had the foresight to have it entered into the computer's memory banks), see any dramatic presentation you want, hear any recording you wish; you can make love to the galaxy's most beautiful women, many of them long dead; you can write, compose, paint...

What's that?

My favorite was Rosemary Clooney.

Never mind; she was before your time. Or mine, for that matter.

You can write, compose, paint, make sculptures; or you can just wander by an unpolluted stream in a virgin forest. You can experience anything you've loaded into the computer. It's all in the mind, of course, but, then, what isn't?

No, I didn't mean to get solipsistic with you. Sorry.

Anyway, I was drifting along, a light show playing hazily in my mind to the faint susurrus of space while the *Kimono* sped on its way to El Nair, Far from the continuous radio noise near inhabited planets, one could hear faint communications from long dead races, from long dead pilots of one's own race:... *I do have lights in sight on the ground.... Is Professor Weisberg still at the Academy?... This program was brought to you by Cheerios,... The lights show up very well, and thank everybody for turning them on.... This is Sissy Face Control....* In fact, some pilots look for brambles of static, hidden pockets where no manmade radiation can reach. I've never been a static addict myself, but I've felt the temptation of natural radiation, unpolluted by civilized and organized wavelengths. The only signal of any strength was that of the laser beacon from Babe Ruth to El Nair, fore and aft of the *Kimono*, but even that was so attenuated it could not overwhelm the ancient murmurings of space.

The dragon. Yes, the dragon.

Well, I was drifting along when this dragon appeared. Just like that. No warning. Just, zonk!, there it was.

I've talked to other pilots since then and they say that's the way it always happens, the dragons just pop out of nowhere, Some people think they come out of another dimension, some kind of hyperspace, and that there's really lots of them, but they rarely appear in our space.

It looked just as Sam Hall said it would, a thin sinuous bright green dragon with glowing red coals for eyes. The light of distant suns seemed to magnify a thousandfold as it reflected off the shifting atoms of its tenuous scales. It writhed in space like a cloud caught in the wind, but its writhing brought it closer to the *Kimono*, purposefully. The twin eyes winked on and off like evil variable stars.

It scared the shit out of me, I mean to tell you! Literally. Not much, because I'd managed to gain control of my sphincter since my last run-in with the Pleiades Pirates. But I wasn't quick enough and the dragon leapt for and swallowed that little morsel of exhaust emission, licked its chops, and waited for more.

You wouldn't think that a dragon could look like a hopeful puppy, especially with glowing coals for eyes but, so help me Fomalhaut, that's what the dragon did. And when it didn't get any more, it opened its mouth and a long tongue of hard radiation belched forth, smelling of sulfur. I laughed as the plasma field that protected the *Kimono* from gas clouds at relativistic speeds easily deflected the radiation. For a few microseconds, the umbilicus between Babe Ruth and El Nair was snapped, but it was quickly restored.

Now I was in a bit of a spot, but I wasn't too worried. In fact, the whole situation was kind of humorous. Here I was deep in interstellar space, being trailed by a space dragon. Though trailed isn't quite the word: it had wrapped itself around the *Kimono* like snake around a tree. It quite obviously had every intention of hanging around, looking for more handouts. I couldn't go near any gravitational masses or I'd be contributing to the demise of an endangered species, which was quite a serious crime at the time, but I had plenty of time to worry about that.

Not that I could have killed it anyway. I had already come to like the little critter, I even gave it a name—St. George.

Never mind, It would be too much trouble to explain. But when you pilot spaceships for a while, you stuff your brain with a lot of useless knowledge. Sometimes you get mental indigestion and they have to use a brain pump on you, But it's all there, somewhere in your personal magnetic core.

No, not yours. Unless you put it there.

Well, I'll be damned! Yes, St. George and the Dragon! I don't know why it'd be in *your* core. But that's cute.

Every now and then, old St. George would belch a little more radiation on me, disrupting the laser thread for a few microseconds. Thinking about the problem I slipped off into a restless slumber, hypnotized by the flashing red light the computer kept sending me.

My cargo this trip was Babe Ruth's championship baseball team, on their way to El Nair for the District 3 semifinals of the Third Millennial World Series. They were the defending champions, of course. They had won 746 straight games, their last loss occurring when their center field (named Babe Ruth, of course) had stepped in a gopher hole.

The whole *team* was named Babe Ruth! This always caused problems whenever they made substitution: "Babe Ruth pinchhitting for Babe Ruth." It was suspected that sometimes they took out one of their stars and resubmitted him as a pinchhitter later in the game. But how could you know?

No, they were in cryogenic cabinets too. Not as compact as mine, of course. But human beings rarely traveled awake in those days, when the space lanes were still wild. Just explorers and pilots like myself. Even between El Nair, and Babe Ruth, there were still several unsavory patches, not fit to be seen by an athlete who must stay simon pure and in condition. Besides, it took several years to make the trip. (That was back before the tachyon drive had been perfected, my dear.)

That lovely blinking red light the computer kept sending to me reminded me of those stalwart athletes I was transporting to El Nair, Why, you ask? Why, indeed? I asked myself the same question. I had no answer. I asked the computer.

Listen, dummy, it said to me, we've run into an area of high radiation, higher than the plasma field can cope with. Do something about it!

It was one of those emergencies that required the help of a human mind. A drifting, half-asleep human mind, the dragon! That's what it was, the dragon, belching radiation at the *Kimono*, was overwhelming my plasma shield and endangering my athletes. And furthermore it was endangering *me*! Under that sporadic bombardment, I was drifting off again, unable to control my consciousness.

With that thought firmly in mind, I made a mental effort to pierce that haze and succeeded, long enough to realize that the computer was right. My internal radiation was rising, slowly but steadily, toward dangerous levels.

I was in trouble.

You see, the *Kimono* belonged to Odyssey Space Lines, Inc., and they had a contract with Babe Ruth that gave them exclusive transportation rights, And they capitalized on it in their advertising: "Travel on a Babe Ruth Liner!" "Make Your Home Run with the Team That Carries Babe Ruth!" "Strike Out for the Unknown on a Babe Ruth Exploratory Cruise!" And those were the least offensive ones.

If I didn't get the Babe Ruth baseball team to El Nair on time, they'd forfeit their Galactic Championship and their value to Odyssey Space Lines, Inc. would be zero.

And my value to Odyssey would be even less.

Of course, that was rapidly becoming the least of my worries.

Every time St. George belched, radiation particles crept or sped through the *Kimono*, depending on St. George's position. If he was at the head of the *Kimono*, our relative speeds approached 2c and those particles were gone faster than any computer could count. But if St. George was at my tail, why, that radiation would creep through so slowly that several particles could gather together in a cell long enough to throw a stag party with films of bombarded nuclei and all.

I was, as they say, in trouble, and already drifting back to sleep.

Wake up, you crumb! The computer shot at me, meanwhile adjusting my adrenalin level.

I woke up.

At first I tried evasive maneuvers, but that only made things worse, With each maneuver, I'd use a little more fuel and St. George would gulp up the exhaust and come back, hungrily looking for me. Hell, they couldn't have been more than appetizers for him. He was waiting for the main course.

Get past St. George? Hell, I couldn't get half past the dragon!

It appeared the only thing to do was to wait him out, coasting as far as possible, in the hope that St. George would get hungry and go look elsewhere before he'd belched us up to the danger point. I wracked my drifting mind for another solution but it was harder and harder to concentrate. Old memories came drifting through my brain to say a brief hello then go floating on out.

I had to do something! I fought my way back through the haze, giving myself a beautiful migraine. The computer cheerfully informed me that the situation had changed: one of the suns along my course had chosen this time to go nova.

As the old saying goes, it never rains but it pours.

What? No, of course it never rains in space, What I meant was...

oh, never mind.

I was headed straight for those expanding gas clouds, full of Cherenkhov radiation. What with my already weakened plasma shield, there was no thought of trying to plough on through. I would have to change course and skirt the nova. That was not a particularly difficult maneuver, even in my now somewhat punchdrunk state, but it would tie St. George still more closely to my metaphorical bootstraps.

Bemoaning my fate and wracking my brain for some way to lose St. George, I queried the computer for the requisite course change. That's when I had my moment of genius. Could we skirt through one of those ionized shells without exposing Babe Ruth to too much radiation? The computer assured me we could, giving me a skimming tangent that barely touched the outer shell.

When I fired the engines for the course change that was necessary, old St. George's eyes lit up like Betelgeuse itself at its brightest. Chomp! he went, chomp, chomp, gulping greedily behind me as I led him on.

At least he wasn't belching while he ate.

When we reached the outer shell of expanding gasses, St. George ignored the nova gasses and kept greedily gulping down my rich exhaust, As soon as I turned off the engines, however, to coast back out, he began munching all around him, wolfing down oxygen, helium, nitrogen and ammonium ions in gay abandon.

I sometimes wonder what happened to old George. For all I know, he's still munching his way through that noval cloud, I hope he doesn't get heartburn.

Yes, that's all there is to it.

I'm sorry. You can't expect a climax with every story. I'll try to do better tomorrow night. But first, come over the to the window, my love. Look up there. Yes, a little to your right and up a bit. Now, if my cesium clock is accurate, in approximately 2.6 seconds, you'll see... ah, there it is! Right on time. Yes, flaring up nicely.

The last time I saw that light, my love, was uncountable years ago and now here it is, shining down on us on the night of my tale. If we could magnify it impossibly many times, perhaps we'd see the shadows of a spaceship and a dragon against those rapidly expanding gas clouds.

The name of the star? I believe it's called Eta Draconis.

Shall we go back to bed? Unplug me before you turn off the lights, will you, dear? Thank you.

On the Planet Planet

The Lord Jestodream ap Twilight, Lord of the Instrumentality, shuffled through the dust of the Planet Planet. He was an old man, nearing his thousandth year, but he was still vital. If his steps were shorter and less certain, he still walked with his chin high. His face was one of craghewn nobility, and his pale blue eyes were still clear. He had seen many years, thanks to the drug santaclara, also known as stroon, and he had been many places. His step was less certain now and his hands trembled occasionally; sometimes even his whole body would tremble. But still he kept shuffling across the plain, his shoes covered with its fine dust. He kicked aside rubies and diamonds; he kicked aside garnets and fine amethysts. He wasn't interested in mere baubles. Soon, soon, he would have the one last piece to complete his collection. The most important one, the original. This would be his last trip to the Planet Planet.

Beside him, helping him occasionally as he faltered, were his faithful underpeople companions: the lovely, feline C'Tabby; the earthly, sturdy H'Dobbin; and the faithful, trusty D'Rover. Although the underpeople had achieved their independence long ago, these three had stayed on with him as servants, friends, and companions. They had been with him on all his visits to the Planet Planet, and they were with him now on this final one.

He had been to all the planets, seen all the Earths, New Earth, Reformed Earth, Earth Renewed, Terra Cognito, before he finally met the go-captain Alcatraz, who had told him about the Planet Planet. And so he had come here and he had bought them and collected them, but the original, the first, the *Old* Earth, had evaded him till now. It was the only one left, the last Earth for him to collect and carry home. Soon it would be his, and he would have the only complete collection of Earths in the galaxy.

The sun shone down on the four figures plodding across the dusty plain. It was not the original sun of Manhome but a golden orange sun, hot but not unbearably so. Strange crystalline formations rose up from the desert, but the travelers approached none of these.

"Soon, huh? Soon, boss?" D'Rover growled.

"Yes," the Lord Jestodream ap Twilight said. "We should be there soon and then Old Earth will be ours."

"That will be nice," C'Tabby purred.

"Can you see it yet, C'Tabby?" H'Dobbin whinnied. His soft brown eyes looked at her with admiration. "You have better eyesight than any of us."

"Not yet," she said.

"I can smell it," D'Rover barked. "It's near, near."

"Soon," the Lord Jestodream ap Twilight said. "Soon."

Finally they came to a large cube sitting in the middle of the plain. Each edge was 2.45 meters long; it was a dull buff in color and featureless except for a door in one of the sides. The four travelers walked around it, inspecting it for other features, but there were none.

"This is it, isn't it, huh, boss?" D'Rover said. "I can smell it. This is it, isn't it?"

"Yes. This is it," Lord Jestodream said softly.

"What do we do now?" H'Dobbin neighed.

"I think," the Lord Jestodream said slowly, "I shall knock."

And he did so. Three times upon the door on the side of the cube. And from inside a small tinny voice, like the humming of bees, a multiple voice, answered in unison, "Come in."

The Lord Jestodream opened the door. The inside of the cube was filled with a warm, comfortable yellow light. And suspended in the center of that yellow light was a large globe, exactly 2.35 meters in diameter, rotating slowly, imperceptibly, except at the poles. It was Old Earth, the Last Earth, reduced and crated for shipment to the collection of the Lord Jestodream ap Twilight.

He rubbed his hands together gleefully. "Yes, yes," he said in a cracking, wheezing voice. "This is it, my friends. I now have the only complete collection of Earths in the galaxy." He closed the door and began lifting a corner of the cube.

"Here, let me help you, sir.," D'Rover said.

"You can put it on my back," said H'Dobbin, "as you did with all the others."

"No, no," the Lord Jestodream said. "This one I will carry myself. This one is special. This is the Last Earth and I will carry it myself. The Last Earth is Man's burden, not that of the underpeople."

And so they staggered back across the sands, the Last Earth on Man's back, on the back of the Lord Jestodream ap Twilight, while his companions D'Rover, H'Dobbin, and C'Tabby helped him, keeping it balanced and surreptitiously taking the weight off the old man's shoulders.

World's End

There were four of them: Leo had arrived via transcendental meditation—he was the intellectual of the group. Otto, being a scientist, used an electro-mechanical contrivance/conveyance. Debrah tripped on three different drugs simultaneously. Karl was the last to arrive, having used cabalistic designs of the Black Arts. His origin was uncertain.

They had never met before or heard of each other.

"Cataclysmic," said Otto.

"Far out," quoth Debrah.

"Interesting," mused Leo.

Karl said nothing, merely stroked his Satanic beard.

They were on a bluff overlooking the city, though none of them could remember its existence before. Otto and Karl were standing; Debrah was sitting on the ground, hugging her knees; and Leo was in lotus position. The noise of a laboring combustion engine made them turn around.

Rumbling up the deteriorating roadway was an old school bus, painted with psychedelic designs in day-glo paint, filled with a horde of motley-costumed clowns in makeup and day-glo paint, one of them a rough-hewn man of the mountains, another heavily-muscled man monotonously tossing and catching a hammer with the single-minded energy of a speed freak.

"We're dead," Debrah said. "We must be."

A ragged shadow bisected the river, leaving them in cool darkness while the city glittered in the sun, crystalline facets suddenly shattering their eyesight.

Here, so near the world's end, the ants on the other side of the river were frantically constructing buildings taller and taller, searching in a babylonic array for the heavens. Cranes and derricks pierced the skyline, lifting girders into place one by one.

At an invitation from one of the pranksters, the four entered the bus. A phonograph was playing old Grateful Dead records. Most of the people in the bus were sacked out. The hammer-tossing driver came in:

"You dudes want to play some basketball? We need a couple more to make up our teams."

The four looked at each other.

"Not me," said Leo, "but I'll watch."

"And I'll cheer," said Debrah.

"What about you two?" the driver asked.

"Sure," said Otto.

"If you really need me," said Karl.

"Great! Let's go!" He traded the hammer for a red-white-and-blue basketball that was stashed under the driver's seat and they all went back outdoors.

"Groovy," said Debrah. "Who'd have thought I'd ever meet them?"

In a few minutes, the game was going. The bus driver and the man of the mountains were captains, with Otto and Karl on opposing teams. There were also two young women playing on opposing teams. They played in an old abandoned playground and the ball took unpredictable bounces as it was dribbled on the cracked surface.

A tall black man took the first shot of the game, a jumping push-shot that bounced off the top of the rusted iron rim to the black board and back down again through the hoop.

"Three points!" the black man whooped gleefully.

"No fair!" the bus driver cried. "You weren't far enough away."

"Damn honkies. Always got to play by the rules." And he stole a pass from the bus driver to Otto and swished it from half-court. "Satisfied?"

As Leo watched the match from the sidelines, he saw another man join the spectators on the other side of the court. He was short but muscular, built like a high school halfback, with a shock of curly black hair. He wore a plaid short, work pants, and railroad shoes. His face, with the shadow of a smile at the corner of his lips, tugged at Leo's memory but the literary scholar was unable to place it.

When the game came to an end, the bus driver came over to grip the newcomer's hand casually, as if they had never been dead, then pulled him over to introduce him to the man of the mountains. The camaraderie in the action jogged Leo's memory loose.

"Ti Jean!" he said hoarsely.

He watched in envy as Debrah, who had already ingratiated herself with the pranksters, went up to talk to the newcomer.

"Far out," he heard her say.

"It's not fair," he mumbled.

Otto and Karl came over and Otto mussed Leo's hair. "What's the matter, kid? You should've played. It would do you good to get a little exercise."

"It's the end of the world," Leo said.

"Sure."

"It is!"

"The end of the world is coming all the time," Karl said.

Otto looked across the river to the city. "Is that why we're here? Why we all arrived at the same time? All of us?"

"The bus, everybody. Its judgment day. The heavens will split and the trumpets will blow and Jehovah will come down," Leo said.

"More than likely, the Russians will lay a fat one down on the city."

"Four of us, at the same time and the same place. And the bus, the people." Leo looked across the court to the animated conversation between the newcomer and the bus driver, who was tossing the hammer again.

Otto followed his gaze. "I wonder if they've got some binoculars in the bus."

"Binoculars? What do you want binoculars for?"

"To look at the city."

"You don't need binoculars. You scan see everything clearly enough. Look at that sign." Leo pointed to a building with DOOM spelled out in big red letters across its top story.

"I want to see more," Otto said. "Come on."

Leo followed behind him, suddenly shy. The newcomer saw them coming and said, "Hello, Leo. I've been wanting to meet you. I've heard a lot about you."

"Me?" Leo asked incredulously.

"Certainly. Come on." The newcomer led Leo toward the bluff, where everyone was looking down on the city.

"It's the end of the world, isn't it?" Leo asked.

"Every day the world ends."

Meanwhile the bus driver had wordlessly handed Otto a pair of binoculars then said, "You really don't need them, you know." He followed Leo and his newfound friend, carelessly juggling his hammer.

Otto looked up to see Karl standing nearby, watching him. "Do you know what's going on here?" he asked.

"Perhaps. I'm not certain. Use your logical mind, Otto. Try the scientific method."

"I don't see how it applies."

"All right. Let me set some points for you, bring your attention to some facts:

"Primus, we have Debrah, a hippie of sorts, wouldn't you say?" Otto nodded. "Now where do we find her? Smack dab in the middle of the people who represent her ideal life style.

"Secundus, these very people contain the link between them and a previous generation, whose figurehead is one of the giants of modern literature, just the sort of romantic figure to become a demi-god for Leo."

"You mean, these people are just figments of our minds?"

"Say, rather, that were called forth by Debrah and Leo."

Otto shook his head. "You've got some imagination, Karl."

"So have you, to judge by the device that brought you here."

)OOO(

A party had begun on the palisades overlooking the city. Debrah and the pranksters were passing joints among themselves and listening to old Jefferson Airplane records. Someone was projecting disjointed motion pictures against an impromptu bedsheet movie screen. Joints passed eagerly from hand to hand. Otto saw two pranksters, slaves to habit, exchange joints. Sitting on the ground, Leo and his friend drank sake from delicate china tea cups as they talked, Leo eager and animated while his friend was more reserved. The driver walked from group to group, from Leo to Debrah, from the man of the mountains to the small muscular man in railroad shoes, the hammer flipping end over end like a metronome. For all the shouting, the earnest conversations, the blare of the record player, the air was quiet and clear, as if it were the eve of a holiday for which no one had been prepared.

"Who's that? I haven't seen him before."

Karl smiled as Otto pointed to a man who stood in front of them, facing the party, his back to Karl and Otto.

"No, it can't be!" Otto's voice was a whisper.

The old man turned, his entire face a smile, from the wrinkled brow below the tangled halo of white hair through the gentle eyes down past the brush mustache to the expressive mouth.

"Ah, Otto!" the Germanic voice said. "I would like to talk you. About your machine. You must tell me how it works, the theory behind it. It is a problem I have wrestled much with."

"Yes. Yes, of course." Otto's mouth and throat were suddenly dry and he had to clear his throat. "I'd be honored to. It's very simple, really."

"Of course, of course. All profound things are."

They left Karl and walked along the edges of the party, the sockless old man in his shaggy sweater and his baggy pants and the young scientist in his grease-stained tee shirt and his bell-bottomed levis.

Karl, forgotten so easily, smiled as another piece of the puzzle fell into place.

I'm the last one, he thought.

The sounds of the party were suddenly drowned in a loud ominous cracking sound. Karl looked up to see the sky splitting into two perfect eggshell blue hemispheres. The ah! And oh!s of the others turned to gasps and cries of fear at the deep flickering redness of the gap, a red that was just intense enough to hurt but not painful enough to force them to turn their eyes away.

The cracking complete, a low drone came from the gap. Karl could see a small dark spot moving, barely visible against the red background, growing larger and taking shape.

The old man pointed to the dark winged shape with his pipe, saying something to Otto that Karl couldn't hear. The drone grew louder, becoming recognizable as the four engines of a World War II bomber.

Now Karl could distinguish the markings on it, the browns and greens of camouflage and a lady painted on its nose, the name Enola Gay.

The bomber came down over the city, sweeping low for her bomb run. The crowd on the cliff watched, unable to tear their eyes away, as the single ludicrously small bomb floated slowly down, growing smaller, lost in the city's jungle, to be replaced by a glowing, growing hemisphere, brighter, brighter than the full moon, brighter than a naked incandescent bulb, growing brighter and brighter then stopping. It was bright, it hurt the eyes, but it was not blinding. The hemisphere engulfed the city but, even before it was finished with that task, it was sending a stem upwards, growing and changing shape.

Karl looked away, the afterimage of the holocaust still bright on his retina. He was alone on the palisades. The others, all, were gone. Then, as the afterimage faded , he realized that Debrah, Otto, and Leo remained.

He looked back at the cloud. It was fully formed now, leaning toward the bluff, its murky cloudy tail twitching lazily behind it as the grinning horned figure reached for them with four taloned hands.

A Sky the Color of Anger, A City Full of the End of the Universe

"Holy J.C. Christ!" I said, looking at the desolation in front of me. "You don't really expect us to give a concert here, do you, Charley?"

Before our agent could answer, Bass rolled up to me and said, "It's a great honor to play here, Fred."

"And it's going to all the networks, baby." (Charley had picked up his English from radio and TV... and me.) "The technicians are down in the circle now and the curtain goes up in two hours. Is your gutbucket tuned?"

Spider strolled over and I scratched his soft blue underbelly. He rubbed a couple of his legs together in the series of scratches that I had learned to interpret as "Thanks."

"What about The Axe?" I asked.

Bass emitted a series of sounds that sounded like Spider's legscratchings and Spider answered. "He's just gotten back from the city," Bass said, "and supervised the setting up of The Axe. He says everything is fine."

"Where is this city?" I asked. "Can I see it?"

"Come on," said Charley. "I'll take you over in the flyer."

)OOO(

I often wonder just what I, Fred Harmon, folksinger and guitar player, am doing wandering the universe with three creatures from other planets who play weird instruments and with an agent who looks like a human being but isn't. And just as often, I know I wouldn't trade this life for the Earth. It'd be pretty damn stupid to trade a universe for a mere world, wouldn't it?"

But now we had left our galaxy for a solitary world in the middle of emptiness. One world surrounded by a dozen suns so that there was never a moment of darkness. Even I, knowing nothing of the mechanics of star-travel, knew that we were in the middle of the nothingness between galaxies.

The planet was a world of reds, like the Mars of the science fiction books. Here and there an occasional streak of yellow whipped across the sky but most of the sky, most of the planet's surface, was a deep, angry red. It sounds monotonous, I know, but somehow it wasn't.

And then I saw the city—a ruined derelict of a city—towers of cinnabar tattered by the wind, minarets of crimson piercing carmine clouds, engines of garnet rusting on the vermillion ground. And in front of the city, gleaming an incongruous ebony and silver, was The Axe.

Charley set us down on the edge of the circle. Around it, scarlet towers formed a semi-circle, the back of our stage. My guitar case and Monkey's tabla case were with The Axe in the circle. The drifting sands inexplicably stopped at the perimeter of the circle.

A three-and-a-half-foot mantis came up to me and chittered. "He wants to put a recorder on you, Fred," Bas told me. I had already figured that out for myself, having been recorded so many times by now.

I stood still while he plastered the antenna on the back of my neck and arranged sensing pads over my vertebrae, the corners of my eyes, and several other spots on my face. Then a cosmetician, a wonderfully humanoid female, covered the wires and pads with makeup so that they couldn't be seen. I made a date with her for after the concert.

"Well, I said, "shall we tune up and a get a rehearsal in?"

Charley put his hand on my shoulder. "Sorry, Fred, but we're gonna have to play this one by ear."

"Out here in the middle of nowhere? The acoustics will be terrible. Where's the audience going to sit? Out there?" I waved my hand to indicate the fiery desert.

"Not exactly," Charley said uncomfortably.

"Look, will you clue me in to exactly what's going on here? I know I'm not the hippest cat in the universe and that I've got a lot left to learn and without you guys I'd be lost. All right. But I've still got a right to know what's going on."

"Relax, Fred." It was Monkey, our tabla player. "It's kind of difficult to explain things. It's sort of custom, you might say, but we're just not allowed to rehearse on the stage. There's only one performance every hundred years or so. It's a great honor to be asked to perform."

What could I say? These cats are the greatest musicians in the world, I mean, the universe. Bass, who plays through the incredibly variable cavity of his mouth (and so is also therefore the only one of us capable of communicating directly with Spider); Monkey, who plays an instrument that sounds something like an Indian tabla or drum, but which has more tonal control and a greater range; and Spider, who plays The Axe, an instrument that looks something like a jungle-gym and which is played by alternately strumming the bars and blowing through holes in them. It is the most beautiful instrument I have ever heard. Fred Harmon, who is me, plays a simple guitar. And Charley, our agent, is humanoid but not an Earthman.

Together we've played quite a lot of gigs and made a lot of recordings and now here we were giving a concert on a dead planet.

)OOOC

I sat on a stool in the middle of the circle. Charley and the rest of the technicians were in a starship high above our heads, recording our sensual impressions. Bass was in a tub of his planetary liquid on the roseate earth; Monkey had one set of hands poised over the keys and over the tuning pegs on the bowls of his tabla; and Spider had clambered into The Axe, six of his twelve legs resting on stop holes while the others were poised to pluck rods. We were the only living creatures on the planet.

In my head, Charley's voice began to chant: "Five, four, three, two, one, roll 'em."

There was a moment of silence then the tabla began, starting on two notes an octave apart, Monkey bringing them slowly together, one going up, one down, sometimes sliding back to the previous note, but eventually, inevitably coming together. When the two notes became one, Spider plucked The Axe. Bass joined in and I started an E chord in the fifth position, slowly backing down into first position.

I hear you call.

How long I had been hearing them I don't know but soon I became aware that we weren't alone. Behind us, humming, crooning, soaring, a chorus of voices was pulling us closer together, singing a song without words, gently tearing the sky into salmon and rose, claret and rouge.

I looked around at the buildings, tall towers of plum-colored crystal: they were wavering, insubstantial, disappearing.

The sky was a kaleidoscopic rainbow; the ground was peppered with crystalline trees of ebony and silver. Spiders strolled among them, carefully pruning the trees for the finest limbs, to make the most eloquent instrument in the universe.

The Axe pervaded all: an organ, a trumpet, a flute, a violin, instruments that have not been invented anywhere else in the universe. A symphony of them played in the silver-and-ebony forest.

Calling me.

Bass underscored the melody, running double notes in different directions and bringing them back again, thrumming and moving to the foreground briefly, picking up the melody and tossing it to the sky.

A planet of glycerin seas and saffron clouds, where gray blowfish-like creatures swam through coral cities and sunned themselves on atolls. A planet where all the languages of the universe are spoke and taught. A planet of scholars.

I see you shine.

Towers of green ivory. Four-armed pot-bellied capuchin monkeys whose comicalness is belied by the infinite sadness and gentleness of their eyes. The smell of blackberry pies baking in a porcelain night. The whisper of starships forever coming and coming, going and going, the sound of the galaxy's nexus.

Across this land.

An unseen spotlight focused on me: I went up into fifth position and back down again, through minors and majors, single solo notes and full chords.

The planet was Earth now, the coffee houses of Greenwich Village, the guitar shops, the hock shops, the soaring sequoias, the crashing surf on the Monterey coast. Every place I had ever been, every woman I had ever known, every ice cream soda I had ever drunk.

It was Washington, D.C., and I had never seen the Jefferson Memorial so clear and lovely as I did then; it was Paris and London, the slums of Tijuana, the Himalayas, places I had never been in my life.

The music was out of our hands now, taken over by the unseen chorus, which built fugues and cantatas, paeans, and dirges. We continued playing but we were background, accompaniment.

Earth was left behind and we entered all the worlds of the galaxy. Some I recognized, most I had never seen before. They were murky and dark, bright and shining, cool and hot; and all were beautiful, all were home. I spent an hour on some, a few seconds on others, a lifetime on many.

The chorus was becoming weaker, thinner, as though there were fewer voices. From uncounted, innumerable throats and unimaginable vocal apparatuses to mere millions, thousands, hundreds.

And the chorus was one clear voice, still loud and defiant, and the planet was a quiet world capable of sustaining only a few hundred intelligent beings, froglike creatures who died at the rate of about one every seven hundred years, who lay quietly on their desert planet waiting for the rain to fall, contemplating the mysteries of the universe.

Then that one voice was gone too, beyond the galaxy to the end of the universe, and the planet was silent and the skies were quiet, waiting, receptive. Nearly seven hours had passed. I sat on my stool, filled with a great contentment, and I knew that the others felt the same way.

We knew that we would be here for the next concert.

Timedipping...

ABOUT THE AUTHOR AND THE WRITING OF SCIENCE FICTION...

Timid Bank Clerks and Other Writers

It may seem incredible but, although I'd been reading science fiction since I was 14, I didn't have the slightest inkling that the world of SF fandom existed until I was nearly 30 years old.

It began with the April 1968 issue of *If*, where I read in their SF Calendar feature that there was to be a science fiction convention, the Disclave, at the Regency-Congress Motor Hotel in Washington, DC. Since I was living near Washington's Dupont Circle at the time, I thought about attending. I even checked to find out where the Regency-Congress was. I turned out to be on New York Avenue (Routes 1 and 50) leading from the north into Washington, a route I took regularly, as it was on the way to my work at Goddard Space Flight Center, as well as to and from Annapolis town, where my beloved Jenny was a senior at St. John's College.

In the end I decided not to go, because Jenny didn't want to go and I knew that, at the end of the school year, we would be parting and going our separate ways. So my introduction to SF fandom was delayed yet a little longer. Strange the ways of fate.

In that same issue of *If* and that same "SF Calendar," there was another notice, about a "Writers' Workshop in Science Fiction & Fantasy," to be held at Clarion State College in Clarion, Pa. The visiting staff would be Judith Merril, Fritz Leiber, Harlan Ellison, Damon Knight, and Kate Wilhelm. The coordinator was Robin Scott Wilson. I sent off a letter, asking for more details. Since I had seen stories in *Galaxy* and *If* by Robin Scott, I assumed that Robin Scott Wilson was a woman writing under her maiden name. I wondered about it, however, since there was a friend of friend in D.C. at the same time, an Australian, who was named Robin, male and a pretty fair country picker.

The Workshop was to be held for six weeks, and attendees could sign up for two-week sessions, although it was recommended that one sign up for the whole period. Somehow I got the impression that everybody would be there all at once, and I signed up for the middle two weeks, because I couldn't take six weeks off from work.

Despite the fact that I'd been reading SF for sixteen years, I was still unfamiliar with most of the names. In fact, the only ones I was really familiar with were Fritz Leiber and Damon Knight, who had been regular contributors to *Galaxy*, which was the only SF I read from 1953 to 1966, except for an occasional novel like *Starship Troopers*. In 1966, I started reading *Analog* and *If* and some of the other magazines. I quickly put down *Amazing* and its reprint sisters.

I guess I had heard of Judith Merril, although I don't know where. I had read some of Harlan Ellison's stories in *Galaxy* but I couldn't remember anything about them even though I did recognize his name. And I had never heard of Kate Wilhelm at all.

I had no idea what any of these people were like, what they looked like, or anything. I had never met a science fiction fan or a writer of any kind in my life, and only a few people who even read SF.

So, on Saturday, July 6th, 1968, I left Washington for my big Writers' Workshop, following the scenic and picturesque roads of western Maryland and Pennsylvania. I got to Pittsburgh around four o'clock and took a motel room in nearby Harmarville. In the evening I went into Pittsburgh, searching for the new *Ramparts* and *Analog* but I couldn't find a newsstand worthy of the name. I also called an old friend, Larry Wolken, but there was no answer. I wandered around Forbes Avenue near the University of Pittsburgh, getting slightly high off the old campus vibes, remembering the year I had been in the Champlain Shakespeare Festival in Vermont. It seemed half of the company was from Pittsburgh's Carnegie Tech and I wondered what had happened to them in the intervening eight years.

I left Pittsburgh the next morning at 9:25 and drove through the coal towns that line the Allegheny River. I got to Clarion around 11:00 and called Robins' house, asking for Mrs. Wilson. The girl who answered asked if I wanted her father. It turned out that Robin Scott Wilson was male and my face in that phone booth was red!

He met me at the campus and this man I'd been writing to as Mrs. Wilson for about two months looked like he could have been a linebacker for the Green Bay Packers. When I started to apologize, Robin laughed, explaining that he had gotten a big kick out of my letters.

Enough for Robin Wilson's sense of humor.

It was Robin, or perhaps I should say Dr. Robin Scott Wilson, who had started this whole thing. He had quit the CIA a year earlier to teach English at Clarion. He was tall but filled out. He was 39 at the time and hadn't published his first story until he was 30. So there was hope for me. He is a gentle man (except for his sense of humor) and an excellent teacher, with the right proportions of firmness, enthusiasm, and friendliness.

It wasn't as I had thought it would be, with all the "famous" writers there at once. Robin had run the Workshop for the first week then had been joined by Judith Merril for the second week. Fritz Leiber was due for the third week but he hadn't arrived yet. Harlan Ellison would conduct the fourth week, Damon Knight and Kate Wilhelm (Mrs. Damon Knight) the fifth week, and the final week, Robin would wrap things up by himself.

Robin took me to Becht Hall, where the Workshoppers were settled in. I had thought of taking a room off-campus, especially if I could have convinced Jenny to spend the summer with me. But I didn't and so I roomed in Becht Hall with everybody else. Becht Hall was a rambling old wooden structure from the early days of Clarion State College. The Workshoppers had the structure entirely to themselves. The first floor contained a few offices, most of them closed for the summer, and the guest room where Judy Merril, Fritz Leiber, et al would stay. The women roomed on the second floor, which meant it was mostly empty, and the men were on the third floor but spent a lot of time on the second floor. After all, that was the floor the refrigerator was on.

While climbing to the third floor with Robin, carrying my guitar, suitcase, and typewriter (Robin must have carried one of them), a rather chunky woman with frowzy hair came down the other way. Robin stopped her. "Judy, this is one of our new Workshoppers. Grant, this is Judy Merril."

I had the feeling that anyone named Judith should look like a prom queen, shy, petite, and demure. Judy Merril was about as demure as a friendly Saint Bernard. She was a witchy-looking hag with hair going in all directions—but a wonderful hag, with a tongue of acid trying to etch away a proverbial heart of gold. Now that her time as a guest lecturer was over, she stayed an extra two days to enjoy the students and go swimming. She was full of life and a joy to be with.

[Now that I know more about Judy Merril, I feel embarrassed about describing her as a hag. She apparently was a very good-looking woman when she was younger. But to my young 30-year-old eyes, she resembled the hag of folklore. My deep sincere apologies to her spirit.]

Shortly after I got settled in, Fritz Leiber arrived in the little red car (a Datsun?) he had driven across the country. The original illustrations for *A Spectre Is Haunting Texas*, which had just been published in *Galaxy*, were taped to his windows, and he had driven across Texas with *A Spectre Is Haunting Texas* prominently displayed on his windshield. Since this was in the dying days of the Lyndon Johnson administration, that took guts, to say the least.

Fritz is gentleness incarnate. Even then, he had been an SF writer for a long time. He was in his 50s or 60s, well over 6 feet (6'8"?) and thin, emaciated almost, with a huge voice, an actor's voice, white hair sweeping back from a high forehead, and dark bushy eyebrows. In other words, he looked exactly like the protagonist of *Spectre*. He usually wore a bow tie and loose light jacket. A gentle patient man, almost beyond belief, capable of being a child and mixing easily with the younger people at the Workshop—fencing, singing, playing tissue-paper-and-comb. I liked him immediately, not a difficult task at all, and consider him the gentlest of all the people I've ever known. I'll never be able to read another one of his stories again without a bias for the man who wrote it.

)OOO(

My main reason for coming to the Workshop was that, although I had been writing ever since third grade and had been reading SF since I was 14, and I had a degree in math and had worked at Goddard Space Flight Center for six years, I still could not write science fiction, although I had written other types of stories without any trouble. So I came to the Workshop in hopes of finding out why I couldn't write SF.

That evening, the sound of typewriters clattered across the Clarion campus and I sat down and wrote a story about a blues guitar player who gets picked up by an alien agent to become part of a band—the other three members being aliens from different planets. It was inspired by an old Emshwiller *Galaxy* cover I had always liked. I titled it "Saint Louis Tickle" after one of Dave Van Ronk's tunes. It later became the first chapter in "The Interstellar Ragtime All-American Jazz Band."

I never had trouble writing SF again.

)OOO(

Most of the students at the Workshop were about ten years

younger than me. The youngest was a 17-year-old high school student, Allan Freedman. The oldest was a retired Navy doctor, Dave Belcher. Dave worked on one story during the entire time I was there, a long 60-odd page piece, "The Price," that eventually was published in *Orbit*. Other students included such unpublished writers as Ed Bryant, Jim Sutherland, and Neil Shapiro. There was as at least one student, Patrick Meadows, who had been published in *F&SF* and *Analog*. Pat was a Long Island high school teacher a few years older than me and we hung around a bit together.

Monday I went to my first Clarion Workshop session. Although Becht Hall was old, most of the buildings on the campus were recently-constructed buildings of brick and glass, and there were very few students there that summer. The only ones I remember were those at the summer theatre in the old chapel (probably the oldest building on campus) down the street Becht Hall.

We met every morning, five days a week, from nine to twelve in a classroom several buildings away from Becht Hall. There were approximately twenty students, most of them neither from the town of Clarion nor the college. (I think there were three Clarion students at that first Workshop.) The first morning (actually the third Monday morning of the Workshop), Robin Wilson laid down the rules of the Workshop for the newcomers and then I guess Fritz Leiber gave us a short lecture, though now I find that hard to believe.

The rules were simple: everyone was expected to write at least one story a week. Robin would have the stories photocopied and they would be distributed for everyone to read. Each morning, Robin and the guest lecturer would choose several stories to workshop. Then the students would give their criticisms of the stories, what they liked, what they didn't. We were encouraged to give constructive criticism and got rapped hard for any vicious or destructive criticism. Robin and the guest lecturer would be last, so as not to influence the students.

The person whose story was being criticized was supposed to keep quiet until everyone else was finished. That wasn't always easy.

Frequently the criticism would be contradictory, one person liking what another thought was bad, which only pointed out the subjective nature of criticism. Robin managed to tone down the classroom situation by having us sit in a circle, although no one could forget who the professor and who the pro was.

On Tuesday night, Judy Merril's last night before leaving for Toronto, she inked "To Fritz. With Love. Judy." on the back of Fritz Leiber's hand.

Becht Hall had two front porches and the Workshoppers frequently congregated on them, reading stories and talking, while two or three typewriters tapped away in the rooms upstairs. One of the people on the porch, perhaps beginning to feel guilty, would drift off to his or her own typewriter, while one of the typists would come down to take a break.

Someone brought a Ouija board and Workshoppers, led by Jean Sullivan, tried to contact the dead. Some of them even succeeded. There was a rumor that there was a ghost in the college chapel where they held the plays, so one night, after the play was over, Fritz led a number of the Workshoppers on a ghost hunt. They were unsuccessful.

Fritz also conducted fencing lessons on the lawn in front of Becht Hall. No one wanted to fence with Andy Fitzpatrick, who seemed to be more interested with going in for the kill than fencing with finesse.

I drove up to Mars, Pennsylvania, but no one else seemed interested. Can you imagine them? Twenty fledgling science fictions writers and not one of them interested in going to Mars. Maybe they had the right idea, however—the Viking landers found more signs of life on Mars than I did.

Clarion was a small town in the middle of Nowhere, Pennsylvania. There was, in addition to the tiny campus, one movie theatre, a couple of churches, and about ten shops on the town's main street. The nearest town of any size, Oil City, was about twenty miles to the west. [I returned about forty years later to find a thriving city, a large campus, and practically nothing left that I could recognize.] The Workshop became a little community unto itself, with a few tendrils into the rest of the college. George Zebrowski got involved with a girl who was in the drama troupe and Pat Meadows managed to find a very attractive divorcee, Dee, but the rest of us stayed in our own little community.

)OOO(

After "Saint Louis Tickle" was workshopped, I rewrote it, incorporating a number of changes that been suggested as well as some other ideas that their comments had sparked. Fritz Leiber was surprised at the changes, stating that he found it very hard to rewrite a story so completely.

Two days later, I wrote another story, "Fountain of Force," based on an article on black holes [by Kip Thorne] in *Scientific American* earlier in the year. [Several years later, George Zebrowski rewrote it and sold it as a collaboration to one of the *Infinity* collections, and was later reprinted in Jerry Pournelle's *Black Holes* anthology.]

At the end of the week, halfway through the Workshop, Robin gave a party at his house. We played bocce ball, badminton, volley ball, fenced, played guitars, and sang in his back yard. I took many pictures, both still and motion. The next day Fritz was gone and we were to fend for ourselves for the weekend.

Pat Meadows, George Zebrowski, Jim Sutherland, and I went to see the college players in "Blithe Spirit" at the chapel. It was pretty bad but afterwards we went to the cast party.

I brought my guitar and, while we were singing, the girl who played the lead kept watching me. But, with my usual savoir-faire, I didn't know what to do about it.

Pat Meadows and the director of the play got into a discussion, learning that both of them had taught high school English, Pat in Peculiar, Missouri, and the director in Normal, Illinois!

Sunday night Harlan Ellison (O great white myth!) was supposed to arrive. If I had known practically nothing about Fitz Leiber, Robin Scott Wilson, or Judy Merril, I knew even less about Harlan Ellison, nothing about the myth and the stories that had grown up around him. I had read only a few of his stories that had been published in *Galaxy*. Because I knew he would be one of the visiting lecturers, I read a collection of his stories on the trip from Washington Clarion. The collection included one called "Repent, Harlequin! Said the Ticktockman," which I had read when it had first appeared in *Galaxy*. I didn't particularly like it originally and I didn't like it this time. In fact, I immediately forgot it, although I was trying to remember it. After all, it had won a Hugo, whatever *that* was. But if I forgot that story easily, I was floored by "I Have No Mouth and I Must Scream," which also had won some kind of award I'd never heard of, a Nebula, I think. There wasn't even one of Harlan's usual introductions in this collection but I didn't miss it, because at that time I knew nothing about Harlan's usual introductions. For some reason (perhaps it was the name Harlan), I pictured him as a timid little bank clerk with pince-nez glasses, like T.S. Eliot. Well, I was right. Harlan Ellison *is* little... but in height only.

If I knew nothing about Harlan Ellison when I arrived in Clarion in 1968, I knew quite a bit by the time my first week had ended, although he had yet to arrive. I soon heard stories, about how when he had first met Isaac Asimov back in the Fifties, when Harlan Ellison was a nobody, just another teenage fan (although I still didn't know about fandom, even at Clarion), he had gone up to Asimov and said, "You're Isaac Asimov? You're *really* Isaac Asimov? You're *nothing*!" (Although that's the usual fan-story of the meeting, Harlan's version is different. According to Harlan, he said, "You're Isaac Asimov? You're *really* Isaac Asimov? You're not so much." Not said in derision but in wonder that this man whom Harlan had expected to be eight feet tall with muscles of iron turned out to be a chubby man of ordinary height with thick glasses. Although Harlan has a slight tendency to exaggerate on occasion, I tend to believe *his* version of the story this time.)

I also learned that he had just edited *Dangerous Visions*, which was supposed to be a collection of SF stories that other editors wouldn't touch with a ten-foot pole because they broke too many taboos. I had never heard of *Dangerous Visions* either before coming to Clarion.

At eleven o'clock Sunday evening, he had still to arrive at Clarion. Most of the Workshop went down to the bus station to meet him where, supposedly, Jim Sutherland greeted him by saying, "You're Harlan Ellison? You're *really* Harlan Ellison? You're nothing."

Grant Carrington, being the stubborn iconoclast he is, went to bed. Damned if I'm going to be anyone's sycophant.

So I didn't meet Harlan Ellison until the next morning, when we all congregated for the Monday morning session. By now, of course, I knew that Harlan Ellison wasn't a timid-looking bank clerk with pince-nez glasses. In fact, he was a muscular little guy with a shock of dark hair, a pair of horn-rimmed glasses, and a pipe. He was wearing a shirt that exposed his hairy chest. He was, in other words, the romantic picture of the Hollywood writer, playing to the hilt with stylish boots and all.

The first story we workshopped that day was by Evelyn Lief. Harlan took Evelyn's story, cut her into little shreds, and left her bleeding on the floor. Harlan and Evelyn both tell the story in his introduction and her afterword to her story in *Again, Dangerous Visions*. It was a performance that left us all gasping in agony for Evelyn, for our future selves. It was a vicious performance that had Evelyn in tears, a complete turnaround from Fritz Leiber's gentleness and the eager friendliness of Judy Merril. We were all stunned, even Robin, I think, who had probably expected Harlan would be a little more gentle in this situation that he had been at the Milford Conferences.

We took a fifteen-minute break and everyone clustered around Evelyn, trying to console her. We all suspected we would each need some of the same ourselves before the week was out.

The coffee break over, Robin turned to Harlan and asked him which story he would like to workshop next.

"This one," he said, grinning with vicious sadistic glee, venom dripping from his fangs. "'Fountain of Force,' by Grant Carrington."

I sat there as the story made the rounds, most people saying nothing, only a few comments. I haven't the slightest idea what was said, waiting only for it to reach Robin and Harlan, waiting in dread for that moment when the axe would descend on my neck and I would crawl bleeding back to my typewriter. I said not a word, made no protest at anyone's comment.

It finally reached Harlan. He looked around at the twenty students circled around him. "Okay. Who's this Grant Carrington? I want to know who I'm talking to." Fearfully I raised my hand. "Man," he said as my heart began beating wildly, "you've got talent." I bumped my head on the ceiling and Ed Bryant and Jim Sutherland had to grab me by the ankles and drag me back to the ground. Harlan then proceeded to tear my story apart and tell me what was wrong with it, in no uncertain terms. But he said I had talent! Harlan Ellison said I was a writer! That handsome man with the Ipana smile and the classy duds, five-foot-six in stature perhaps but a mile high in heart. He said I had talent. I couldn't wait to get back to my room so I could dust off my sycophant uniform.

"All right, kids," Harlan said when he had finished demolishing my story. "The fun's over. Judy Merril and Fritz Leiber brought you sweetness and light but now Uncle Harlan's here and the fun and games are over and it's time to get down to work. I want a story a day from each and every one of you. One thing that was missing in all the stories I read except Grant's was hard science. So tomorrow's assignment is a hard science story." There was a community groan. "Except for Grant. I want *you* to write me a story with real people and feeling in it."

That night, for some reason I can't possibly explain, I wrote a pornographic SF story, "Penultimus." The next day I went for a walk to the grocery store with Evelyn Lief and Lynn Marron. I didn't know whether or not I should turn the story in to Robin to have it photocopied. "What's so bad about it?" Evelyn asked. "Let me read it."

"I don't know if I should." I still had rather chivalric and romantic notions about ladies, despite the fact that a couple of years earlier I had lived with a former hundred-dollar-a-night call girl.

"Come on. I'm not a kid."

I reluctantly forked it over and Evelyn began reading, passing pages to Lynn as she finished them. "Oh, my God!" she gasped. A few moments later, Lynn, said, "Oh, no!" and began to laugh. Evelyn grinned. "You reached that part, did you?"

When we got back to Becht Hall, we gave it to someone else (Jim Sutherland, I think) and watched him read it, laughing at his reactions. It was a whole new art form: Creative Reading! Give someone a copy of "Penultimus" and watch him/her read it. Harlan finally came out on the porch. "What's all the noise?" he asked.

"Here. Read this." Evelyn shoved "Penultimus" in his face. Harlan began reading while we all sat around smirking, eager to watch the great Ellison's reactions.

He started page two and said, "I'd better read the rest of this in my room." And that was the end of Creative Reading.

I was eventually convinced that I should submit it to the Workshop; even Harlan saw no reason why I shouldn't have it photocopied. So Robin collected it along with the rest of the manuscripts and dutifully turned it over to the lady to have it photocopied. And the shit hit the fan. Robin hadn't looked at the manuscripts but the Xerox lady did and it wasn't long before the president of the college had a copy of "Penultimus" in his hand and Robin Wilson on the carpet. Fortunately, the Workshop was also important to the president so the matter ended there.

Except for a small lecture by Robin to the Workshop in general, without mentioning names, about our responsibilities and the fact that Clarion was a small town and not as cosmopolitan as New York, Los Angeles, etc. and we should be careful not to offend the natives. He also took me aside, mentioning that he thought I was mature enough to avoid doing things like that. "After all, the rest of them are just kids, but you ought to know better."

["Penultimus" eventually got published, as "The Ultimate Lay," in *Cavalier*, perhaps the most I've ever been paid for a short story.]

The next day a bunch of us got invited to another Clarion party, being given by a Clarion student named Patti. In addition to several of the Workshoppers, there were a number of students there as well, mostly Polish, and Pollack jokes were being told left and right... by Pollacks. Harlan Ellison came along and immediately cornered the only really attractive girl there, Cindee. She and he made a couple for the remainder of his stay.

The only other girl worth looking at was Patti, the hostess, who supposedly had been a model. A bunch of us, including Ed Bryant, Jim Sutherland, and myself, clustered around her but somehow an 18-year-old Amazon named Muriel attached herself to me and, when she had to get back to her dorm, she wanted me to walk her home. I immediately declined the honor but the Workshoppers wouldn't allow me to let this poor defenseless judo expert walk home alone in the dark. Ed Bryant, bless his black-hearted soul, pushed me out the door with the admonition, "Come on, Grant. Be a man."

Muriel took me down every dark alley and road she could find, while I walked nervously as far from her side as I could. If I could have walked on the other side of the road, I would have.

"I think you're so cool," she said.

Cool? If I'd been any cooler, I'd have been an ice sculpture.

Finally, despite all her peregrinations through the dark streets and alleys of Clarion, we wound up at her dorm, where I couldn't avoid her kiss, and then I walked quickly back to the party, wondering if I would be able to avoid her in my remaining days in Clarion.

Back at the party I tried to gain Patti's attentions but failed. She was a fairly attractive large girl with big breasts, the outline of her nipples clear through her sweater.

But if I struck out with Patti, so did everyone else. Harlan went home with Cindee, George Zerbrowski with his girlfriend from the drama group, and Pat Meadows had his divorcee, Dee. The rest of us went home alone.

)OOOC

As I said, Harlan was a lot cooler than I had expected. (If he'd been any cooler, *he*'d have been an ice sculpture.) I had been determined to dislike him but, by the time he left, I think I would have walked through hell for him if the price was right. He's just the opposite of Fritz, being 5'6" or so and very active. On opening day, he told us that he had waded through the worst tripe he'd ever read when he read our stuff.

He had us writing a story a day. And, to show us that it could be done, he wrote a story a day himself. I remember two of them. One, whose title escapes me, was about a group of people trudging across a desert. They finally come across the Empire State Building, half-buried in the sand. One of the characters, a whining dislikeable person with oily hair, was named Grant.

The other story I remember was titled "The Pitll Pawob Division." When Harlan had arrived at Pittsburgh's airport, his typewriter was on another plane. The airline promised to send it to Clarion as soon as it arrived. "What do you mean?" Harlan screamed at the ticket attendant. "I'm a writer. That's my means of making a living." He marched into their office and took a typewriter. "I'll return this to you when I get my typewriter," he informed the secretary. She called the airlines manager, who eventually allowed Harlan to take the typewriter, on which was a piece of embossed tape with the words, "Pittl Pawob Division." He didn't know what it meant but he wrote a story around it just to show us it could be done.

My own stories were "Penultimus," "Nothing Personal," and "Will the Real Harlan Ellison Please Stand Up?" and "A Sky the Color of Anger, A World Full of the End of the Universe." (Pat Meadows threatened to write a story titled, "I Have No Scream and I Must Mouth off.") "A Sky the Color of Anger" was written for a painting by a friend of Neil Shapiro's which Neil had brought with him from Rochester. The painting showed a shattered city in the background with a few rusted vehicles in the foreground. The predominant color of the painting was red and "Sky" was a sequel to "Saint Louis Tickle," the first story I had written at the Workshop. We all were supposed to write a story around that painting but not many Workshoppers did, since Harlan would be gone by the time the stories were to be workshopped. (Harlan's desert story was written around the painting.) When Harlan saw the title of my story, he asked, "Are you trying to make fun of me, Carrington?" I assured him I wasn't and, when he read the story, he agreed. The title originally was supposed to be the first line of the story but I liked it so much I decided to use it as the title, something that admittedly wouldn't have even crossed my mind if I hadn't seen the titles of some of Harlan's stories.

)OOOC

I had one more run-in with Muriel. A couple of days after the party, I was walking down Clarion's main street with our gofer, a regular Clarion student who had somehow attached himself to the Workshop without being a member of it. It was he who had gotten us invited to the party where I had met Patti and Muriel. As we walked past a gas station near the campus, I noticed the car getting gas was driven by Muriel. "Keep walking," I said to our gofer.

But as we passed the gas station, I heard Muriel call out my name. "Just keep walking," I said without looking back. The gofer smiled and took me down a narrow alley between two buildings as I heard Muriel's car start up. We walked slowly down the alley, hoping that she hadn't seen us dart down it. It was too narrow for a car, just a sidewalk, a path, really, between two buildings. Muriel's car zoomed past the mouth of the alley then, about half a minute later, it went past the other end of the alley. Apparently she hadn't seen us go down the alley, for she didn't returned and I never saw her again.

And that was the first and only time in my life I've ever been literally chased by a woman.

Friday was to be my last night in Clarion. I went to the town's lone movie theatre to see "Wild in the Streets," which most of the Workshop had already seen. As I left the theatre and walked back to the college, I ran into Patti and Dee coming the other way, and I walked to Patti's apartment with them. I didn't get back to the college that night and, the next day, I drove back to D.C. with Patti. After a night in my apartment, we went on a quick sightseeing tour of the town (Patti especially wanted to see the Kennedy grave), then I drove back to Clarion, taking a wild road through the Pennsylvania mountains, a winding road with many switchbacks, a joy to drive in my Renault Caravelle.

The next few days I returned to the Workshop but I was no longer truly a member. I paid two more weeks' tuition to Robin but I didn't stay at Becht Hall. As the morning Workshop session ended, I went back to Patti's apartment. But she treated like a puppy dog, someone to trail around after her as she went to see her friends, someone to obey her commands, and that soon got on my nerves. She was living quite well on food stamps and cadging extra groceries and other necessities any way she could, and I think she taking only one course at the college. Like most of the regular Clarion students I met, she was from Pittsburgh.

We spent one evening at the apartment of some of her friends, a veteran and his very attractive Mexican wife. She was very intelligent

and she told us about seeing a flying saucer while riding a bus in
Mexico. She said he never believed in them until she had actually seen
one herself.

On Tuesday night, Patti, Cindee, and I went for a walk behind the
Clarion graveyard. There was a small pond down there and we sat and
talked. Cindee said she came down there often to get away from the
hustle and bustle of Clarion to think.

But I couldn't take the way Patti was treating me and so
Wednesday afternoon, after the Workshop session, I packed up my
Renault and drove to D.C. I got one letter from Patti and never heard
from her again.

Meanwhile, in my last three days at the Workshop, I had met
Damon Knight and Kate Wilhelm, who were a great couple—Damon
slight, with a pepper-and-salt goatee; Kate, good-looking, with looks
to last. Her hair was beginning to turn white even then, although she
couldn't have been any older than her early forties. Their young son
Damon, about three years old, was with them and, instead of staying
in the downstairs room at Becht Hall, they took up quarters in several
rooms on the second floor, just down the hall from the refrigerator.

Damon, of course, was well known as the leading critic of SF as
well as the co-founder of the Science Fiction Writers of America and
the Milford Writers' Conference, on which the Clarion Workshop was
based, However, it was Kate who was the most respected critic at the
Milford Conference, a quiet woman whose criticisms went right to the
core. Supposedly Kate was the only person whom Harlan would sit
quietly and listen to while she tore his stories to shreds.

)OOO(

Despite the rather sour taste left in my mouth by staying those
extra days with Patti, the Workshop had been a good experience, lots
of fun, and one that gave me more confidence in myself, not only as a
writer but also has a human being. That confidence was to be
destroyed in the ensuing year but Clarion was my first contact not
only with successful writers but also with other would-be writers who
had genuine talent and desire to write, rather than the dilettantes one
usually meets in creative writing classes. My whole romantic outlook
on writing had to change as I saw that writing, more often than not, is
just plain hard work, a job... but a job that finds its best rewards in
those rare moments when it is not plain hard work but a pure joy.
Unfortunately those rare moments are only earned and worthwhile
after the hours and days of plain hard work, the times when, as Robin

Wilson put it, one is "crapping rocks." But even those rocks can turn out to be diamonds and sapphires... or at least some pretty quartz.

Tiptoeing Through Tulane

Ah, visions of Joanna Russ, Chip Delaney, Harlan Ellison, Damon Knight, and Kate Wilhelm! Not to mention Robin Wilson, Jim Sallis, and Piglet. The Tulane Science Fiction Writers' Workshop in New Orleans, direct descendant of Robin Wilson's Clarion SF&F Writer's Workshop.

Ah, Monroe Hall! Home for six weeks. Also the home (at various times) of a group of Mormons and some military types. All kinds of strange doings at Tulane—a square dance convention, a Three Dog Night concert, yes, yes.

The tone of the Workshop was set on the first Monday night when three of us (Gerry Conway, Steve Richardson, and myself) went down to the French Quarter with Carol, a friend of Jim's. While she and Steve sat in the Seven Seas (which became the Workshop's home away from home), Gerry Conway and I walked around the Quarter, looking at the strip shows (from the sidewalk), the portrait artists, looking, in general, at another tourist trap. The Quarter does have something I've never seen anywhere else. Picture a peep show emporium like those in Times Square. Girlie pictures. Drool, slobber. But the façade of this place is like the waiting room of a movie-picture whorehouse—plush seats and draperies, all open to the populace and tourists walking by. (No, I did *not* go inside.)

Back to the Seven Seas for a beer then back to the Tulane campus, bouncing along St. Charles Avenue in a VW at something in excess of the posted speed limit.

Ah, you guess it! Yes, the flashing blue lights of our friendly New Orleans Police Department. Courteous. Helpful. Reverent. "Up against the wall! Get out of the car. Where do you work? You were doing 75 miles an hour." (Since when do you search a car for speeding?) "What's this? A pack of cigarettes. Must be marijuana. Look at them hippie types, long hair, mustache. Writers? Uh, wait a minute, writers, huh? Mumble, mumble." Would we write up an expose of the NOPD? Maybe we were agents for *Playboy*. Or, worse, *Reader's Digest*. "Now, listen, speeding's serious offense in New Orleans. Not to mention possession of marijuana. Now we're going to let you go this time. Just be careful in the future." (Play the police movie. Let them do their thing.) "Yes, sir. Thank you, sir."

Ah, yes, the friendly, courteous, helpful New Orleans Police Department. That was the last time I had to deal directly with them myself but several others in the Workshop fell afoul in the same manner, though no one ever got busted. I guess long-haired people get hassled even in Eden.

Week Number One: Robin Scott Wilson is there. Who is Robin Scott Wilson, you ask. Well, Robin (or Professor Wilson or Doc of whatever else you wish to call him) founded the Clarion SF&F Writers' Workshop in 1968 and is well loved by all. Robin, an ex-CIA agent with a James Bond car, is big, a bit on the heavy side, likes his beer and his stories, and now works for the University of Chicago. His expertise at circumventing academic red tape helped Jim Sallis through the ever-hectic first week. And the, to top it all off, he's interviewed on the radio and hands the interviewer (who keeps calling him "Doc") the biggest line I've heard on the air in a long time. Yes, yes, Robin can spin them out, all right.

Gerry Conway calls the radio station. (It's a listener call-in show.) "Ah, I'd like to know what you think of Bill Dean Glick, Dr. Wilson. He's gathered quite a following with his underground novel, y'know." (Billy Dean Glick being a character in one of Piglet's stories.)

"Ah, yes, Bill Dean Glick is a writer of enormous obscurity."

Week two. Joanna Russ. Sweetness and light. Strangely enough, 'tis true. This same Joanna Russ with whom I had a screaming argument in Damon Knight's kitchen two years earlier (I was absolutely dead wrong) and I get along marvelously. Strange woman. But I turn opposite pole from how I'd felt about her. Love-hate, yes, yes.

Jim Sallis gets sick and is hospitalized for the rest of the Workshop. Piglet gets sick and is hospitalized with a tube down his throat. And comes out of the hospital with a blonde on his arm.

Colds and sniffles abound. The Midnight Indian gets drunk and pisses on the refrigerator. Dave Skal writes mad manic pieces about the inside of his skull.

Things are beginning to get rough. The Midnight Indian has taken control of the Workshop, such as it is, in Jim's absence. (And at Jim's behest.)

Chip Delaney arrives before Joanna leaves and they both go out and around and around. Chip will stay three weeks. During Chip's week, he tries a bunch of experiments: lectures and developing our own languages and syntaxes. He assigns people to criticize others' stories, both those they like and those they dislike. All these experiments fail, but is it because they are bad experiments or because the Workshop just isn't hanging together?

Not everybody wants to be a writer. It's different this year. The red tape and economics of a university require a certain number of people to attend. The number is set at 25, which as least five too high in the first place. Then applications are slow to come in and the English Department accepts anybody who applies, including a 14-year-old whose uncle is on the Board of Trustees and several who are just killing time or getting a summer school credit.

In the end, there are 28 attendees.

Don't get me wrong: there were some fine writers there and some awfully nice people who weren't writers at all. But there was a definite lack of seriousness about writing. And there has *always* been a dearth of seriousness about other matters whenever SF fans and/or writers get together.

So-o-o-o... throw a few towels, ketchup, and beer cans in the hallway. (I bled all over the hallway after walking on a flip-top, totally oblivious to the fact I was bleeding to death.) Roll toilet paper out on the Frisbee field below Monroe Hall, spelling out a few obscenities. Sleep late in the morning and thereby skip class. Regularly.

O yes, much goes on. Especially at night and the early morning. In the Seven Seas. Even some writing.

I was taking the elevator down from the sixth floor of Monroe Hall, where the men were endormed (the women were on the seventh floor), about to go shopping or go for a drive or some such thing. Chip Delaney was in the elevator with me. He was going over to the Student Union to rent a movie projector for the world premiere of his film *Orchid*. I walked over with him, we talked awhile, and he invited me out to dinner with him that night, if I would provide the transportation. [If I remember his words correctly, it was something like "Let's get away from the kids for a while."]

Gladly, Chip.

So we bombed down to the French Quarter in my Opel GT to have oysters Rockefeller and oysters something else, which was the first either of us had had oysters Rockefeller and oysters something else. Chip paid. Then we walked around the Quarter, down Royal Street. I was leading Chip to the Seven Seas, where we had a couple of beers. Chip paid.

Then we went across the street to the Morning Call for beignets and chicory coffee. This is a particularly strange New Orleans habit, to go to the Morning Call or the Café du Monde for beignets and coffee. Both establishments are open 24 hours a day and that's all they serve: chicory coffee and beignets. [When I came back to New Orleans in 1979, the Morning Call had moved to Metairie.]

The coffee is about half chicory and many people don't like it. But it resembles Turkish coffee, of which I was very fond and so I often went there early in the morning.

Beignets are basically unsugared doughnuts, really, except they are served so hot at the Morning Call that you have to let them cool. They are shaped like jelly doughnuts without the jelly, and considerably lighter and fluffier. Powdered sugar is provided in a little tin shaker so that you may sugar your own doughnuts as well as yourself and anyone in the vicinity.

Then Chip and I walked down Bourbon Street, past the penny stores, the bars, the strip joints, the head shops, rapping about this that, mainly about Chip's movie and how it had gotten started (he met the producer at a party) and about how it was filmed and how Adolphus Mekas (his technical advisor) had told him it was impossible to do two shots he want to do. But Chip decided to try them anyway and, to his own surprise that that of Adolphus Mekas, they worked.

A couple of days later, the world premiere of Samuel R Delaney's film *Orchid* took place on the fifth floor lounge of Monroe Hall, Tulane University, New Orleans, Louisiana, etc. Chip had just received the first color print, and his producer (the mother of one of the Workshoppers) was there. In addition, three other people associated with the film were present: the cameraman and two of the actors, all three of whom were in the Workshop.

Chip says "orchid" is the Greek word for the male sex organ and that it is symbolic. The only relation that the film has to science fiction is that it's by Chip Delaney. Chip calls it fantasy. All right.

The film follows a late middle-aged man as he leaves his office, where a child has been playing with his compasses and other such work objects, only to disappear when he looks at them. He goes out on the street and is accosted by a guy doing interviews with an unplugged microphone then is swept up by a group of freaks and gets involved in a number of apparently unconnected activities, including a nude scene a la *Hair*. (That is, it's a nude scene, not a sex scene.) The movie ends with a long monologue by the interviewer, talking to the lead actor (the middle-aged man). What does it all signify? I don't know, having seen it twice and listening to Chip talk about it, but it *does* seem to have a thread of something (significance? Plot? I don't know) running through it.

It was all done with a hand-held camera and there are two mirror shots that are very effective. It was also shown at the Noreascon and has been on view at several other places since.

I wasn't around when Harlan Ellison arrived. It was Friday night and Marilyn Lessentine was throwing a party. I had been accosted in the Quarter by a good-looking Jesus freak representing a church group called The Process. [Someone once told me that Charles Manson had belonged to it once but I don't know if that's true.] On Friday nights they had "telepathy developing sessions" so naturally I was hooked. Well, I didn't develop any telepathy and I blew a few dollars but it was a groove anyway and there were a lot of nice people there.

But there's a whole 'nother song, *my* song, and has nothing to do with the Workshop.

Except that I was at the "telepathy developing session" when Harlan Ellison arrived. He came to the conclusion that the Workshop was in a mess (a right conclusion but apparently for the wrong reasons) and that only Harlan Ellison could straighten it out.

So Sunday night we had a Synanon Game. Now, once before, in Clarion in 1969, Harlan had led a Synanon Game. It wound up tough and dirty, Harlan wading in with both fists flying and a few others (yours truly included) following behind to mop up when Harlan took a breath. But there were only ten or fifteen involved in that game, which lasted two or three hours, after which everyone felt purged and clean, empty of the hostilities which had been building.

This was different. For one thing, the feeling of unity, of community, in the Clarion days of yore was not nearly so present in this group. (Do not blame the group entirely for this, or the administration at Tulane; at Clarion, there was a need for community, namely, the rest of Clarion was up in arms against us! So we banded together out of necessity. But at Tulane and New Orleans, we were but a minor drop in a very large bucket, not even a nuisance much less a Cosmic Menace.) Also, about 25 people took part in the game, including several who were more or less pressured into it. (No one entered the Clarion game in 1969 unless they were vitally interested.) It wasn't pressure of the threatening kind, more on the level of "What kind of fink are you? What have you got to hide that you don't want to be in the game?"

And 25 is just too many. Harlan couldn't carry the game by himself and he wasn't getting much support from the rest of us, including yr obdt srvt, so the game dragged on for six hours, with many people escaping unscathed.

Human nature being what it is, many of us who were untouched by the first game, felt hurt and deprived so we pressured Harlan into another game. Harlan wasn't here for most of it, since he had managed to latch onto Miss Louisiana or Miss New Orleans or Miss Bayou or some such, a blonde of the usual glamor-contest looks who was a grammar school teacher, so he let Justin Zittler be the executioner for most of the game.

After another six-hour game, with much fewer people, but also without Harlan's rapier jabs for most of the time, we split. Most of the group went down to The Seven Seas, it now being approximately four in the morning.

Behold, there is a third-story porch near The Seven Seas, and Lo, the sun is about to rise. Somehow several people get onto the porch (by invitation) so they could see the sun rise over Mrs. Sippi. Steve Herbst decides to join them. The hard way.

He shinnies up the porch support and is on the porch below when the owner of the porch gets a little bit riled by these beardless hippies and comes out swinging a baseball bat.

"You should've thrown him a knuckleball," someone suggested later.

)OOO(

Somehow, with Harlan's help, the Workshop managed to pull itself together. The little cliques, if they didn't dissolve, at least opened up somewhat and we began to learn about each other.

Was it the result of the Synanon Games?

I doubt it. It was just Harlan. Something about the man, call it charisma if you will, or just his unboundable enthusiasm, his refusal to take anything from anyone, and his habit of dumping on someone until they rear up on their hind legs like a man instead of a worm. Yeah, he's got it all right. I hate the man's guts but I love him dearly.

Then in one day both Harlan and Chip are gone.

Harlan of course disappears with all the fanfare. Miss Delta goes out to the airport with him and he says farewell to all, unlit pipe clamped between his General Tom Thumb teeth.

Chip sneaked out at dawn. I wouldn't have known except I was awake and saw a light in Herbst's room. (Does Steve Herbst ever sleep?) His roommate, Sheldon Light, was borrowing Steve's old battered automobile (Oldsmobile? Buick?) to drive Chip to the bus station, where Chip was to take a bus to San Francisco. After finishing up some business there, he would go up to Seattle for Vonda MacIntyre's SF Workshop at the University of Washington.

AS So I went along at five in the morning and Chip had coffee and breakfast with Sheldon and me then boarded his bus. This is my vision, my last vision, of Samuel R. Delany, author of *Nova*, *The Einstein Intersection*, and *Babel-17*:

This same Samuel R. Delany is wearing a pair of jeans and a plaid shirt. His Afro hairdo is long gone; his mustache is thick and dark; and all he's carrying onto this bus for his 2000-mile trip across the country is a little bag, not even a suitcase, but a carryall, a flight bag bursting at the seams, yes, with his underwear and dirty clothes, but *that's all he has!* No typewriter, no suitcase, no Opel GT full of guitars, no trunk full of books etc. like us aspiring writers who haven't published anything have brought with us to New Orleans.

And I envied Chip more than I've envied anyone in a long time. Not because he's the author of three very fine books but because this is a man who travels light, friends, and let me tell you, from my own experience up and down both coasts and across the nation, up to Canada and down to Mexico: that's the only way to travel.

So. Cheers, Chip, may our paths cross again and often.

)OOO(

Which brings us to Damon and Kate. Before that Sunday sun which had dawned on the bus terminal in New Orleans had set again, Damon Knight and Kate Wilhelm (Mrs. Damon Knight), along with Number One Son Jonathan (of approximate age five), arrived from the Golden Coast of Florida.

These last two weeks, when Damon and Kate were in control, as much as anyone could be in control, the Workshop was rather quiet, a combination of exhaustion due to Harlan's week, the steady and quieting influence of the Knights, and the fact that everyone was broke (except yours truly, who, in gremlin fashion, had hoarded his money till the last week).

Oh, there was the usual Frisbee and strange smells at odd hours and trips down to The Seven Seas and the Morning Call, and Patrick Huyghe found a used book store where he picked up a copy of Volume 1 Number 1 of *Galaxy* for 10 cents, but came the last Friday and a couple of tables were set up on the sixth floor hallway, loaded with French bread, cold cuts, pickles, etc. ad nauseam, and we all gorged ourselves and talked and partied, and people began drifting out until, by the end of that Friday night, about half of the Workshop was left.

The Workshop ended on a very symbolic note. There is a tale concerning a bunch of us sequestered in Steve Herbst's room, lit by candles, smoking a little of the Evil Weed, and Little Scott calling the dorm manager because he thinks the dorm's on fire but the dorm manager isn't in, so he leaves a recorded message (you figure that one out if you can—I still can't and I certainly couldn't that night) and then Justin Zittler tells him to call the manager and cancel the fire call.

But Little Scott won't until Justin tells him what it's all about and, when Justin finally does, Little Scott wants to call the Kampus Kops and for three hours there's this strange scene, straight out of *Dragnet*, with the heads giving Little Scott the third degree instead of the cops doing it to heads. Meanwhile I'm grinning my psilocybin grin and Joe Manfredini and I are shaking our heads at the seriousness with which the others are dumping on Little Scott and wondering just how much he is putting us on, which he has done in the past and well.

Many hours later the dorm manager comes through, looking at the mess in the sixth floor hallway, mustard and ketchup and pickles and flip-top cans and cold cuts scattered about and around, and we tell him that it was only a fire in a waste basket which had gotten Little Scott scared, and he accepts it, eager to be away from the zanies.

But I don't think I'll tell the story.

And, before the night was gone, half of the Workshop was also gone, on their secret trips across the country to their homes and colleges or whatever. Saturday the rest left, leaving only yours truly and the Knights. Sunday morning the Knights left and on Monday I loaded my Opel GT once again and was on the road to Florida, but that is a whole 'nother song.

And all that was left of the 1971 Tulane Science Fiction Writers Workshop was a little ketchup on the sixth floor of Monroe Hall.

)OOO(

Somehow, in the midst of this, some writing was done. Steve Herbst and Dave Skal managed to sell stories to *Orbit* and other stories were sold to Harlan. Out of the newcomers, those who hadn't been to a previous workshop, there are two names to watch for: Lisa Tuttle and Art Cover both impressed Ellison—in general, Art Cover impressed the hell out of just about everybody. (How would *you* like everything you wrote to be a Cover story?) Scott Edelstein (Big Scott) has sold a poem to *Eternity* since the Workshop and of course there are the other names, those from previous Workshops: Russell Bates, Dave Skal, Steve Herbst, Mel Gilden.

Russell, in particular, being Kiowa, has a heritage he can cash in on in these days of concern about the American Indian.

And, surprisingly, we made a little dent in New Orleans. That was easy to do in little Clarion but I didn't think we could do it in New Orleans. But they knew us at the Cuban restaurant, at a Mexican restaurant in the Quarter, and of course at the Seven Seas. The dent is smoothed out now and forgotten, of course, but we were there. We did it.

Afterword

Most of the stories in this collection were written in the 1970s and 1980s and I regret to say that some of them have a bit of moss hanging on them. As I've reread them from the distance of a couple of decades, the influence of the 1950s magazine *Galaxy* has suddenly become very obvious to me. Forget Heinlein, Asimov, Bradbury, and Clarke; my science fictional influence was H.L. Gold.

The title of the collection is not quite correct—there are no stories herein that take place in Annapolis. For that, you have to go to "Annapolis Town" in *Time's Fool and Other Stories*, the previous volume of my work published by Variations on a Theme and Brief Candle Press.

Past and Present

"The Pied Piper of Gotham" (*Plume & Sword*, November 9, 1964) was the second story of mine that was published in a magazine that wasn't the literary magazine of a college (and I was on the editorial board of both of those). It is a bit overwritten and has a few too many "said-bookisms" and some of the other excesses of a young writer. (For the record my first non-college published story was a rewrite of Chaucer's "The Pardoner's Tale"—I was even more arrogant then than I am now—and it appeared in *The Canadian Forum* in 1959. Since I was in love with *West Side Story*, its characters were street punks.)

"Just a Five-Dollar Man" (previously unpublished, written in 2001) is my attempt to be the blues guitar man I'll never be, with a little bit of recreating part of the Psychedelic Sixties.

There's not much to say about "Yours For the Future" (*The Diversifier*, November 1977) except to note that the sentence suggesting that Larry Niven take classes at Caltech comes from the fact that Larry and I shared classes there in 1956-57, even though he doesn't remember me at all.

Wow! What a trip it was rereading "Night on Old Baldy" (*Weirdbook 14*, 1979). This is fantasy, encroaching a tiny bit on horror, not territory I've spent much time in. The title comes from Mussorgsky's "Night on Bald Mountain," one of my favorite classical pieces, in fact the piece (thanks to Disney's *Fantasia*) that got me interested in classical music in the first place. The story comes from

Peter Stampfel's "Spring of '65," from the Holy Modal Rounders' Good Taste Is Timeless album. And the names of the families in Jackdaw Valley come from those whom I was working with at the Savannah River Ecology Lab from 1977 to 1980. Finally the figure in the wood comes from Francis Bacon's "Figure in a Field" that used to hang at the top of one of the staircases in Washington D.C.'s Phillips Gallery. Whether or not it works for you, the reader, is up to you but for me rereading it was a trip through so much of my life.

The inspiration for "A Shakespearean Incident" (*Fantastic*, October 1975) came from a dream I had that is now completely forgotten.

"The Interstellar Ragtime All-American Jazz Band" (*Eternity*, 1979) has a long history. It began as "Saint Louis Tickle," which I wrote the night I arrived at the 1968 Clarion SF&F Workshop, before I had even gone to class. After rewriting, it was published in *The Diversifier* (May/July 1978). "Saint Louis Tickle" then became the first chapter of IRAAJB, which Stephen Gregg published in his magazine, *Eternity*, in 1979.

"The Timedipper Who Stayed" (previously unpublished, written in 1979) is really just a fantasy, even if it involves the Timedippers of my Chewing Gum & Rubber Band Universe. Other than that, I can't remember exactly what inspired it.

"Ask Lafferty" was published in 1979 in *At the Sleepy Sailor, A Tribute to R.A. Lafferty*.

The Future

35 years after writing "A Simple Twist of Fate" (*Eternity*, 1980), I'm surprised I could write anything like it. It was obviously inspired by the opening lines to the Bob Dylan song of the same name, but other than that I have no idea where the inspiration came from. At the time it was written, the Morning Call was at one end of the French Market and the Café du Monde was at the other end and the ugly building that housed the Jax Brewery announced its presence near Jackson Square by a sickeningly sweet miasma that hung over that section of the French Quarter. By the end of the Seventies, the Morning Call had moved to Metairie and the building that had housed the Jax Brewery now was full of little boutiques, so everything foretold in this story should have happened by now, which I guess makes it now nothing but a fairy tale, a casualty in the folly of writing SF stories that could come true in your own lifetime.

"The Key" (*Amazing*, June 1992) was written in the early 90s, inspired by wanting to go back to the years when I had lived at Hopkins Street in Washington, DC, working at Goddard Space Flight Center, playing music, and making love. One of the nice things about being a writer is that you can rewrite your past. Making an interesting story about it, though, is a whole 'nother song.

"Younger Than Springtime" (*Best Erotic Fantasy & Science Fiction*, 2010) is a more recent effort, written in 2004, pared to the bone, another fantasy inspired by my years at Hopkins Street.

"The Gogfather (unpublished, written in 1979) was written at Stephen Gregg's request as a follow-up to "The Interstellar Ragtime All-American Jazz Band." He accepted it for *Eternity* but the magazine folded before he could publish it.

The Distant Future

"Hark, Hark, the Quark!" was published in the March 1980 issue of *Isaac Asimov's SF Magazine*.

The inspiration for "There's No One Left to Paint the Sky" (*Amazing*, May 1972) comes from a line from the Patrick Sky song "The Loving Kind" from the album Reality Is Bad Enough.

"His Hour Upon the Stage" (*Amazing*, March 1976) was on the 1976 final Nebula ballot for novella. Running against Ursula LeGuin, Isaac Asimov, Joe Haldeman, and John Varley, I probably didn't vote for it myself. Why throw away my vote? I was too busy trying to breathe and stop the nosebleed from the rarified atmosphere of the company I was in, probably the only time my name will ever be mentioned in the same breath with people of that stature.

The inspiration for "Nothing Personal" (*Eternity*, 1973)? I don't remember, except maybe from my years of riding herd on those big old dinosaurs from IBM and Univac. More importantly, it began a friendship with *Eternity's* editor Stephen Gregg that lasted until he died in his early 50s. I miss Stephen; I miss him a lot. I miss our long talks about music until the early hours of the morning, I miss learning about new music from him, and I miss his laugh, which I can still hear. I wish someone would put together a *Best of Eternity* anthology.

The Really Distant Future

"Carrara" was published in the February 1975 issue of *Eternity*.

"Half Past the Dragon" was supposedly a cover story for the November 1974 *Fantastic*. However, after seeing Joe Staton's painting of a dragon encircling a spaceship at Ted White's house for the second time, I realized that I had failed to remember it also contained the Earth and the moon, and that the spaceship had NASA on it. Ah, well. I had a lot of fun filling the story with puns. It was republished in Germany, and I have to wonder how many of the puns survived translation, and if the final pun made any sense at all in German. The title comes from Donald Colvin's September 1953 *Galaxy* story, "Half Past Alligator."

Somewhere in the mid-1970s, Scott Edelstein (I think) was trying to put together a collection of last man on Earth stories in the style of various SF writers. I chose Robert Sheckley and Cordwainer Smith. When the collection didn't happen, I was able to sell my Cordwainer Smith parody, "On the Planet Planet" to *The Diversifier* (October 1976). (Instead of a last man on Earth story, it's a last Earth on Man story.) I apparently had a bit of fun with the said-bookisms for the underpeople.

"World's End" (*Night Voyages*, Fall 1981) is another fantasy story. It was a surprise for me to revisit it. While not an unmitigated success, it's a much better story than I had thought at the time. I guess Gerald Brown, editor of *Night Voyages*, saw more in it than I did at the time and maybe he was right. Maybe. If I were to write it today, it would be very different. Maybe I will.

"A Sky the Color of Anger, A World Full of the End of the Universe" was written at the end of my second week at the 1969 Clarion workshop. Someone (either Neil Shapiro or Jim Sutherland) had brought in a painting and Harlan Ellison had us write a story around it. At that point I had written "Saint Louis Tickle" but not "The Interstellar Ragtime All-American Jazz Band" (which "Saint Louis Tickle" would become the first chapter of) so there is some contradiction between "A Sky the Color of Anger" and IRAAJB, sort of an alternative universe to an alternative universe.

There's not much to say about "Timid Bank Clerks and Other Writers" (*Knights 20*, March 1979) and "Tiptoeing Through Tulane" that isn't already said in the articles themselves.

Finally we have the little untitled piece of whimsy that follows this afterword. It was the result of an exercise at a song-writing class at The Writers Center in Bethesda, Md., led by Cathy Fink and Marcy Marxer. We were supposed to spend five minutes writing about "The Best Cup of Coffee in the World." This, with only a little bit of rewriting, is what came out:

A Damn Fine Cup of Coffee

I was born under the worst cup of coffee that ever there was. It came from Seattle, of course, in a refrigerated boxcar full of angry, insane Angus cattle what did things to that cup I can't even begin to describe. Their horns delivered tons of sugar into that poor tiny cup, and they doused it with perfume (and you don't want to know what Angus perfume smells like). Now how it got from that boxcar to the hospital is a whole 'nother song but let's just say it got there. Well, actually, to tell the truth, there was a hobo on that train in that same boxcar, a hobo by the name of Woody Houston, who just happened to have a guitar with him, and he started playing Bob Dylan songs even though Bob Dylan hadn't been born yet, and them there Angus cattle stampeded out of that boxcar, leaving Woody Houston alone with that poor mangled cup of coffee, which by now was covered with a large pile of sugar and other stuff, which Woody dug through and extricated the cup and dusted off its britches and spooned out half a ton of sugar so now the cup was feeling a lot better though still not very good. "I know just what you need," Woody said. "I've got these friends of mine who will fix you up good as new." Now these friends just happened to be my parents but they were in no mood to fix up a cup of coffee, no matter how much in need it might be, because right then my mother was busy giving birth to me and I was giving her trouble, practicing to do what the good Lord sent me here to do. But Woody was having none of that. He slapped me across the bottom, sending me flying across the room as he sang "I'm the trouble-bustin' man." And he sure busted my chops, let me tell you, which is why to this day I don't have no chops, though I've been playing guitar now for all of 15 minutes, which I guess is all I need for fame, right? What? Oh, the coffee. Well, sir, my father broke out a bottle of Old Frothingslosh and dumped it in, making it one damn fine cup of coffee.

Visit
briefcandlepress.com
to read about the author,
and upcoming publications

www.ingramcontent.com/pod-product-compliance
Lightning Source LLC
Chambersburg PA
CBHW020610180626
46810CB00007B/2707